# KINETIC

## THE LUMINARIES

S.K. ANTHONY

Copyright ©2013 by S.K. Anthony
Cover Design: http://www.maeidesign.com
Copy editing by Melissa Gray
Proofreading by Lynda Dietz
Book interior design by JT Formatting

www.**skanthony**.com
Printed in the United States of America
First Edition: August 2013

Library of Congress Cataloging-in-Publication Data

Anthony, S.K..
      Kinetic (The Luminaries) / S.K. Anthony – 1st ed

      ISBN-13: 978-1492128755
      ISBN-10: 1492128759

      1. Kinetic (The Luminaries) —Fiction. 2. Fiction—Fantasy
      3. Fiction—Urban Fantasy

*For my loved ones.*

# CHAPTER ONE

*MIDNIGHT, FINALLY THE fun begins.* While I was stuck here looking everywhere but at my date, I'd caught on to the robbery happening across the street. He was busy babbling as the two men seemed to be messing with the alarm system. They were dressed in all black, their hoodies covering their heads, and their sunglasses screaming hello to me. I'd been sitting there with my jacket on, ready to go, for the past thirty minutes, and all this guy wanted to do was talk about some company he'd acquired with all his extra-millionaire money. These two couldn't have had better timing. If I had to sit there listening to Mr. Chatty for one more minute, I would die of boredom.

"Excuse me. I need to use the ladies room." I grabbed my purse and got up.

"Yeah, yeah." My date flashed a smile while I tried my best not to roll my eyes.

I walked out of the restaurant, not even giving Mr. Chatty a backward glance. My heels clicked against the pavement as I headed toward the jewelry store, and suddenly, I wished I was wearing something a little sluttier. I adjusted my black leather jacket and pulled my fitted red dress higher to show more leg. I knocked on the door and waited a beat, but none of the robbers answered. *How rude.* I yanked the door from its hinges and leaned it against the wall. I made my way in and found them at the back of the store. I looked at one man, whose mouth dropped wide open when he saw me.

I smiled, "Hey."

"Looky, looky here," the other man said, coming out from the office to my right. "Sweetheart, I don't know if you noticed but the store is closed."

"Ah, yes, I noticed. The thing is, I was over there..." I pointed to the restaurant behind me, "with this blind date, David something or other, and he was talking my ear off when I noticed you two—ah, gentlemen—coming in here."

"Are you a cop?" the first man asked as he reached for his gun.

"Do I look like a cop?" I pushed my hip sideways, trying to look some kind of interesting. "You guys will probably need a hostage if the cops show up, though, so I'm offering myself." I reached for a necklace and put it on while checking myself out in the mirror that was conveniently placed on the counter. My new layered haircut really emphasized my caramel highlights and almond eyes. *I like it.*

"Is this a joke? The alarm is disarmed. We don't need you. I mean, you're hot, mamacita, but you've gotta be crazy," the second man said.

"Well, no," I answered as the men continued filling their bags with jewels, "but I am looking for some fun tonight, and you two look like you are up for it, know what I mean?" I bit my lips and started pulling down the zipper of my jacket. The two men came toward me like magnets, so I did what any respectable girl would do: I waited until they were close enough and then grabbed them by their necks, delighting in the sound of their heads colliding with each other. They dropped to the floor, unconscious. I proceeded to toss one man on top of the other and sit on them while I called my NYPD friends to come over. I didn't bother tying them up, nor did I worry about them regaining consciousness. Even if they did, try as they may, they wouldn't be able to stir one inch from under the whole five feet and 110lbs that was my body. Yeah, I'm special like that.

"HEY, ANNIE, SO what happened with your date?" Beth asked me the next day at work.

"Nothing. It was quite boring until these two guys came into play."

She gave me a wink, "Ah, you had yourself a threesome."

"More like I ditched one for two, you know how I roll," I said, grinning.

"I heard. Glad you got to kick some ass."

I shrugged. "It was a simple robbery, nothing a little head banging couldn't fix. They were at the right place at the right time to save me from Mr. Chatty."

"Hey, there's always Derek," she said. "What? Don't give me that look, you like him."

"He is just a friend, Beth. Yes, we hang out and he's nice, but he's also our boss. Besides, I'm not interested in dating. I just want to go out there and use my hands to beat the crap out of assholes."

"Okay, okay, I got it. You'd think a little vacation would have loosened you up a bit."

"Well, I don't see why it would. I just stayed home, watched the news, and cringed that I wasn't able to help the whole time."

"Of course you did," she laughed. "I have to go, but I'll call you later," she said with a wave.


I MADE MY way back to my office and worked on boring paperwork all morning. The *bing* on my computer screen alerted me to a message. The digital envelope took over the whole screen and opened up with its message: *Ms. Fox and Mr. Cole, please report to duty immediately.* I dumped the papers into my drawer and went to get my instructions.

I STOOD WATCH at Worldsafe, location confidential. I had gotten here through the portal controlled by my good buddy, Andrew Cole. He was suave like that. He could go wherever, whenever, all he needed to do was open his portal and walk right in. And if you were his friend, like me, you got to ride along. Worldsafe was considered the most secured location in the world to store your belongings: money, documents, nuclear formulas, urine. Whatever you thought would be dangerous for the outside world to find, you could keep it here. It was for rich people only. The leaders of the world probably kept all their illegal belongings here, along with their extra-marital kids' identities, and their countries' secrets. I didn't actually know the content of the safes, but as you can tell, I liked to guess. That's not why I was there, though. I was there because my boss, Derek Lake, had sent me.

Security had been breached, and only Luminaries were cleared to work on the case.

So now here I was, standing with my back against the heavy, layered steel armory door. It stood at ten feet tall, six feet wide, and fourteen inches thick. It had combinations and keys, and it took two ex-marines to pull it open. It was the only entrance and exit to the vault. The surrounding walls were made of even stronger materials, I'd been told. It didn't matter to me. The reflection was quite terrific, so I turned to adjust my lip gloss while one of the ex-marines shook his head in disbelief.

"Can you believe that?" he whispered to the other. He got a shrug in response, and I couldn't help myself.

"Come on, big guy. At least I'm a change of scenery for you." I gave him what I thought of as one of my best smiles in the spirit of keeping peace.

"You're less than one third my size! Where is that guy that you came with? Or even the other girl? At least she's taller and older."

"Andrew is standing guard outside the building, and Beth is walking the lobby *and* not that it's your business, but she and I are the same age."

"You look like you just came out of high school."

"I graduated years ago, but trust me, I'm the one you want here."

"We don't need anyone else here. We've been guarding Worldsafe for years, and nothing has ever happened. Besides, I can fit you in my pocket," he laughed.

"You can try to put me in your pocket, dude, but you'd be sorry," I challenged playfully.

"Oh yeah?" the other guy jumped in.

"You have no idea." I walked over to them and raised my hands up to their chests. "Try to push me."

I felt the pressure, but really? It felt like a joke. I

gently nudged them, and they both fell backwards. "Satisfied?"

As they gawked at me, the screams from two levels up reached my ears. The lobby was under attack. I could hear the crashing sounds of glass breaking and the cacophonous sound of something blowing up. Right before the smell of burning wood hit my nostrils, one of the guys went to check out the corridor that led to us from the stairway. His partner started following protocol, which involved him opening the vault to lock himself inside. He entered the codes, and as I pulled the door open for him, the other guard's body came flying towards us, landing at the feet of his partner.

The sizzling of fire in the air didn't stop me from ushering the guard inside, but instead of following through, he lunged at me, catching me by surprise. I was trapped under him when I saw another figure run into the vault. Shit! The guard was choking me, his elbow on my neck, while the intruder ran after the safes. I pushed against the wall with my left leg and sent the guard blasting away from me in one swinging motion.

Coming to my feet, I ran into the vault and found myself at the bottom of what seemed like three floors. It was filled with storage units, all next to each other. It reminded me of prison cells, each of them with their own armored doors. I smelled more smoke coming from above, so I ran up the first set of stairs and let my nose guide me. I saw the figure trying to melt one of the armored doors, and I launched myself at him. He was ready for me, though, so I found myself thrown across the room like a ragdoll. I pretended to be injured as he approached me, and when he was close enough, I kicked his feet from under him and he fell, hitting his head on the concrete floor. I jumped on him and pinned his hands down just as he looked up at me.

And there he was, Nick Logan.

My ex-husband.

I stared at the face I'd once loved, now with a patch covering his left eye and scars running all the way down his jaw. They were almost hidden under his days-old beard and wild, dark hair. His deep hazel *eye* looked at me, empty, daring me to speak first. I punched him.

"What? No kiss?" he said. "It's been years."

"You cold-hearted murderer," I said between clenched teeth.

"Annie, you are getting weaker." He licked the blood splatter from his lips and gave me a half smile. "If you are going to kill me, darling, do it now," he told me as he tried to push my hands. But we both knew any attempt to escape me would fail.

I knew what I had to do. Orders were clear... KILL ON CONTACT.

The thing is, it was Nick.

Before I knew what I was doing, I'd released my hold. He got up and rubbed his mouth.

"What did I tell you about giving second chances?"

"You won't hurt me," I said.

"Honey, you are so wrong! I wouldn't even blink an

eye, no pun intended," he smiled. "Next time you won't be so lucky. If you ever get the chance again, take it." He shoved me down and gave me a hard kick in the ass. He started to leave but turned instead, his smile still plastered across his scarred face. "If you can."

I watched him leave and took a deep breath. I had to give this some thought. I wondered if there was any excuse I could come up with that the Organization would believe. I was going to be in so much trouble. And it was possible they would even strip my abilities away. Although my job could be mentally exhausting, I knew that, deep down, I couldn't give up what made me, me. I was a badass, I liked using my extensive training to bring down the bad guys of the world, and what had I just done? I'd let the worst of them walk away. I came into this Organization to serve a purpose, and I had never regretted it. Until now.

Nick had taken advantage of all the knowledge he'd gained when he was part of the Org. He was guilty of kidnapping, attacking government buildings, killing a lot of people, and was considered enemy number one for all Luminaries. But while I had no respect left for him, I couldn't hate him. Not like the rest of them did. This was the man with whom I had exchanged wedding vows, the man who was once my whole world, and he had to be taken down. But he still had enough power over me that I'd let him go. *Stupid heart.* I never wanted to be one of those girls again, the ones who live for love or die for it. No, love no longer had any place in my empty chest.

The problem was, I'd found my heart staring at me through one eye, and I'd lost my shit.

# CHAPTER TWO

"ANNIE! ANNIE! ARE you okay?"

I couldn't concentrate enough to recognize the voice that was calling my name. I was in shock from seeing Nick.

Beth placed a hand on my shoulder. "Annie, you're scaring me. Why are you staring at me like that? Did he hurt you? Wait here, I'm going after him."

That's when I realized that she was leaving. "NO!" I screamed. "I don't want you to go alone, Beth. I don't know what he's capable of doing to you, and he's probably too far away already."

"You realize if there's someone who can catch him, it would be *me*, right?" she asked.

"Just stay here. He's dangerous."

"Sure thing, babe. Just breathe. No one else is here. Are you going to tell me what happened?" She stooped down by my side. I remained on the floor, lying in the same spot I'd been when he'd kicked me.

"I'm not even sure I know what happened."

"Okay, are you hurt, though? You didn't answer me," Beth said, and helped me up.

"No, I'm not hurt."

She frowned. "I didn't mean physically."

"No."

"Did you let him go?" she asked.

"It's not what you think, I—"

"Save it. Just stay quiet."

"What? Why?" I started to panic that Nick might have returned.

"Shhh...."

I turned and saw Andrew coming from behind me. He picked me up in his arms and asked Beth to watch his back as he opened his portal. The swirling of mist starting from his hand widened into a space big enough for him to pass through. His tunnel, as we called it, felt somewhat peaceful, as if all my worries were for nothing. It was just like Andrew, full of serenity.

"You can put me down, you know," I said. He was well over six feet and had such a muscular body that I felt like a baby bunny in the arms of a giant.

"I don't want to take any chances. You were actually hurt, and we both know that's not normal."

"I'm not hurt."

"Okay," he said. He set me down and we walked on in silence.

Five minutes later, I was sitting in my office with a

nice cup of hot coffee. I loved coffee. It was almost a sin how much I drank it. I was waiting for everyone to arrive so we could start our meeting. I still had no idea how to explain what had happened, but since I'd brought it on myself, I figured the right thing to do was to go with the truth. If they decided to exonerate me, I would consider myself very lucky. I couldn't argue that I didn't make a big mistake, but I would even beg, if I had to, for them to let me stay until this fight was over. Everyone deserved a second chance, right? Maybe I was biased, but I thought I did.

*Everyone report to the conference room.*

And that was my cue from the intercom. I popped a mint, wiped my sweaty hands on my jeans, and went to face judgment.

Derek stood at the head of the large oval table with a look of concern on his face. He was staring at me, and I couldn't help but feel ashamed of my actions. Derek had taken over the head position when his dad, Dr. Derek Lake, had decided to step down three years before. That was the same time Nick had walked out on me, not that I was keeping track.

"Listen up everyone," Derek said. "I must inform you that the *devil himself*—sorry, Nick Logan—has made a move again by attempting to steal something. Lucky for us, he wasn't able to retrieve the object he was after. We are not sure what's in the vault, but rest assured, we will find out. Two guards were hypnotized and slightly injured, but they will be fine."

"Annie, perhaps you should give us your account of the events," Lisa said, clicking her tongue as all eyes fell on me.

"Yes, of course," I began. "As you already know, Beth was in Worldsafe when the power went off. Derek sent me along with Andrew to help secure the vault while the back-up generator was still going strong. We were each in our positions when the attack happened."

"I was right behind her," Beth chipped in, giving me a side wink, "and I saw when he tried to hypnotize Annie. She was too fast for him, so when he failed, he blasted her with a jolt of current just like the guards. Lucky for us Annie is tough or she would have been seriously hurt."

"Hmm," Lisa made a sound.

Beth ignored her and jumped up from her seat. She walked around to where Derek stood and faced everyone. Her expression changed, and I could see the fear in her eyes. "It was different…it wasn't just shock waves anymore: he can spurt fire from his hands."

"Fire?" Derek asked.

"Yes, I saw it when we were fighting in the lobby. He asked me to step aside, and when I didn't, he started setting fire to everything." She started pacing around. "He aimed straight at me, and if I hadn't been so fast he would have burnt me, but instead, he hit a bag—I'm guessing he brought it with him—and it blew up. It was disturbing…he just kept laughing."

"Maybe it was the lighting that made it look like fire?" I asked.

"No, Annie, trust me on this one, you didn't get a chance to see it. Anyway, after that, I stayed with Annie instead of following him. I didn't know what was wrong with her. She was stunned and wasn't breathing."

Well, that explained the smoke inside the vault as well. *Interesting.* Poor Beth. Now she was going to have to answer for me. I mean, I can get hurt and die like anyone else, but I'm strong and can take my share of beating and endure bad injuries. Now she'd have to explain why she didn't leave me, knowing I would most likely be all right.

"You let him get away? That's so like you two," Lisa said, slamming her hands on the desk. "Very irresponsible, Beth. You should have killed him."

"So I was supposed to let Annie die, then?"

"Look at her. She is healthy and living," Lisa answered, lifting her right eyebrow.

"Beth, you did the right thing," Derek said as he turned to point at Lisa. "You need to let it go. With Nick spurting fire, we don't know how strong his first beam might be now. She didn't know if Annie was all right, and I expect you would have done the same thing in her situation."

Lisa's lip curled up while looking at me, and she sneered, "Of course...*who wouldn't?*"

THE FOLLOWING MORNING, I woke up with a headache, and I noticed that the light was blinking on my house phone, indicating I had a message. I couldn't believe I hadn't heard it ring, much less heard the message as it was being recorded. I went to make some coffee. I hated making it. Somehow, it never came out good enough. Making the coffee used to be Nick's job. Ah, well. I went to the phone and pressed 'play' and heard Beth's voice:

*"Hey you, I'm coming over with breakfast. See ya!"*

God, I owed Beth! She had really saved me yesterday. I didn't want to think about what my fate would have been otherwise. Beth and I had become best friends when I'd joined the Org eight years ago at the tender age of fifteen. She had started three months before me, and we were both assigned to Lisa. Our dislike for our dear coach might have strengthened our friendship, but we didn't like to give her any credit. Lisa hated me now because I had Derek's attention, but back then, it was all about hating Beth. She'd made our lives a living hell during training, but she'd made fun of Beth a lot for growing up on the streets. Unlike us, Beth had always been on her own and didn't even have the privilege to say she had other orphans to call a family.

Lisa was gorgeous and she knew it. She had green eyes, long red hair, and the bitchiest attitude I'd ever been witness to. Lisa was envious of Beth's beauty, even though the two of them were like night and day, except for the fact that they both had green eyes. She just needed attention, and if anyone rivaled it, they were in for a war. She was three inches shorter than Beth, who stands at 5'11", her own yellowish-green shaded eyes stunning against her brown skin. Beth rocked a boy haircut like no other. I always joked with her that she would always have a job as a model if she ever decided to leave the Org.

Thankfully, we were reassigned to Jenny within the year. That was absolute luck. Jenny was the most compassionate person ever, and she had the biggest heart. She showed us the ropes, and to this day, I went to her when I needed any advice. She was twenty-six, only three years older than I was, but she'd joined when she was thirteen, so she was already considered a pro by the time we got there. I remembered how scared Beth and I had been when our time came to be altered. We didn't know if we would react to the injections or not, and we both really wanted to join the Org. Not everyone could be altered, and those who couldn't were the people who would be sent back to normal life. Their memories would be erased so they would know nothing about our work at the Org. And for those who became one of us, the only unknown was what kind of power each person would develop.

Jenny assured us that we were the right type and told us that she had found us herself. That made us feel better. We doubted Jenny would have made a mistake. One of her gifts was that she could sense the potential in people to become Luminaries. Her other gift was healing, which I was secretly jealous of. I got robbed, I think. The only ability I'd developed was strength. I was incredibly strong and quite durable. Okay, I guess that's not too shabby, but that's it, nothing else. It used to be a bitch to control my strength, but I had it down now, thank God. And Beth? Well, she got to move around extremely fast. The tests they'd run on her clocked her speed at about seventy miles per hour. She could run, jump, and attack as fiercely as a cheetah.

I heard Beth's keys as she unlocked the door and looked up when she got into the kitchen. "How does a BLT sound to you?" she asked with a smile.

"Perfect."

"Good. Please, tell me you have coffee. I didn't want to risk a drop in my new car," she said as she went straight to the table and sat down. "How come you didn't answer the phone? You look like you just woke up."

"I did just wake up, and I didn't hear the phone." I got two coffee mugs and the milk from the refrigerator. "Beth, I wanted to say thank you."

"You got it, babe. I knew you would be hungry. By the way, I got us a big order of home fries to share. We need all the calories we can get."

"I wasn't talking about the food," I said.

"I know what you meant."

"Good, and why exactly do we need the extra calories?"

She frowned. "We need to start working out with more intensity, that's why. Both of us lost it yesterday. Annie, he could have hurt us. We had the chance to end this ourselves, and we let him slip away. I was shocked when I saw how much he's changed and…his beam…fire…whatever. Wow! It was something else. And you? What's your excuse? Whatever happened, we can't have that again. Will you tell me why I lied?"

"I don't even know."

She went to get ketchup for the home fries. She didn't take her eyes off me, though, as she said, "Look, I don't want to pressure you. Please think things through and let me know when you're ready. But I deserve an explanation, if I don't already know..." she said with a sigh.

"I couldn't do it. I wanted to, I knew I had to, but I couldn't. I had him pinned down and weakened and I…I—"

"It's okay, Annie, no one has to know. Honestly, I'm not sure I can do it either. I couldn't kill him. The best I could do would be to capture him for the Org to decide his fate."

"How come?"

"Because I know how much it would hurt you."

I nodded. "It's Nick, you know? I think I would hold a grudge against anyone who actually does it, so I thought about it last night. It has to be me."

"Unless it's Lisa."

"Hmm, she might be just about the only other person I'd be okay with killing him. I already can't stand her. But I don't know," I shook my head. "The way he looked at me, I swear I could see a glimpse of the old Nick.

Maybe I can help him."

"I don't know about that, sweetie. He's too dangerous to allow him to just hang around. You know all the things he's done and how much he's hurt people. How much he's hurt *you*."

"Can you believe he kicked me?"

"What?"

"He knew it wouldn't hurt me, but still, it felt like he'd spit on me. The action alone…it pissed me off!"

"What's up with his face?" she asked.

"I don't know. He looks scary, though."

"I was going to say horrible, but yes, scary, too."

"Whatever—he deserves it," I said.

We spent the rest of the afternoon watching movies and didn't even think about working out, as usual. We always planned to but never got around to it. We preferred to enjoy our rare moments of girl time by watching chick flicks, instead. And it was exactly what I needed after the day before.

"Annie?" Beth interrupted my thoughts. "Do you have any idea what Nick was after? Worldsafe is supposed to be top secret. We only learned about it a few months ago, so how did he know about it?"

"I don't know. I don't even care what he wants or why he's so eager to get it. The only thing I can tell you is that no place is secured if regular people run it. You and I both know he can be very *persuasive*. I swear, I could kick him!"

She laughed, "You just want payback for him

kicking you."

"Dammit, I do!"

"I'd like to see that," she raised an eyebrow before finishing with, "*if you can.*"

"Very funny, Beth." Ever since I'd told her the details of my encounter with Nick, she'd been cracking jokes at my expense. "You can stop now."

"Fine, party pooper."

I noticed she was busy texting on her phone and asked, "Is that Andrew? Tell him thanks for yesterday."

"It's Derek. He just wants to make sure you're okay."

"Of course he does." I took a deep breath.

"He cares for you, Annie…he's not going to wait forever."

"Well, I went out on a date so it should be obvious I'm interested in dating anyone but him."

"One blind date doesn't say that. Derek is a good guy. You need a good guy."

"I might strangle him if he annoys me too much."

"Nick annoyed you," she pointed out.

"Yes, but most of the time, I found his annoying habits adorable, and Derek just gets under my skin," I said. *He's too darn possessive is what he is.* "I don't know… I don't think I'm into him. He's too short."

"He is not short! Annie, 5'9" is tall for you. Well, anyone is," she laughed. "He's cute, too. Don't act like you don't find him attractive."

I shrugged. "He's all right."

"I can imagine your olive skin with his sandy hair on your kids—adorable!"

"Funny, Beth."

She laughed. "Cute, Spanish, blond babies."

"Cut it out if you don't want me to break your arm," I threatened.

"Okay, okay. No one else will treat you right, you know."

"I thought you didn't like Derek for me."

"I don't know what to think, but I know you care about him, and I want to see you loved. You might be too depressed if you lose him, too. I've seen you go down that road before, Annie, and I don't want to ever see you like that again."

"I don't have the heart to love anymore. Anyway, I can survive on my own."

"You won't be too lonely?"

"I have you."

"Oh, man…lucky you," she grinned.

My phone rang. I looked at the time, almost nine o'clock. I was sure Derek couldn't wait any longer. Beth answered the phone while I ran away to the bathroom. I really didn't want to be bothered with him right now. When I came back, Beth was getting ready to leave. She'd told him I was already sleeping and that he could talk to me the next day. She left saying that she couldn't leave Andrew abandoned all day.

Beth and Andrew were great together. And they were my best friends. Although complete opposites, they complemented each other like no other couple I knew. Andrew was very big and muscular, and I secretly feared he would crush Beth with just a hug. He wouldn't stand out as best looking in a crowd, but he was very charming. Most importantly, he was good for Beth, and I couldn't have been happier that she had him in her life.

I didn't have any difficulty sleeping that night. I woke up early on Sunday and went on my morning jog. Beth was right, Nick had gotten stronger somehow. I really couldn't understand how he'd developed more powers, but that was the least of my worries. I had to get my butt moving if I planned on being the one to take him down. I actually hated jogging. Nick was the one who had gotten me started, the bastard...obviously, he had always been evil.

It's not like I needed to work out. I just liked having as much resistance as possible and moving as fast as I could. Mostly, I needed to clear my head before going to work, especially when I had so much on my mind. It sometimes seemed that Derek could see right through me and knew when something was bothering me. Ugh, I was sure he would insist on having me checked out to make sure I was one hundred percent fine. The more I thought about it, the more I began to think I was ready to give him an answer. He'd been great, and very patient with me, and I was beginning to realize that if my empty chest was not otherwise occupied, I'd keep wallowing in my pain over Nick. Yes, it still hurt, but I refused to keep giving him power over me.

I spent the rest of the day visiting my little friends at Sweet Orphan Home. It always made my day to put a smile on their faces. Both young and older kids were always excited to see me. I never failed to bring some goodies to help satisfy their sweet tooth. And my older keeper friends always appreciated the extra supplies I donated to them, also. Having lived there myself, I knew the difference just one caring person could make. I just wished I'd had one back then.

# CHAPTER THREE

AS SOON AS I walked out from the diagnostic center on Monday I saw Derek waiting for me. "Everything is fine. Just like I said."

"I had to make sure, didn't I?"

"If you say so."

"I do say so. I know you can handle yourself, Annie, but the way Beth described it, how different it was…let's just say that it's better to be safe than sorry. Come with me to my office, will you?" he said, escorting me down the hall.

"Uh, sure." I hesitated. "You need something from me?"

"I need to talk to you, but not here. Why don't you go up and wait for me? I'll get us something to drink."

I watched him turn around and go through the corridor and decided to stop by Beth's office before going to Derek's. Unfortunately, she wasn't there. I should have known he would have sent her out on an assignment already. He tended to keep us separated anytime he gave me an ultimatum about this being the last time he'd swallow his pride and ask me out. The drama king. He simply didn't like that I talked to Beth about my personal life, or his.

I took the elevator to his office and walked past his desk to look out the window. It was a beautiful view of New York City. The skyline really was something to be admired. Out of the corner of my eye, I caught sight of something that was moving. *This frigging guy had stalking tendencies!* He had a picture of me as his screensaver! I didn't even recognize it, but I knew it had to be new because my highlights were only two weeks old. Was he having me followed? Maybe it was good that he wanted to talk. I'd just tell him I wasn't right for him and end it now.

I heard the door opening behind me. "One large coffee with milk and sugar, just the way you like it."

"Thanks, Derek." I turned to look at him.

"Why don't you come over to the sitting area?" He had a separate section at the back of his office, but at the moment, his chunky mahogany desk seemed like the most appropriate place for our conversation, so I took a seat there.

"No, I'm good here." He looked disappointed as he walked over. "Actually, I'm glad you wanted me to come to your office, Derek."

"You are?" He took another glance towards his

private section. *Ugh, this guy.*

"Yes, I think we need to talk."

"Good. Here, have your coffee, and should we say ladies first, then?"

"Um, I know what you want to talk about, okay? I assume that you are going to ask me out again. I just—"

"Well, you're wrong." He pushed his chair back and crossed his arms over his chest. The thing with Derek was that he was too proud and didn't handle rejection well. "This is business, Annie, but if you think we have time to talk about your heart's desire, I need to cut you short. Life is not all about you."

"I didn't say it was, Derek. We were going to talk about it over the weekend, but with everything that happened, we didn't even see each other."

"So you thought I wanted to talk about that right now. I mean *right* now? We have a crisis on our hands, Annie. Look around. Do you think I want to focus on you?" he smirked.

"I guess not. Just get to it, then."

"What is Nick after?" he asked, his face red.

"I'm sorry?"

"What is he after? You have to know. He must have mentioned something to you when you two were close," he said this like he'd just swallowed an onion.

"I haven't seen Nick in three years. How do you expect me to know what he's been up to since?"

"If you can think hard, maybe you'll remember if he ever shared his dreams and hopes about destroying all of us…or whatever it is he's after. A slight memory? Anything," he pushed.

"I have no idea what he is doing or why."

"I hope that's true, Annie. You'll be in a lot of trouble if you're holding back information from us."

"What? I can't believe you even said that."

"So you wouldn't protect him for any reason, right? I mean, you can't possibly still love him. Or do you?"

"No."

"Then why won't you go out with me? Like a real date? I'm tired of us being just friends," he said.

"I thought this wasn't about my personal life."

"Well, now it is. Give me a chance. It's all I ask for. If you don't have any more feelings for him, then there's no reason why you can't try to be happy with me." His brown eyes pleaded with me.

"I'm not right for you."

"How do you know what's right for me?" he asked as he walked around the desk. He sat on the chair next to mine and played with my hair. Before I could say anything, he went on to caress my neck.

*Seriously?* I pulled away. I could see the disappointment on his face, but I really couldn't force myself to be romantic with him. I just didn't feel anything with him, and I knew it shouldn't be like that. He deserved better, like someone who didn't mind him stalking her. I was about to bring up the screensaver picture, but I decided I had already upset him enough. Pick your battles and all that.

"I don't know what's right for you, Derek, but I know it's not me."

"One chance?" he asked softly.

"Don't you want to be with someone who wants to be with you? Who feels butterflies when you hug her? Who—"

"All that will come with time, I promise. How do you know you won't like my kiss? You haven't even let yourself think about me that way. Honestly, tell me you don't look at me as just a friend."

"Well, yeah, that is the truth. You *are* just my friend," I said.

"But we could be so much more. At least give me one date before you make up your mind. Come on, what's one date?"

"You go from telling me our meeting is not about us, to accusing me of hiding information that could possibly mean the end of the Org, to persuading me to give you one date. Do you ever give up?"

"Sure," he said, smiling. "I give up once I get what I want. And we will talk about our date later. For now, I need to get to another important meeting."

"Okay, but please don't get your hopes up."

"Oh, *I will,* and you should, too."

"Bye, Derek," I said, and walking out the door, I took a big gulp of coffee, burning my tongue in the process. Had he just boiled this? My poor mouth.

What was I thinking, letting him talk me into a date? I had no idea. I know I'd thought about giving it a shot yesterday, but really, I had just wanted to keep my mind off Nick, and that wasn't fair. But then again, maybe Derek was right, I might surprise myself and really like him. Beth thought I could like him, and if anyone would know, it was her. She must have been pushing me for a reason, unless she was just screwing with me. Gosh, I hated this. Where was she when I needed her?

I went to my office to see what my new assignment would be. I really needed to focus on something other than Nick and Derek. I walked in and felt a chill creep up my back. Everything seemed to be just as I'd left it, but something felt strange.

My desk was in the far back left of the room. My papers were stacked neatly on my desk. The drawers were locked. My sitting area was facing the fireplace with the pillows in the same order I'd left them. My computer was powered down. My coffee maker was dirty. Shit, I didn't clean out the grounds, and my mug was smelly. *Gross!*

I liked my office a lot, and found it to be very relaxing. Everything was locked away and had a clean look. Of course, this didn't mean I was organized. If you dared open my compartments, you would see everything was piled with absolutely no order.

Oh my God, that was it! My papers on my desk were too neat. And I was missing some sticky notes I'd left for myself. Someone had gone through my things. Well, the things on my desk, anyway. There was no way they could get into my drawers.

As I was walking out the door to demand a confession from whomever had disrespected my privacy, I noticed it. Right by the window, I saw a picture frame, the one that held an old picture of Nick with his arms wrapped around my waist. The one that was supposed to be locked up in my drawer. I immediately closed my office door and ran to pick up the frame. The window had been opened, too. I hadn't noticed it before. It had to have been Nick, but I couldn't believe he'd been here…no, there was simply no way…I…He would have been sensed, he would have been caught, and oh gosh, he would have been imprisoned, or even killed. Not that I cared.

I looked into every compartment in my desk, and everything was in its place. My drawers were in order except for the frame that I held in my hand. The picture was gone. The only person with motivation to take it would be Derek. He would be too jealous knowing I kept it with me, but he had no way to know I had it, nor any way to get it. The only other person who knew my combination was Beth, and she wouldn't take my picture. Unless she thought she was helping me to get over Nick? Not likely. I didn't know who it had been, but I knew I couldn't mention the picture just in case he had really been here. I wondered if they would tell me if he'd been caught. I knew the best thing would be to end his life, and I really couldn't be mad at them if they did. It would hurt, though. All I knew was that I had to find out who had been in my office. I needed to rule out all possibilities of

Nick ever having been here.

I sprinted out the door and saw Lisa being rolled to the clinic by Jenny. When I asked what had happened to her, Jenny mumbled some words I couldn't hear and started twirling her beautiful blonde hair nervously. I knew she was hiding something from me.

"None of your business what happens to me," Lisa said.

"No, I guess not, but I can see you'll be fine. You're just as bitchy as you were before."

She lifted her head up and asked, "Why were you running? Something out of the *ordinary?*"

"Yes, actually. Someone's been snooping around in my office."

"Oh, I know," she said with a quick smirk.

I went towards her with full intentions of wringing her neck. "Lisa! What the hell were you doing in my office?"

I felt my arms being pulled back as Lisa and Jenny disappeared into the clinic. I was so upset, I didn't care if she was hurt or not, I just needed some answers.

"Take it easy, Annie. She needs to recover before you tackle her. You do realize she's injured, don't you?" Derek said from behind me.

"That witch snooped around my office, and you want me to be calm?"

"If you want to be angry at someone, then you should be angry at me."

"Derek, tell me you didn't put her up to it."

"Breathe, Annie."

"Derek!"

"I did ask her to see if something was missing from your office."

"How dare you? I can't even trust you!" I went to punch him, but he was fast at getting out of the way.

"Let me explain. It's not what you think—"

"Explain my ass!" He grabbed my hands and drew me close to him, a mere inch separating my face from his. When my anger boiled inside me like this, I tended to break things. I concentrated on breathing very slowly, because the thing I had in mind to break at this very moment was his head.

"If you don't shut up, I will kiss you," he said, smiling as I just stared at him. "Good, that's more like it. First, I have to tell you that we weren't snooping, we were protecting you. Second, it was just a quick check this morning when I asked you to meet me in my office."

"What do you mean—?" He brushed his lips on mine, and I turned my head away before he could move in closer. He just smiled while I clenched my fists. If I hadn't been trying hard to control my temper, I would have hurt him *so bad* right then.

I pushed him off me. "This is sexual harassment!"

"I told you to stay quiet," he admonished, ignoring my comment. "Now, Beth was going to visit you before she left on her assignment. She was about to go in and heard a noise inside, but found someone holding the door shut. She couldn't even budge it. We know it wasn't you since you were in the clinic."

"Why do you think Lisa blocked Beth from going in? I'll tell you why. Because she was up to no good. She never is!"

"Lisa was with me, Annie. We don't know if someone was in there or not. Beth asked me to come check it out with her, but you were getting out from the clinic at the same time, so I sent Lisa with her."

"So who was it, then? Who did they find?" I asked.

"No one. The door opened easily for them, and Beth said everything seemed normal. She left to scope the area, and she hasn't been back yet. Lisa rearranged your papers to annoy you."

"It really did get under my skin. You're the boss, tell her not to touch my papers ever again."

"Will do," he said.

I frowned. "So why is she hurt?"

"Beth slammed her into the wall for saying something stupid."

My lips curled up. "That's my girl."

"Is everything else in its place?"

"Yes, I think so. I didn't have a chance to look properly, but everything looks okay."

"Let me know if—"

"Yeah, yeah. Oh, and Derek?"

"Yes?"

"Don't ever kiss me again without my permission or I will break you into pieces."

"Looking forward to having my bones mended,

then," he said with a big grin.

"Bye, Derek."

"Wait a second, hold up while we try to figure out if something is going on here. If someone was hypnotized," he gave me a serious look, "I'd rather you not go out on assignment or be alone for too long."

"Why do you say hypnotized? Who do you think was here?"

"I can't discuss anything further with you, Annie."

"Oh, no, no. You'd better answer me, Derek."

"It's just a precaution. If you'd like, we can talk some more about this over dinner tonight."

"Tonight?"

"Pick you up at eight o'clock."

"We didn't say it would be tonight."

"We didn't say it wouldn't be." He walked away, smiling.

I went back to my office and knew there was nothing I could do. I had told Derek I wasn't sure if anything was different in case we found out it had been someone in the Org. The only problem was, they seemed to think it was Nick, too. Why would he want my picture now? Did he still care about me, after all? I would probably steal his picture if I didn't have one, too. Can't say I blamed him. We had been so happy back then. That picture represented our best days. Maybe he just wanted a memory of great times. Or maybe he missed me. *Oh, get ahold of yourself, Annie!*

I decided to get on the computer to finish my report

on the events at Worldsafe. I needed to keep my mind busy. I had too many things going through it. Nick. Derek. Lisa. Beth. My office. The picture. Dinner. *Sigh.*

I finished writing my report and reading everyone else's. Well, that didn't make sense. According to Derek's report, Beth hadn't been scheduled to go to Worldsafe until today, but he'd sent her a few days early. He never rescheduled...unless he knew something was up. He had sent Andrew and me to keep an eye on her in case anything had gone wrong. Only Andrew hadn't realized they'd moved up the date. If Derek was expecting a break-in then he must have known what was hidden there. So why was he questioning me about what was there? Knowing Derek, he must have just been checking to see if I knew, too. And the sneaky bastard had the nerve to accuse me of lying to protect Nick.

I called Beth to see if she was back, but she didn't answer. On my way home, I stopped by her office again. Nothing. My note was gone, too. Where was Beth hiding? It was so unlike her not to check up on me. I was so gonna kick her ass when I saw her. I know, I like kicking and punching a bit much. It's an addiction.

# CHAPTER FOUR

I WAS READY by seven thirty. I didn't go out of my way to look pretty. I just threw on a black pencil skirt with a white-laced top and my ballet flats. I didn't want Derek thinking I was trying to impress him. God knows, he was already so full of himself.

I tried calling Andrew since Beth was still not answering.

"Hey, Annie."

"Andrew! I'm so glad I got through to you."

"Actually, Annie, I can't talk now. Can I call you back later?"

"No, wait, I'm looking for Beth."

"I'll have her call you in a bit," he said.

"Is she okay? I haven't been able to reach her."

"She's fine. I'll have her call you. I promise."

"Okay, talk to you later, Andy."

"Yeah, later," he said, and he hung up.

I was starting to wonder why she hadn't called me or touched base with me for the whole day after my last incident, when the bell rang. Oh boy, Derek was ten minutes early. I thought of making him wait, but I figured it was best to get this over with. I opened the door to find him looking around the front patio.

"Are you planning on coming in? Staying out? Or going straight to wherever it is that we're going?"

"Hello to you, too." He had changed out of his usual suit and tie, and the more casual khakis and short-sleeved dress shirt looked nice on him.

"See anything interesting out here?" I asked.

"Oh no. The only thing interesting for me right now is you."

"You are so cheesy, Derek."

He laughed, "Yes, I know." He moved away from the entrance and bowed while swaying his hand so that I followed it straight to the car. "Let me just get the door for you."

"Thanks, Mr. Gentleman."

"You are very welcome."

I watched him walk around his black Mercedes-Benz E350, his eyes focused on the outside of my house. He slid in next to me and had just started to drive when my eye caught Beth trying to get into my house through my dining room window. She must not have had her key handy.

Before I realized what I was doing, I gasped out loud, "What the hell?"

"What? What? Do you see something?" Derek slammed his brake and started to get out of the car. I didn't know what Beth was up to, but I wasn't about to get her into any trouble. I was sure she would give me a good reason later. At least, she'd better.

"No, no! Derek, what are you doing? Get back in the car. I was just wondering what the hell we are doing. I really don't want to give you any false hope."

"That's why you screamed?"

"I didn't scream."

"Jeez, Annie, you scared me there!" He buckled his seat belt. "Why are you so afraid?"

"I'm not afraid. I just don't want to hurt you."

"I think you're scared that you might actually fall for me. Admit it, I intrigue you." He drove off.

"Well, a little bit, yeah."

"Let's just have a nice, quiet dinner. We'll enjoy each other's company, maybe a drink, dessert, and then I'll take you home. And I'll only lay a finger on you if you ask me to. How's that?"

It suddenly crossed my mind that he wanted me out of my house so they could search it just like they'd searched my office. "What if I asked you to turn around so we can have a relaxing dinner at my home?"

"I'd say sure! But don't hold it against me if the intimacy makes me want to put my hands all over you." He pulled the car over. "Is that what you want?"

"Yes, I think so."

"You want my hands all over you?" he asked me,

shock spreading across his face.

"Funny! No, I want to go home and have dinner there. That's it."

"Okay, let's go. Do you want us to pick up the food first?"

"No, drop me off, and you go pick up the food."

"What are you in the mood for?" he asked.

"Surprise me."

"Fine, let me just make a quick U-turn and you'll be home. Be sure to change into a nice baby doll for me. I like those a lot."

"Ha ha, you're just full of jokes tonight, aren't you?"

"No, I'm just in a much better mood now that I know we'll be in the privacy of your house."

Maybe he didn't know about Beth after all. I could be so paranoid at times. He dropped me off, and I got out so fast I slammed the door and barely even heard him yelling for me to be careful with his car. I ran to the house and turned around to make sure Derek had left before I started calling for Beth.

"Beth, I know you're in the house. Get your ass out here right now."

"Are you alone?" I heard her mumbling from my right. Having an open concept layout made it easy to keep track of anyone in the house. She was in the kitchen.

"Yes. What the hell do you think you're doing?"

She walked out to meet me, and I noticed she was limping. There was a trail of blood behind her.

"Beth, what happened?" I ran to her. "Oh my God!

Let me call Andrew—he needs to get Jenny here so she can heal that for you."

"I did," I heard Jenny's soft voice say from behind me. She came down the stairs with a few towels in her hand. I helped Beth sit on the bottom of the stairs since it was closer than the couch.

"What's going on? And why is she still hurt if you healed her?"

"I did the best I could with Beth, and trust me, it's much better. She's lost a lot of blood, but I haven't healed her enough. I feel like I'm going to faint from trying to fix her up. She still has some broken bones and internal injuries that I didn't check because I was so focused on the blood loss, and I don't know how to heal her. I'm just too weak. I was about to call Derek to come and help."

I held on to Beth, who was almost blue, and grabbed the towel from Jenny, noticing she looked exhausted. When I lifted Beth's jeans up, I could see a long opening from her hip down to her knee, and her skin was very purple-greenish. I could see Jenny had done quite a lot of work on her already. I could also see the pain on Beth's face as I tried to fold her jeans up, so I just ripped them off from her butt cheek down. Being strong really was helpful.

"I'm sorry we came here, Annie. It was just the closest place to where we were, and…I didn't think you were home." Her green eyes were blinking wildly. It was a lot to handle.

I had to keep talking so she would stay alert. "So I wasn't supposed to find out you got hurt?"

"No, but that's because she wasn't supposed to get hurt," Jenny answered for her. She came closer and got on her knees. "Let me try to heal her again."

"No, Jenny, you've used up all your energy for today. I don't want you getting sick. I think I can manage some pain."

"Beth, shhh, you rest." Jenny turned to me, "I can give it one more go, Annie. Will you help me?"

"Sure. Beth, let her try one more time. I need you to feel better before I hurt you for not letting me know you needed my help."

She gave me a faint smile.

Jenny had Beth lie on the floor, and then took her leg in her hands. "The outside healed, but for some reason, I can feel the inside is still very wounded. And your ribs, too, Beth. I just don't know which to tackle first." Jenny placed her hands on the leg, and I could see the white waves transfer from her hands into Beth. Jenny didn't do this for too long before I had to pull her away because she, too, was turning very pale.

"You're too weak, Jen. That's enough," I said.

"Just one more minute. I can feel it getting better. I'll stop if I can't handle it, I promise."

"Jen, I can't let you do that. I'm going to call Andrew so he can take you two to the Org. You need to get the proper care. Or even Derek. He is close t—"

"Actually, Annie, I want to try something. I'm going

to try pulling energy from you and using it to boost me up. Hopefully it will work, and I'll be able to heal Beth."

"What? How?"

"I don't know yet. I just want to try it. Can I?"

"Umm, yeah, okay."

She put her head to mine, and we placed our hands palm to palm. I could feel the currents coming out of my body and going into hers. I knew she could feel some pain from my intensity, but since it was my energy, I knew the pain wouldn't be too bad for her. When she finally finished, her cheeks were rosy again, but we must have been a while because neither one of us had noticed that Beth had passed out. Her wound had opened, and once again, she was losing blood.

"Jenny, hurry!" I screamed in panic and watched as Jenny went to work. She was stronger now and was able to use her hands instead. She worked it fast, massaging her fingers inside the cut, and as it healed, she worked her magic outwards as well. I could see that it wasn't working fast enough, though, because Beth's eyes kept rolling back into her head. I went behind Jenny and placed my palm on her forehead so she could take my energy and give hers to Beth at the same time. When she was finished healing Beth, I was too nauseated from all the blood. The last thing I remembered was seeing Derek walk into the house.

I opened my eyes to find Derek and Jenny over me. They had me lying on the couch. As weak as I felt, I saw Derek's hand above my body sending his healing waves into me. I pushed him away.

"Derek, what are you doing? Go help Jenny! I'll be fine."

"Don't worry about me, you just fainted. How are you feeling?" Jenny asked.

"Hungry, actually, and a bit disoriented. Why is the room still spinning?"

"Ah, well, that's perfect. I've got our dinner right here. Jenny, why don't you get Beth and leave? You've had a long day."

"How long was I out?"

"About five minutes. You can handle everything else, but a little blood makes you faint?"

"I can't stand blood. Don't pretend this is news to you." I pursed my mouth, "Oh my gosh—Beth! Where is she?" I realized she wasn't around.

I heard her running toward us. "I was making a mess of your closet. You didn't want me going home with my ass hanging out, did you? Imagine what Andrew would think!" She was smiling, and I could see she was her usual self. She seemed completely healed.

"You're all right!"

"Yes, Derek finished healing me." She turned to both Derek and Jenny, grinning. "You healers are just too handy."

I frowned. "Are you wearing my brand new jeans?"

"You owed me for all I know, so these jeans are my payback."

"I owe you? What for?"

"Helping you decorate with my blood," she said, matter of fact.

"They look better on you either way, like a Capri but good." I smiled and got up to give her a hug. "How did you get hurt?" I saw the three of them look at each other quickly and noticed Derek shaking his head.

"I'll let you know, Annie. Why don't we let them go home now? They're very tired."

"Yes, Annie. We'll talk tomorrow. Thanks for saving my life, by the way. If you hadn't let Jenny try to use your energy, I don't know if I would have made it to the facility in time."

"Of course we would have. We would have called Andrew!"

"Yes, ladies. Everything would have turned out for the best. Why don't I walk you out? Annie, sit here and don't move."

I watched him walk silently to the door. He wished them a good night and closed the door behind him. He went around the house and cleaned up all the blood with the towels Jenny had brought down. When he finished, he picked up a bottle of wine and came over to the living room. Most people thought it was too simple, but I loved the dark chocolate furniture against the pale cream walls. The heavy sofa clashed beautifully with my contemporary simplistic style. I was just glad the blood was gone, and more so, that I hadn't had to clean it myself.

"I'm getting the plates and utensils so we can get on

with our date."

"Okay, I'm bringing the food over to the table, then. Don't give me any funny looks, I'm fine."

He nodded and went into the kitchen. I took the food to the dining room, which was between the kitchen and the living room, and emptied the bag. I was pleasantly surprised to see he'd chosen Italian. My stomach started growling so loudly it was embarrassing. I had been so busy all day, I'd forgotten to eat.

"Derek, this is great. Thank you."

"Sure," he barely answered when he came with the plates. "Where are your wine glasses?"

"Oh, I'll get that. Can you grab some water for me, though?"

He went to get it and came back in no time. "I'm such an idiot, I should have thought to give you water after you fainted. I'm not thinking straight. I'm so sorry, Annie."

"It's fine, I'm good." I debated on asking him, but I had to. "Derek? Is that why you asked me to go out with you tonight? You knew something was going to happen?"

He looked tired. "What? No, Annie, don't talk like that. I asked you out because I wanted to make you realize that you can have a great time with me. I know you're probably thinking I wanted to keep you safe, but trust me, I had no idea they were still out on assignment. Had I known they were hurt, I would have stayed at the Org." He sat across from me.

"Yeah, of course."

He continued, "I called Jenny before I left to come here, and she said they were about to leave the stakeout so I didn't ask anything else. How could I have messed up like that?"

"Don't stress yourself out, Derek. They know how to take care of themselves. Maybe something came up after you spoke to her."

"Yes, I'm sure it was after. I should have left my phone on, though. I turned it off so no one would interrupt our date. I wasn't thinking."

"Where were they? What were they doing?" I asked.

"Eat, Annie, you need to. I have to find out all the details myself, and then I will talk to you about it, I promise. I just want to relax the rest of the evening."

"You call this relaxing?"

"No more questions about tonight, Annie, please."

"Okay. Can I ask you something else, then?"

"Go ahead."

"Why did you send Beth to Worldsafe two days earlier than previously scheduled?"

"Oh, yes. I see you read the reports. I got a call from…uh…just a call that they were having problems with their power lines, and I was asked if I could send someone to help stand guard while they fixed it. Why do you ask?"

"I don't remember you changing plans without a meeting before. I thought maybe you expected Nick to show up for whatever reason."

"No, I had no idea it was Nick who would show up.

My assistance was requested, and I complied, end of story. Why does he always have to come up? Can't we have a conversation without his name being mentioned?"

"I'm sorry. You're right, let's forget these past couple of days." I poured some wine into our glasses and smiled at Derek. Gosh, he really was handsome. "To…I don't know what to toast to."

"To new beginnings, new opportunities."

I knocked my glass to his. "Cheers."

He gave me a breathtaking smile, and I thought that maybe, just maybe, I could make this work. We had a surprisingly nice dinner. He talked about growing up in the Org as a normal child and seeing all these amazing people doing so much good. He couldn't imagine doing something with his life that didn't involve doing great things, too. And the best part was that I could see the passion in his eyes when he talked about it. I didn't push for him to tell me what Beth and Jenny had been up to when they got hurt. Why bother? I knew he wouldn't tell me.

# CHAPTER FIVE

I MADE IT to the Org bright and early. I'd woken up feeling very tired but also anxious to find out what Jenny and Beth had been up to the night before. The only person I met there was Andrew.

"Good morning, Annie. He knew you would be early."

"Derek?"

"The one and only. Come on, we're not staying here. Big man thinks it's not safe so we're going somewhere else," he said.

"Do we have to wait for anyone else?"

"Nope, you're the last. Derek made everyone come in at five o'clock. Before you get mad at Beth, Jenny, or me, he said you needed your rest—and we agreed—so we didn't call you in earlier. Now, come on, we need to get out of here."

"I can't possibly need more rest than Beth and Jenny

after last night."

"Yes, you can. You were the one who was drained. And it was you who helped make them better."

I went into the portal with Andrew and felt that familiar peace wash over me.

"I did nothing. I just sat there and then I fainted."

He laughed, "I heard."

In no time we were in an office that I certainly did not recognize, but that had Derek written all over it. An oval table was in the middle of the room. It looked a lot like the one from our conference room at the Org. Hang on a minute…it was the same one. Why was it here? Everyone was sitting around, not daring to break the silence. I saw Beth coming my way with two cups of coffee in her hands, and she walked around slowly, stopping to give one to Andrew before she handed me the second.

"How are you feeling?" I asked her.

"I'm better, thanks." She sat next to me, putting me in the middle of them.

Derek walked in and our eyes met. "Now that everyone is here, I think we can start." He stood in the center of the room and began, "There are a few new faces, so please get yourselves acquainted after the meeting. I've prepared a file so everyone can read and be aware of what's going on. You'll have time to familiarize yourself with it when I'm done. As all of you know, we've been dealing with a very dangerous enemy for a few years now. He is someone most of us once considered a friend. If he attempts to contact you—any of you—" he looked at me, "you should know he is not to be trusted. He wants nothing more than to use you. And don't be fooled, when he's done with you, he will kill you."

He stood up and swayed his hand to make a board appear. "This man," he said, pointing to a picture of Nick, "is a killer. We all know he has already taken down a few of our members. He is after a very powerful weapon. The details of this weapon will be given to only those who need to know about it directly. If he gets his hands on this weapon, not only will we all be in danger, but we also know he will use it to kill a lot of innocent people. We know this based on his past actions. He wants power. More power than we already know he has.

"It is our belief that he has found a way to enhance his Luminary abilities. We know he can manipulate people with his mind and that he can shoot a laser beam from his hands, but as of the incident that happened five days ago, we have a witness who says he can also spout fire. We got intel that he was going to be in a building close to the Org last night, and I sent two of our people to check it out. He hurt them. Lucky for us, Jenny was there, and with the help of Annie, she was able to heal the injured person. Annie is very strong—"

Lisa cut in, "Oooh, that's news. Annie saved the day! Thanks, Annie, you are so, *so* valuable to us." She placed her hands over her heart.

"Lisa, stop it," someone said from the back.

"No, no, let's have everyone thank Annie. She helped her best friend last night. Gee, how surprising! But let's not forget that she allowed Nick to escape from Worldsafe. And now she is the reason we are all in danger." She threw a pencil at me.

"You're crazy! How is it my fault?" I asked, catching the pencil and crushing it.

"Enough, Lisa," Derek stepped in. "Annie, Nick is after you. We know this for sure."

"No, he is not. Wouldn't he have taken me when we were at Worldsafe, if he were?"

"I stopped him, Annie," Beth answered. But I knew it wasn't true since I was the one who had let Nick go. He could have easily taken me, but he didn't even attempt to.

Derek started again, "One of the ways we know that Nick has been able to enhance his power is that he seems to now be able to channel other Luminaries' powers and use them."

"That's impossible," I yelled.

"Is it? Just last night, you let Jenny channel your energy to heal Beth. And whose idea was it, Annie? Any chance you might have practiced this with Nick in the past?" Derek asked.

"What? No! I didn't even think it was possible," I answered, surprised.

"So why did you have Jenny do it last night, then?" Lisa asked.

"It was my idea. I figured since I can put energy into people, why not take it?" Jenny cut in and answered

Lisa's dirty look with an eye roll.

"Let it go, Lisa," Derek said. "Annie, the same idea applies to Nick. He can put ideas into people's mind using his form of energy. Now he can take them, and he wants yours. We're sure he went into your office the other day because he figured your guard would be down and no one would really be protecting you…and he was right. Good thing you were late so he didn't get a chance to kidnap you. We are assuming he tapped into your residual energy from your office to stop Beth from opening the door."

*What the hell is this guy talking about?*

"It was even luckier that no one got hurt, but it did make us aware that the Org is no longer a safe place for us to be in order to conduct our investigations. From now on, we will be meeting here. We are, believe it or not, at the Org's secret location: right under the old Org. Anyway, Annie, you are going to be under our protection 24/7."

"No, I'm not."

"Yes, you are. No arguing. Now that you're all up to speed, I'm going to take Annie to my office to give her further details. I will be talking to each one of you afterwards. In the meantime, please read—no, *study*—the files in your hands. Annie, follow me."

I went behind Derek as he walked to the stairs. "What? No elevators?"

"We do have elevators, but I'd rather take the stairs to make sure we're in the open."

"I thought you weren't worried since our location is so secured," I said.

"It is, but we never know when there could be a traitor."

"Well, who else knew this was here?"

"My dad, of course and myself, and…" Derek hesitated, "Andrew."

"It sounds like you don't trust Andrew."

"To a certain extent, I do, but he was the asshole's best friend, wasn't he?"

"Yes, he was, but he's very trustworthy. You know he would give his life for the Org. Your father saved him."

"He is a good guy, I know, but Lisa brought up a good point."

"Which is…?"

"How is it that Nick made it into your office undetected if he didn't have someone on the inside?"

"Lisa? Really?"

"I know, I know. She pointed out that he made it in and out of your office too fast to have done it with no inside help, and we all know Andrew is the best at that." He paused to look at me. "I guess if I really believed that myself, I wouldn't have trusted him to bring everyone here. But if something happens here, I certainly will not have him take us to the other secret Org location."

"How many secret Org locations do we have?"

"Just two," he answered.

"*Just?*"

"Keep it to yourself."

"Uh-huh. Isn't that too many? Like overboard?"

"For the kind of work we do, you can never have too many back-up plans. You know how my dad is…he's the most meticulous, controlling, and obsessive person I've ever met."

He had some nerve judging his dad, when he was just as OCD. We went down two sets of stairs and made it into an office without any windows, which honestly, made me feel a bit claustrophobic. He walked past me and took a seat at his desk while I waited for him to begin, purposely not saying any words or making any eye contact.

"I have to say a few things to you, Annie. First off, I have to say I'm sorry."

"You're sorry for what, exactly?" This was already interesting. This man never apologized.

"You're not making this easy for me, huh?"

I shook my head from side to side.

"Okay, well, I guess I'll continue now. May I?"

I nodded, this time with a smirk.

"All right, Annie, here goes. He really is after you. Nick wants you for two reasons: one, your power, and two, he is still in love with you."

"Ha! That second reason was funny."

"The 'he is still in love you' part is not a matter to laugh about, Annie. He does love you. In our negotiations with him, he—I—"

"Negotiations with him? You're in contact with him?

How?"

"He has reached out to us, Annie. He emailed us through various, funky emails. He's really good with computers, you know that, so we haven't been able to track him. He's good at covering his tracks. The IP addresses have been re-routed through several countries. That guy really gets on my nerves."

I couldn't help but smile. Nick was really good. Too bad he was using his talents to hurt people.

"Okay, go on," I said.

"So all he keeps asking for is you."

"What does he want from me?"

"You are the most powerful Luminary because you're full of energy. With you by his side he can continue without needing his monthly injection to keep him strong. He wants us to hand you over to him, and if we do, he promises to stop trying to do anything else. As if we're that stupid. Lisa would have given you up in a heartbeat, but thank goodness she's shared all the emails with me," Derek said.

"Why would he contact her and not you?"

"Why does he do anything?"

"Good point."

"Right, so he wants us to hand you over. I've made it clear that you are well-protected from him. And just so he understands the other aspect, I also made clear that you have forgotten all about him."

"How exactly did you make it clear to him?" I knew where this was going…

"I told him that we are together, to let him know you're mine now. No big deal," he shrugged.

"How dare you tell people we're together? We are not together, and I certainly am not yours!"

"Relax, I know that. And I'm not telling *people*, I just told him specifically so he would leave you alone, in case that's all he wants you for." He stood up and came over to me. "Are you really mad at me for trying to make him leave you alone, or are you mad because you're still in love with him?"

"No, you're right. I'm sorry and thank you. You really are a great friend, Derek, and I do appreciate it."

"A great friend. I guess that's all I am to you, huh?"

"Derek, I don't know. I had a wonderful time with you last night, and I like you a lot. I just don't know if it's wise to get involved with my boss."

"Yesterday was because I was your friend and whatnot, and now it's because I'm your boss?"

"I, umm. . ."

"Save it, Annie. I want you to give me a chance and date me, but things are more complicated now. I care for you a great deal, and no matter how you take this—as your boss or as your friend—I'm demanding that you stay with me until we get our hands on Nick."

"You're kidding, right?"

"No, I'm not kidding. I have to keep you secured, and that is the best way I know how to do it, not to mention the fact that the only person I trust is me, so I want you with me."

"I'm not about to change my life because of him. If Nick wants me, let him come and get me." I snapped my head up and continued, "Actually, that would help you. It will only be a matter of time before he comes for me at my house, and you can catch him there."

"That's a big risk, Annie, and I'm definitely not willing to take it," he said.

"I can stay with Beth and Andrew. They can take care of me, and if someone were to show up, Andrew can get me out of there in no time."

"You're forgetting the part where I don't trust them." He raised his hands. "Control yourself!"

I hadn't realized my hands were in fists.

"Like I said before, Andrew was, and might still be, his best friend. And Beth? Well, I don't know. If you think about it, he could have killed her last night and he didn't."

"Are you serious, Derek? She almost *did* die. If Jenny hadn't been there, we would be planning her funeral right now. He didn't do her any favors. You know that better than I do. You're a healer! And you know we were lucky Jenny and I both were there. Otherwise…I don't even want to imagine what would have happened."

"Okay, calm down, I know you're still shaken up, and I know they're your friends. I've known them for a long time, and they've always shown loyalty to the Org, but I also know they cared for him."

"They care for *me* more," I said.

"Even if they didn't care for him, Nick knows them

so well, he could probably hypnotize them in one second flat to find out where you are."

"Well, that still defeats the purpose," I pointed out.

"How so?"

"Then he can find out I'm with you so it would still be no secret."

"That's where you're wrong, Annie. They don't know where I live. And neither do you, for that matter," he said.

"I've been to your place before."

"No, you've been to one of my places before, but where I'm taking you for safety will be a very secret place."

"Derek, I appreciate your concern, I do, but I'm not going anywhere."

"You don't understand, it's not only you I'm concerned about. There are other lives at risk here. If he gets ahold of you and your powers there is no telling what he will do. Annie, you are the weapon he wants."

"Weapon? The last time I checked I wasn't locked up in a vault, which is where you said the weapon he was after was being kept."

"I just said that so they would understand the danger. Besides, there is obviously something in that vault he wants. I think it's something that will either help him get to you or steal your strength. The only information I received regarding the contents is that it was related to quality control substance. A laboratory storage of some sort."

"Steal my strength? Is that even possible?"

"It's only speculation, but look at us and what we can do. Most people wouldn't think this is possible, and yet here we are. Either way, I'm not sure about the substance. I'm just trying to put two and two together until I get some concrete information that makes full sense. The only thing I know for sure is that you are part of his plans."

"Then I'll stop taking my shots, and there will be nothing to worry about."

"NO!" Derek screamed so violently it had my ears ringing. "You will not stop taking them. You need them to protect yourself."

"I don't see the problem." I let my shoulders fall.

"The problem, Annie," he took a few deep breaths as if to compose himself before continuing, "is that once he realizes you have no power, he will not hesitate to kill you."

"You said he still loved me. I don't see how he can love and kill me at the same time, if it were true." He started shaking his head, but I continued. "You're just contradicting yourself, Derek. Besides, it doesn't matter. He'll probably just think that him taking my powers just can't be done, and he'll probably let me go."

"A man in his state of mind might find love to be a weakness, and he might even kill you so that you don't hold him back. Believe me, Annie, he will kill you." He held my hand.

"Then there will be one thing less for you to worry

about."

"How can you say that? You know how I feel about you," he said, placing my hand on his chest.

I moved away, uncomfortable. "I mean that he can't use me to get stronger without his monthly shots. Speaking of that, I don't understand it, Derek. How is it that he still has powers if he's been gone over three years? He shouldn't be able to do anything."

"He stole a large supply when he left."

"It was never reported."

"No, we didn't report it. We didn't know he would use it to hurt people. Dad thought that Nick just didn't want to part with his powers," he said.

"I thought I knew him, I really did."

"Of course you did. You were married to him, but he fooled all of us. I thought of him as my friend, Annie, and even I got burned."

I laughed. "No, you didn't. You never liked him."

"Okay, not friends like buddy friends, but we were good co-workers, we were partners for a while, and then he started acting hostile against me."

"That's because you were flirting with his wife all the time."

"I was just being nice to you."

"Nice is what you call it?" I asked.

"Okay, I was flirting, but it was because I felt we had a connection."

"I was married!"

"But always, always so beautiful and friendly with

me. I just thought maybe you weren't happy with him, and really prayed that you were secretly in love with me," he said, grinning.

"I wasn't."

"Ouch."

"Derek, don't make this situation more complicated, please."

"If it were someone else, I wouldn't give them a choice, but since it's you and I want you to know that I respect your decision as a friend, as an employee, and as a woman, I want you to tell me what you want."

# CHAPTER SIX

"JUST LIKE THAT?" Beth asked.

"Just like that."

"Wow, babe..."

"Well, okay, not just like that," I said.

"I knew it! How then? Did you have to kiss him into submission?"

"No, but I probably would have if it had come down to it. I'm not into being under surveillance every second of the day. I made him see reason and convinced him without having to sell myself."

"And what reasoning is this?" she asked.

"That if I'm not hidden, we have more chances of getting Nick, since he'll want to come after me."

"So you'll stay in your house, and what? Act as bait with Andrew so he can get you out when the time comes? Gosh, I love my man, he really is so convenient," she said.

"He really is… I have a key chain that will set off an alarm. If I press it, it will notify him and everyone else."

"But you know Derek will have more of us surrounding your house, right?"

"I know, I guess I'll have to accept that. Heck, as long as I don't have to give up too much of my personal freedom, I suppose I'm good."

After filling Beth in on my date and last conversation with Derek, I left to go find Jenny. I still didn't know what had happened last night, but I did know Derek had lied to everyone about at least one little detail. I didn't want to ask Beth since she was the injured party. It had to be Jenny. She would have far more insight on things. She was still in the room where we had all gathered that morning, and she looked lost in her thoughts.

"Hey, Annie," she said.

"*Jenny*?"

She nodded. "You have questions. I have some answers, but not all of them."

"Give me what you have, it's all I ask."

"Come on, I've been waiting for you. We'll talk, but away from the others."

I followed Jenny to the stairway, and we went to what looked like a supply room. This secret Org location was almost as big as the original.

"How did you know this was here?" I pointed around the supply room.

"I didn't. I was just taking the stairs and hoped to find something."

"Oh, it looked like you walked straight here."

"I guess it's the sensor in me," she said as she started twirling her blonde hair, a dead giveaway that she was nervous.

"I thought it only worked with people. I never knew you could sense objects or places."

"No, I didn't, either, but lately I've noticed that I've been better at sensing other Luminaries' powers and getting to what I want when I want it. Don't repeat that to anyone. I need to learn to control it before I tell Derek."

"You got it, Jenny. Now will you tell me what I need to know?" I got a smile in response. "Where exactly *were* you guys last night? I know Derek said it was by the Org, but you guys came to my house, so I'm guessing he lied." I looked her dead in the eye. It was nice to deal with someone as short as I was from time to time.

"Yes, I'm not sure why he lied, since he did tell everyone that Nick was after you." Concern washed over her face. "You need to be really careful. We found Nick by a building that was two blocks away from your house. It was an empty office space on the 6th floor, and it had a very clear view of your house."

"How did you know he was there?"

"Derek was searching for a place he could use as a lookout for you. Lisa was on top of that when she caught a glimpse of Nick. She alerted Derek right away, but after checking out the office space, she insisted she wasn't prepared to face Nick so he called us and off we went," she said.

"Why would you guys try to take him on alone?"

"We didn't. He wasn't in the building, but other people were in there. Nick must have seen them and was standing watch to see who they were."

"How do you know that? You talked to him?"

"Yes, we talked, but it wasn't because we confronted him. It was afterwards. Beth and I just went as lookouts to see what his moves would be. And more than anything, we were supposed to make sure he didn't see us."

"Okay…so that was a fail."

She shrugged. "He was in the café that's in the opposite corner of the building. We were in there too, and I guess he saw us, but we didn't realize he was there. I sensed him and thought it was because he was close, but really, we were only a few tables apart. Anyway, the men who were in the building came down to the café. I'm not sure how they knew they were being watched, but they did. They made a scene. Beth and I decided it was better to take it outside, to make sure no innocent people got hurt. They cornered us in the parking lot, and Nick actually tried to help us. He hit Beth by mistake. Then he held them off long enough for me to get her out of there."

"He didn't hit her by mistake," I said.

"Yes, Annie, it was a mistake. He didn't have to come and help us, but he did, and he was mad at us because we pretty much blew his cover. I'm not even sure if the place was his or theirs. Lisa swears it's the same office where she saw him. Regardless, they hadn't noticed that he had been watching them for a whole week, and…well, we screwed that up for him."

"Screwed that up? Listen to yourself, Jenny, it's almost as if you're on his side."

"I'm not on his side. All I know is that the man explained what I just said, and I didn't sense that he was lying."

"When did you even get the chance to talk to him?" I asked.

"While we were fighting the other guys. Look, he's an enemy, I know, but he wouldn't let them hurt you or us. He caught one of them and was questioning why they were after you, but his friend took advantage of that distraction and came after me. Nick tried to beam him, but Beth came to help me. She was so fast he didn't see her, and she was caught in the crossfire. It was a direct hit by Nick, and he felt really bad. He was actually the one who suggested I try transferring your energy so I could heal Beth faster."

"It was his idea?"

"Yes, that's why Derek is so sure Nick wants you so he can use you," Jenny said.

"Forget Derek for now. How did Nick know we could use each other's power?"

"I don't know, but I'm glad he suggested it. I did question his motives in helping us, and he said he had no issues with us, but that we should know you're in danger, and we should keep an eye on you. Derek thinks he's playing us by pretending he cares about your well-being," she said.

"What? Like appealing to your sensitive side?"

"Yes, Derek thinks Nick staged the whole thing, and that he is saying there's a third party involved so we can waste some time looking into other possibilities while he gets to you."

"Isn't that stupid, though? Try to get more surveillance on me so he can get to me?"

"Not if he gets one of us to take you to him and hand you over."

"Who do you believe, Jenny? Because what I'm hearing between the lines is that you seem to think he saved you guys out there…and that he really wants to protect me."

"I don't know," she said.

"Yes, you do."

She was busy twirling her hair. "I think you want to believe he's still good."

"That's not what I asked. Did he try to deceive you or did he help you? Jenny, you're my friend. Please tell me what you think."

"What does it matter what I think? Ask Beth. She's your best friend in the whole wide world, right?"

"I'm asking you because I know you love me, and because you are the greatest sensor out there right now. So, what did you sense?"

"I think he helped us, and I do believe he wants to protect you, but I'm not sure if he hypnotized me or not. My thoughts aren't trustworthy right now. I'm not about to forget all the damage he's done and all the lives he has taken in the past years. Just watch your back. And I guess it's not my place, but still, I would give Derek a chance. He's good for you, and we know his intentions are good. He loves you for sure, Annie. Nick…well, I don't know. I really, really don't know. I'm sorry."

"Thanks, Jen," I sighed.

"I have to go now. I'm sure Derek is looking for me. If I learn anything else, I'll let you know. And if Derek asks me, I'll tell him I told you everything the same way I reported it," she said.

"Okay." *Oh, Jenny…always the rule follower!*

I went back to the conference area and waited with everyone else who was going in for assignments. Some of them had left and some had come back. The ones who had stayed were gossiping about me. And Lisa, being the instigator that she was, kept fueling their fires. It didn't bother me, though. Being Nick's ex-wife didn't make me guilty of his actions.

It was a long day, but I waited for Derek. I don't know why, I just felt it was the right thing to do. He looked so exhausted when he got out.

"Did you come straight here after you left my place last night?" I asked.

"Yes, I did."

"I'm guessing you're hungry."

"That I am," he smiled.

"Come on, come by my place and I'll make you some dinner."

"No, I want to actually sleep tonight. But you are

coming to my place, and we'll pick up some food on the way."

"Okay, but I'm going home right after," I said.

"Please, don't argue right now. I'm so tired that I'm practically begging you to stay at my house tonight. I don't want to be interrupted at all. No offense, but that wouldn't change even if Nick broke into your place."

"No offense taken," I laughed.

"Will you come and stay the night?"

I don't know what it was, but the way he looked at me made my heart skip a beat, and I couldn't help but say yes.

"I know you talked to Jenny. I just want you to know that everything that happens with Nick involved is only because he has premeditated all the details and is in control of what we know. It pains me to say that since I'm such a control freak, but it's true. I don't know what to do about him, I really don't. All I know is that I can keep you safe as long as you're by my side."

"How can you be so sure of what he wants?"

"Look at this email." He took out his Blackberry and searched for what he needed and handed it over to me to read.

*Derek,*

*My friend. It was really easy to have your people work with me. They just had to think that we were on the same side and fought with me, not against me. Doesn't that piss you off? The irony is that I didn't even have to use my special influence on them. They just trusted me, no questions asked. Isn't that like a kick in the nuts? I am so blessed that my friends will always—and I do mean always—be my friends. You can try to have them on your side, but I worked my magic on them for many years, and whenever I decide to, I can hypnotize them to deliver Annie to me. I have no issues with any one of them. I just want Annie. How is Beth, by the way? Send her my regards!*

The bottom of the email had the same picture I'd seen on Derek's computer, with the caption, 'She is mine.'

"That bastard."

"I've been telling you," he said.

"How did he get this picture?"

"I don't know. He keeps attaching it to all his emails."

*Okay, so Derek wasn't the stalker. That's good.*

"He used Beth to see if the energy transfer would work," I suddenly realized.

"Yes, he risked her life. He is not a good man, Annie. Please don't let him fool you."

"I'm not a fool. Not again, anyway. I fell for it once, but not anymore. Come on, let's go get you some food and a good night's sleep."

"As long as you're by my side, it will be a peaceful sleep."

"Oh, stop it."

"No, I'm serious. I won't have to worry that you

might be in danger."

"Okay, well, I feel better, then."

"You should," he said, laughing.

This time we took the elevator and went all the way to the top floor. It was only three floors, which surprised me. We got out in the lobby of a hotel that was adjacent to the building where the original Org was located.

"You really don't think this is risky? Being in the same spot?" I asked him.

"Yes and no. The risky part is if they try to use this same building to spy on us, but since they can get into the old Org with no problem, I don't see why they would. They'll see that we've vacated. Why would there be any reason to keep watch at the same empty place? There is nothing for them to watch or take."

"You know you're mumbling, right?"

"I'm tired," he said, yawning. "They'll never guess we're underground. Besides, they'll just try to figure out where we are now by following some fake leads I've leaked with the FBI and CIA."

I smiled. "I don't think you're supposed to use your Bureau connections for this."

"I help them, they help me. Anyway, they'll be busy for a while."

"Who are they?" I asked.

"Nick and the people who work for him. Those men who attacked Beth and Jenny, I'm almost positive they were in on it. Regardless, there's no reason for anyone to come back to the old Org."

"They might, you never know," I said.

"I have no doubt the old Org will remain under surveillance by Nick's people, on the odd chance that something was forgotten or left behind in the move. But I can assure you, they will find nothing. Everything has been moved, and what was left, I burned. All Nick will find there is a pile of ashes."

"You burned my stuff?"

"Yours and everyone else's," he said, laughing.

"That's horrible, stop laughing! You should have given us a chance to get our possessions. Poor Jenny is going to have a heart attack. She keeps everything."

"And all of those things were transported to the new Org. Everyone's offices are as they left them, just in a different location. I left chairs and empty things that were not important…those are the only things I burned, I promise."

"How come I didn't get to see my office today?"

"First things first. I had the security team check every single crack in the building to make sure that we were safe and secure. I kept everyone together in the event that we weren't."

"Derek?"

"Annie?"

"I don't know how you do it. How do you deal with the stress of being in charge of all of us, national security, and whatever else? You're only thirty years old. I would go crazy!"

"Not so much national security. Our area of expertise

is only to assist when needed. There are always terrorists and other threats that the government hires us to investigate, but technically, anyone can hire us. We choose to do good with our special gifts. We work with the government and help secure and protect all the secret branches within it. But we could easily work against them if we wanted to. Right now, though, I don't want to work for anyone but ourselves. There's a big enemy who is dangerous to us, and my priority right now is to protect each Luminary. In particular, you."

We reached the parking lot and went to a small SUV that had a bunch of stickers with 'Baby on board' and 'My kid is an honor student' on it. A short, bald guy came and opened the back door for us to get in, and a plump woman joined him on the passenger side.

"Wow, this is interesting," I said. "But what about the others?"

"Andrew and Kevin will take care of everyone else," Derek said.

"Kevin? Who is that?"

"He is a young Luminary, newly turned."

"He can open up portals as well?" I asked.

"Nope, Kevin teleports."

"How long does it take?"

"It's instantaneous."

"Nice." I nodded in approval.

He started laughing and whispered for me not to worry, when I pointed to the driver and his wife. He then grabbed my hand and intertwined his fingers with mine. I couldn't move. It felt so different. Maybe it was because he was so protective of me, the strongest girl, but I liked it, so I didn't pull away.

"Lisa did that?" I pointed my chin at the couple. "She hypnotized them?"

"Yes, that's the work of Lisa."

"So she knows where you live?"

"No, I told them where to take me."

"But she can make them tell her if she wants to," I said, knowing that Lisa loved to use her hypnotizing powers without reservations.

"Yes, but we aren't going there. We're being dropped off at a restaurant where I have my own car," he said.

"If you can transport objects, why can't you transport yourself?"

"Because I'm not Kevin or Andrew."

"Bummer."

"You're telling me," he said with a smile. "My life would certainly be much easier if I could do more than healing and manipulating materials." He took my hand and put it to his lips. "I'll do everything in my power to protect you, I promise."

"I think I can handle myself."

"I know, but you can get in over your head, and as much as you think you're invulnerable, it's not impossible to hurt you."

"True, but it will take a whole lot out of the other person to do that," I said.

"Unless there's blood around," he laughed.

"Funny! Well…without a pool of blood around me, I'm almost indestructible."

"And you don't know how grateful I am for that. I don't know what I would do if something happened to you, Annie."

"You would have your revenge," I said, looking away from his deep stare.

"That, my darling, is one hundred percent true." We didn't need to specify who would be the one to pay.

After we were dropped off, we went into the restaurant to collect the takeout Derek had previously ordered. We got his Mercedes-Benz, which was parked in the back, and made our way to his house. He drove for about an hour, so that would mean he was about an hour and a half from the Org. Making a long drive like that every day would kill me. He seemed quite content.

"How do you drive so far each day?" I asked.

"I don't."

"So what do you do?"

"I stay at my condo, which, as you know, is closer to the Org."

"Oh, well that makes sense, then. I'm guessing you came all the way here because I'm with you. I feel bad now…you would have been eating and sleeping much sooner."

"Yes. But this way I'll be sleeping much deeper. Otherwise, I would be too worried to allow myself to relax."

# CHAPTER SEVEN

IT WAS A big Victorian house, which seemed quite old but full of character. Most of the furniture were antiques kept in excellent condition. The walls were a pale yellow with some wallpaper borders. It had a lot of wood panels in two of the opposite walls, with a mirror in the middle. It looked as though it could have been the dining room, but there was no furniture in it.

"I'm looking for the right table to put in there," he said, noticing that I was staring at it. "I know it looks odd, empty, but none of the tables I purchased seemed to fit nicely, although the one you have might be just perfect."

"Oh, I know the guy who made it. He owns a craft store with his father, and he likes to build furniture on the side as his hobby. I can pass along a referral, if you want."

"That would be nice, Annie, but I was trying to

throw you a hint. I want your actual table, along with you, in this house. Eventually of course. I know you're not ready yet."

I had nothing to say. I was very torn. I liked Derek a lot, stalking tendencies aside, and I knew I could trust him, but Nick had done a horrible number on me. I got by in life by walking around only half alive, and it really wasn't fair to Derek. He was offering me his full love, and all I had to offer him in return was a broken instrument inside, beating as my heart.

We ate and he walked me to the guest room.

"I think this was a successful second date, what do you think?" he asked.

"This wasn't a date."

"For our lifestyles, it kind of was, Annie. We have to take it when we get it." He smiled and turned to look at me. "The only thing that would make it perfect would be a goodnight kiss for the man who is currently keeping you safe from your evil ex-husband."

"You're babbling and you need your rest, Derek. How about a rain check?"

"Of course. You'll find everything you need in the closet. I'm right across the hall if you need me. Sweet dreams."

"And to you," I said, smiling. I actually wanted to kiss him. His brown eyes were so full of understanding when I turned him down, yet again. I would hate being responsible for breaking his heart the same way mine had been destroyed. I couldn't do that to him, I just couldn't.

Still, maybe I did deserve a chance myself. As Jenny would say, there was only one way to find out the outcome of any dilemma: dive in.

Derek slept in until seven o'clock, which he assured me was a late start to the day. For me, sleeping in meant lying in bed until at least ten o'clock in the morning, but I guess to each his own. Maybe it was a sign that we couldn't work out, because if I did give him a chance, and he woke me up at seven every morning to tell me it was late, I would kick him. And my kicks were powerful, so he'd better not expect me to have the same sleep schedule as his...I might just be his demise.

We picked up coffee and breakfast on the way to a different restaurant where the same couple from the previous night waited to drive us back to the hotel. We walked into the Org and went straight to the conference room, finding that almost everyone was there.

Derek walked up to the head of the table. "Good morning. I want everyone to meet a new member of our team. He is only seventeen years old, but has big potential. His skill is the reason why we activated him this early." He picked up his cell phone and made a call. "Kevin, why don't you join us now?"

Out of nowhere, a young boy appeared. He seemed scared but eagerly excited to be there. He was tall and skinny. He definitely needed to start bulking up if he were going to be in the line of fire with us, but then again, he could disappear whenever he wanted to...so maybe not. He had a military buzz cut and dark hazel eyes. His face was definitely a young boy's face, but he had a charm about him, especially when he smiled. In a year or two, he was going to do well with the ladies, for sure.

"Kevin, this is everyone. Everyone, this is Kevin Pierce. Some of you have already met him, but for those who haven't, I will ask you to come up and introduce yourselves to him. I have to leave now. I have an important meeting to get to. Lisa, please stay with Annie and Kevin. Everyone else, you will find that your offices are in this building, along with your belongings. There's a directory that Samantha will give you. If you have any problems, please have her relay the message. If it's an emergency, you have each other." He stopped at the door and looked back to say, "As far as Kevin goes, he is a powerful teleporter. He is responsible for you having your belongings here, so you can thank him. He made it much easier for Andrew and me."

Some people went up to Kevin, welcomed him into the Org, and wished him luck. Lisa, being Lisa, went up and pulled him away and told everyone to leave him alone and to get to work. I waited right where I was. Since I knew I'd be stuck with Kevin and Lisa for probably the whole day, I didn't see any reason to move from my chair.

"Annie, follow me, please. I'll be babysitting you two in my office. Some of us have actual work to do," she said, looking dead at me. I turned away from her.

"Hi Kevin. I'm Annie, welcome to the Org—"

Lisa cut in, "Yes, welcome. Too bad you came at a time where everything is in havoc, thanks to this one here," she said, pointing at me. "If you survive these times, then you're not as flimsy and weak as you look. It would be nice if you could grow a beard so I at least wouldn't want to close my eyes when I look at you."

"No, I'm fine with my face like this. My look is perfect for fooling people, so I'm not changing it anytime soon," Kevin said.

"Just follow me," she said, looking at us with what felt like piercing daggers.

"Good one," I whispered to Kevin, and out of nowhere, he gave me a high five. I couldn't help but laugh. At least he'd keep me entertained while we were being watched by Lisa. "By the way, it's not my fault that we're in this situation."

"Oh, no?" asked Lisa. "Then why are we all hiding here and protecting you from the outside world? Nick is after you, which is why he broke into the Org. He'll probably find this one soon, too." She looked at Kevin. "Nick and Annie were bound together in holy matrimony."

"You're married?" he asked, frowning.

"I *was* married."

"Yes, and now she's seeing the big boss. What they see in her is beyond me. She's so plain," Lisa said, twisting her mouth and looking me up and down, "whereas I take care of myself properly."

"That just makes you high maintenance,

Lisa...another way of calling you a bitch," I said, smiling.

She winked at Kevin. "Well, that I am. Born a bitch, always a bitch...you know how that goes." She turned to me with a smile, surprising me in the act.

"I see what they see. Annie is pretty and she's nice," Kevin chimed in.

"And she can break your neck with her pinky if you dare touch her," Beth said, coming from behind us.

"Oh, wow. You're beautiful!" he said with his mouth hanging open.

"I know. And you are very observant. Kevin, right?" She gave him a smile.

"Yes, ma'am."

"Don't call me that. I'm not that old." Beth playfully patted his head.

"Don't call any of us that, or I'll break your neck myself," Lisa said. This caused Beth to bring her eyebrows together, giving me a puzzled look.

"I dunno..." I whispered to Beth. Lisa being friendly and making jokes was new to us.

"Lisa?" Kevin asked.

"What?"

"You're beautiful, too. You're just mean."

"Thanks, Kevin. Now tell me something I don't know," she said.

"Your stockings are ripped," he said, looking at her leg.

"What?"

"Your stockings are ripped. That's something you didn't know," he said, pointing to Lisa's right calf. She looked at it and said some bad words that maybe she shouldn't have said in front of Kevin.

"Fantastic! Now I have to take them off and throw them out."

"Maybe you shouldn't be dressing all corporate when you're in the fighting business," he suggested.

"I fight with my mind, not physically. Now, you guys, don't leave my office. Beth, you watch them while I go take these off."

"I can help you with that if you want," Kevin said.

"You little—" she went after him. "Don't you respect—"

I held her back from hitting him.

"I thought you weren't into the physical fights much," Beth said, standing in front of Kevin.

"I meant I can transport them off of you so you don't have to leave us," he explained.

"Oh…okay, do that then," Lisa narrowed her eyes and placed her hands on her waist.

He stared at her legs and took a deep breath, closed his eyes, and suddenly, her stockings were in the trash right behind her.

"Okay, that was awesome!" Beth exclaimed. "That's going to be useful when you start dating."

"If you ladies would like to help me practice, I wouldn't mind," he grinned.

"I'm sure you wouldn't mind. You fresh boy, you!" I

said. He was funny. Probably crossing the line too much, but I had to admit he was entertaining. I spent most of the day with him in Lisa's office. She worked on her computer while we joked around and got to know each other. He brought out the wicked teenager in me, which was nice. It had been a long time since I'd allowed myself to just be completely silly and act immature.

"That's it. You are officially my little brother!"

"I'm not that sick in the head," he growled.

"Why do you say that? I would make a great sister," I said.

"Because I doubt I would have a crush on my own sister."

"Well, in that case you *are* sick," I said.

"Relax, I can admire your beauty and your sense of humor without thinking I'd ever have a chance with you. Besides, you're way too old for me."

"You got that right."

"Like, way too old," he teased.

"All right, point taken. And I'm not that old. So how come you don't have a girlfriend?"

"Who said I didn't?"

I raised my eyebrow at him.

"Fine, I don't. But that's all right. For now, I'm just enjoying playing the field."

"What field?" I laughed.

"I got close to a few girls in the training house."

"You're not supposed to be dating there," I said.

"Did you really not date anyone when you were

there?"

"Well, I did. But I married him after I finished training, so that makes it okay."

"But you dated. So you can't tell me anything," he said.

"Okay, you win. I was just talking about policy."

His lip curled up. "Yes, policy you didn't follow."

"You win this one," I laughed.

"Why did you get married so young?"

"We were sure we wanted nothing other than to spend our lives together, so we didn't see any reason to wait. I was eighteen and naïve, what can I say?"

"But now you're divorced."

"Right," I said softly.

"I didn't mean to make you sad. This Nick guy, how can he be so bad if someone like you loves him?" Kevin asked.

"I don't love him. Not anymore. I guess he just enjoyed taking me for a fool."

"I don't think so. No guy in his right mind gets married that young and then leaves his wife hanging," he said with conviction.

"He didn't leave me hanging. One minute we were happy, and the next, he was gone with no explanations, no goodbyes…and now he's after me."

Kevin stared at me for a moment. "Maybe he wants you to join him."

"He knows I wouldn't. He just wants to use me."

"I won't let him hurt you."

"That's sweet, but you can't stop him. Nor should you have to be responsible."

"Well, I have to be with you at all times to transport you to safety at a moment's notice, so you can be sure no one will get close enough to harm you. I won't allow it."

"Don't underestimate him. There is a reason why he hasn't been caught."

"And don't you underestimate me," he said, and touched my arm. I found myself standing on top of the couch instead of next to him. I hadn't even felt him moving me, nor did he close his eyes to concentrate.

"How did you do that?" I asked.

"I transported you, duh."

"Yes, but that was so fast, and you didn't concentrate like you did with Lisa's stockings."

"I know. I'm good like that. Well, not that good. You're a person, so I have to touch you to teleport you," he said. "But stockings are nothing. I just needed to think it and it was done. I only pretended to concentrate before, so I could stare at her long legs without her hurting me."

"I heard that! You sneaky punk," Lisa said from across the room.

"This is a private conversation," he said.

"Not private to me if you're in my office. And by the way, I hope you enjoyed staring at my legs because next time I catch you doing that, I will definitely hurt you."

"I did enjoy it, thanks. They are perfect, which is why I know you won't hurt me. If you hurt every man for staring, which is what you want us to do, then you wouldn't be wearing short, tight skirts."

"Fact one: I will hurt you. Fact two: I do love the attention. And fact three: they are perfect," she smirked.

"What about your legs, Annie? How do they look?" he asked, turning to me.

"You mean in a skirt? Or when I'm kicking you?"

"No, just in general. I can check them out for you and let you know if you need to work on them."

"Her legs are muscular in a manly way," Lisa said.

"No, they're not. They are toned…in a feminine way," I said.

"Whatever! You two are giving me a headache. Now you, transporting guy, get us some food."

"I can't leave you guys," Kevin said.

"I didn't say to leave," Lisa answered. "Just transport some food to us. I want sushi."

"I can't do that. It would be stealing."

"Fine. I'll ask Samantha what we have upstairs, and you can transport it down. Sadly, I'm sure there is no sushi."

After we ate, Samantha brought us each a folder to read. Mine was an email from Derek instructing me to take Kevin home with me, or rather for him to take me home when our shifts were over. Also, he told me I didn't have to worry about spending any more time with Lisa. Every single security detail was covered at the new Org, and if I wanted to work in my office, it was fine as long as I had Kevin with me. He also said he missed me. I guess sometimes this obsessive guy could be sweet.

"Mine says I can set you two free, so please get the hell out of my office," Lisa announced.

We got up to leave, and once Kevin was out the door, Lisa said, "By the way, he fooled everyone, not just you." I looked at her, knowing she was talking about Nick, but she just turned her head back to the computer and continued typing.

# CHAPTER EIGHT

MY OFFICE WAS actually right around the corner from Derek's, no surprise there, and it was almost exactly the same as my old one. I signed into my computer and found another email from Derek telling me to help with Kevin's martial arts training.

"How much self-defense do you know?" I asked Kevin.

"None."

"What were you doing at training all this time?"

"All this time? I was only there for three weeks when they pulled me out."

"Three weeks only? That's odd. Normally we bring new recruits in no older than sixteen. Where were you before that? You have parents?"

"Of course I have parents. Everyone does. I just don't know them. I met Derek's father about a month ago in the hospital," he said.

"The hospital? I'm shocked they didn't find you earlier."

"Yes, Dr. Lake met me there and...it doesn't matter. My foster dad beat me up and left me on the street...at least, that's what I'm told. I don't remember anything before the hospital. I almost feel like he erased my memory when he beat the crap out of me."

"I'm sorry." I heard an alarm going off in my head but wasn't sure what it was about.

"Don't be. I don't remember the beating. I was in a coma, I woke up and my whole life is like new. They caught my foster father, and he confessed to the beating. Apparently, I've been in the system since I was born. My mom was some kind of addict, and she overdosed while pregnant...she died giving birth to me."

"I'm sorry," I said.

"There's nothing to be sorry about. It was a sad life from what I can tell, and I'm very happy to be leaving it behind. In some ways, I feel indebted to my foster father for helping me forget it and giving me a shot at a new life. I'm surrounded by beautiful women like you, Beth, and even Lisa, and the best part is that you all have crushes on me."

"Hahaha, we'd be crazy not to."

"See what I mean? It seems like a good trade off, almost dying and instead living with angel-like creatures."

"Some things are just meant to be."

"Yes, they are. Hey, do you think Beth will give me

a nice kiss when she hears my sad, *sad* story?"

"Ummm, no, but maybe I can convince her to give you a pat on the back."

"Works for me," he said, grinning.

"You should come with me some time to visit other orphans," I said.

"Where do you go?"

"I visit different ones, but I spend extra time at my old orphanage."

"Why? What do you do there?"

"Spend time with the kids. Take stuff for them. Make sure they feel cared for. And send cupcakes once a month so they can all celebrate their birthdays, things like that."

"That's nice, Annie. I know a lot of kids who would appreciate that. It's great that you do that for them."

"I do it for me," I whispered. "Okay, that's enough talking. So you haven't received any physical training at all. This should be fun."

"You sound scary. Take it easy on me, will you?" he asked.

"I'll see what I can do. What did you do in those three weeks, then?"

"They've been training me to use my teleportation powers. They've hardly spent any time explaining what we do here. I'm not even sure if we are good or bad," he joked.

"Oh, hang on. Do you not know about Luminaries?"

"Nope."

"And you didn't think to ask?"

"Yes, but they said it was 'imperative' that I learn to control my skills first."

I had Kevin transport a punching bag and a treadmill from the gym to my office, and I had him running while I went over the basics of what we did in the Org.

"So basically, what you're saying is that we're like the CIA, but with powers?" he asked.

"Something like that, sure. Except we don't work for the government, we just offer our services to them. We spy and do what they want, but quicker than they would on their own. It's one way of making sure they don't shut us down."

"Well, they wouldn't shut us down. They need us."

"Right."

"And Dr. Lake is the one who started the whole Org?"

"Yes, he did. Of the three founders, he is the only one still alive."

His eyes widened. "Tell me it wasn't the powers that killed the others."

"No, that would be Nick."

"Oh…" he turned his head, clearly feeling awkward. "Why is it called the Org?"

"For Luminary Organization. When they first started, it was just a few of them who worked on the experiment. When they discovered what they could do with the formula they'd created, they decided to go by the code name 'the Org,' and I guess the name stuck."

"Boring!"

I laughed as I went to the little refrigerator and got us two bottles of water. Before I turned around, one bottle had disappeared from my hand and, of course, Kevin was already drinking from it. "Do you have any more questions for me?" I asked.

"Yes. How did they know that the substance from the falling sky would give us powers?"

"It didn't fall from the sky, silly. Honestly, I can't believe they didn't at least go over the basics with you," I said.

"Not my fault," he shrugged.

I continued, "In one of NASA's trips to do maintenance on a satellite, they found that what was causing interference was a type of rock. Actually, if I remember correctly, there were lots of chunks of rocks. They hit the satellite and caused some parts to break. They believed it was caught in a meteor shower. Anyway, they brought the rocks to Earth, only to find that they had melted in our atmosphere. After many years of investigating the substance, Larry Lumin, the lead scientist, discovered it had healed some of his cuts. Some kind of accident happened, and his skin had come in contact with it. He realized what had happened and did all sorts of experiments until he came up with the right formula."

"But why would they let him keep the rocks from outer space?" Kevin asked.

"He was a billionaire, so for the right donation, he

was able to own the rocks. As far as NASA was concerned, he only wanted to own a piece of the universe. You know how rich people can be flashy. Anyway, he confided in his good friend, Dr. Derek Lake, who then offered himself as a guinea pig, and the rest is history."

"Who was the third pers—Oh! Wait, I get it. Larry Lumin—Luminary," he said with a little dance.

"Yes, Dr. Lake came up with the name in honor of Dr. Lumin," I said, laughing.

"Who was the third person?"

"A woman. They never mention her name, and the information they have about her is next to nothing."

"I'll bet she was hot, and they were both in love with her, and they couldn't get over their differences so she kicked them both to the curb and—"

"Wow, that's enough. You have an active imagination."

"Oh, come on. What's the gossip on them? You have to know something."

"I don't. I'm not even sure how Nick found out who she was. All we know about her is that there was a female co-founder, and 21 years later she was murdered by Nick Logan. That's literally everything I know about her."

"I'll bet I can find out," he said.

"How?"

"I can transport whatever I want, from anywhere else to me. Of course, first I have to find out where they're keeping that info…"

"Good luck with that."

"What? You're not helping?"

"Do I look like I am?" I raised an eyebrow.

DEREK CAME BACK earlier than expected and asked to have a meeting with Kevin, so Andrew had the job of escorting me home. Once we got there, he followed orders and made sure the house was secured. He waited until Beth came to join him for the night to be my first set of bodyguards.

I spent the next few days locked in my house with Kevin, and I was going insane. Lisa came over to see how I was doing, or rather, to annoy me.

"So why are you here, really?" I asked her.

"I thought you might be bored and maybe you would be up for a little outing."

"Where?"

"Derek sent me to look out for some family over in New Jersey. Wanna come with?"

"Who is this family? And why are you asking me to come with you?" I just didn't trust this girl.

"Listen, you don't have to come. Are you going to eat that?" she asked, pointing at my doughnut. "If not, you can offer it to me. I'm not going to refuse…that would be rude."

"Yes, you are anything but rude, Lisa," I said, rolling

my eyes.

"Just give me that." She snatched the doughnut and took a big bite. "We can have Kevin come with us and get us out of there if we get into any danger."

"I thought we were supposed to be looking after other people, not ourselves," I said and stared her down.

"Yes, but he can get all of us out in no time. What good is he if we can't use him properly?"

"Who are they? The family?"

"The Lumins."

"What? I thought they all had secret identities since their father and mother were killed."

"Yes, but Nick is good at uncovering secrets. Who's to say he can't find them? Derek thinks they might be in possession of their father's research notes," she said. "The older daughter called and said her phone kept ringing at random times during the night, but each time they answered, the caller hung up. They're nervous, so we're just going to do a once-over at their security system. We've already changed their phone numbers."

"You mean you are going to do that, right? I'm no good with any crappy computerized system stuff."

"Yes, and you will have my back," she said.

"Okay, let's do it." I was so excited to get out, I couldn't care less that it was with Lisa. "Kevin!" I turned to find him already standing next to me, grinning.

"One word to Derek and we are all dead, understand?" She looked at Kevin first and then at me.

"Oh, come on, we are the last two people who would

tell him we left the house!" I said.

"All right then, let's go."

We drove up to the front of the gates of what seemed like a mile-long driveway. Lisa touched a button on the wall panel, they asked for a password which she keyed in, and then we waited to be buzzed in. We drove slowly the whole way, looking for signs of any breech, but found nothing. The two middle-aged sisters were standing by the doors waiting for us.

"Hello, ladies," Lisa said.

"Hello," they both answered at the same time.

Two men came out and stood next to them.

"I'm Marie," the taller woman said, "and this is Maggie. Mark here," she pointed to the burly man on her right, "is our bodyguard."

"And I'm Allen, Maggie's husband," the other man said. He seemed to fit well with his wife, both of them slender and with glasses. I stepped up and reached out my hand.

"I'm Annie Fox, and this is Lisa Kinkaid. We were sent from the Organization to make sure everything is secured."

"Yes, follow us this way," Mark said.

"Who is that boy?" Allen asked. To Kevin, he said, "Have I seen you before?"

"No, that's Kevin," I cut in. "He's with us."

"Oh, he looks familiar," Allen frowned.

I looked up at Kevin, and he just gave me a shrug. He wouldn't know either way since he had lost most of his memories.

"These young boys, they all look the same to you," Maggie said. "He's always complaining about the future of our country with boys who walk around with their butts hanging out of their pants." She turned to Kevin. "Not yours, dear. Yours are fine. Your pants, I mean. My husband is just old."

"It's okay," Kevin answered.

"All right, follow me this way," Mark said in a no-nonsense tone.

We walked behind him into the house and made an immediate right. The corridor took us through the kitchen and into an office that was set up with video monitors and several computers. Another man was in there, but he ignored us and went about his day. Kevin and I went to take a look around the backyard and patio while Lisa did her computer thing. After we were done, we met the sisters inside and followed up with some questions for Lisa's report. Since they'd changed their phone number two days before, they had not received any more calls, but they were still nervous.

Lisa was really taking a long time since they had several top-of-the-line security systems. She had to run diagnostics on each and make sure there had been no changes out of the ordinary. I helped her check the video feeds while Kevin went out by the pool in the back to play with the dogs. About two hours in, I noticed the feed from the back fence. The garden looked absolutely beautiful, except that when I had walked around earlier, there hadn't been so many flowers in bloom. This was an old feed being looped over and over. There was a squirrel that ran up one of the trees every two minutes on the dot.

"Were you able to see me when I went to the back earlier?" I asked monitor guy.

"Yes, you and the boy. Why?"

I showed him the feed.

Sweat bubbles formed on his forehead. "Shit!"

I called Kevin, and he immediately appeared by the door. "Get the family out of here, now."

"Where should I take them?"

"Here," Lisa gave him an address, "this is a safe house."

"What about you girls?" he asked.

"Come back for us," Lisa answered.

"No, go get backup. Actually, call Andrew and send him. Go!" I cracked my knuckles and smiled, "Finally, some action. Let's do this!"

Lisa discontinued the feed from the cameras facing the back and turned up the microphones instead. She asked the men for headsets and we put them on. This way, we were all able to communicate with each other and hear what was going on with our surroundings at the same time. I sent Lisa out to the front with the monitor guy, and I took the back with Mark.

Everything seemed quiet, but we didn't see anyone, nor was anything out of place.

"They haven't come here yet," Mark said.

"I'm not sure about that. The loop had been going on

for quite a while, and they wouldn't risk us noticing it for too long. They must already be in the house." I looked around.

"You stay here, I'll go," he said.

"No, you stay and I'll go." I walked away before he argued any further.

I went in and found some shoe prints leading up to the second floor. I hissed into my headset that they were inside and sprinted up the stairs. As soon as I turned into the hallway towards the master bedroom, something slammed into the back of my head. *Ha!* I pulled one of my old tricks and dropped to the floor. I stayed down a few seconds until I heard the footsteps coming to check on me. I saw the knees lowering and counted...*one, two, three*...then I raised my head in full force and caught the intruder in the chin. The dislocation of the jaw squeaked through my ears like cracking ice. I got up and looked at the man. *Well, he was out.*

My headset had fallen off, but I didn't retrieve it. I continued down the hallway, and another man came out from the master bedroom, pointing a gun straight at me. I stopped where I was so he would have to come to me. I heard the footsteps behind me but didn't dare turn around.

"Shoot them," I heard from inside the room.

The man moved the gun to the side and pulled the trigger. The bullet shot past me, so I jumped backwards in an attempt to push down whoever was behind me, but instead, I found myself being slammed against the wall. I saw Mark unconscious on the floor, then looked up to see who was holding me.

"Hello, Anniewee," Nick smiled as he blasted off a beam, hitting the man who was shooting. "We really have to stop meeting like this." He winked with his one eye. Or maybe he just blinked. How would I know?

Another man came from right behind us, and like old times, Nick spun me around so were back to back. He fought that man while I took on another one who jumped down from the skylight in the roof. That was the problem with high trees near a house, we didn't think to look on top of the house. The attackers were coming down by the dozen. He beamed them off, and I knocked them out. I had to be careful not to go overboard and kill anyone. Fighting was fun, but holding back with regular people in the heat of the moment really killed my buzz.

"What's up, Nick? Your people don't know you need me alive?" I asked as I kicked the last guy on my side and sent him back out through the roof he'd dropped from.

"No one knows *how much* I need you alive," he said as he turned to fight two more guys.

I left him and went into the room. There were three of them: two of them huddled at the safe, and the other one ready with a gun. I raised my hand in defeat and went to stand right in front of him. I really hoped he wouldn't shoot since I was cooperating nicely. The click of the safe opening got his attention long enough for me to clock him out. Nick came in with fireballs ready at his hands and told the men to bring the contents to him. I stood there watching, not sure if he would use the fire against me. They handed him the backpack and he turned to look at me.

"Get her!" he shouted as he hypnotized the men, their eyes glazing over as they went into a trance before they both lunged and fell on top of me at the same time. *Gosh, he really has to stop doing this!* One of them had put his gun to my head, but right then, Andrew came and pulled him off. As they started fighting, I wrapped my arm around the other man's neck until he let go of mine. When he did, I kicked him towards Andrew's guy and saw them both fall before I ran off to find Nick.

I jumped down the stairs, finding Lisa lying on the floor with monitor guy hovering over her, checking her pulse. He nodded and gave me a thumb up, which was good enough for now, so I left her with him. I followed a noise and made it into the kitchen, interrupting the little dance going on between Jenny and Nick. He was caught inside the square of the island and the stove and would have to pass by Jenny before getting out. His face seemed to have gained some extra scars since the previous week. His right hand held a fireball, and his left fingers glowed with the beam ready to attack. I went to stand next to Jenny.

"Let me go or I'll hurt her," he said, lifting his chin to me.

"No," she said.

"Dammit!" He walked to the refrigerator and nudged

the freezer open with his elbow. I moved in closer. "Stay away, Annie. I can't control this shit for too long." He shoved his right hand in the freezer, and I heard the sizzling of fire being put out.

"What the heck was that?" I asked.

"NO!" I heard him scream as Andrew ran in between us to get to Nick. "Don't come any closer!"

Andrew didn't stop, and Nick jumped, sliding over the island and landing with the agility of a cat on the other side. Here I was again, left with the choice of letting him go or stopping him, but this time I knew what I had to do. I stepped into his path.

Nick's arm shook as he clenched his fist, the energy swirling around his hand. He looked behind him once and then back at me. His one eye met mine, and if I wasn't mistaken, it held sadness. With a sigh, he opened his hand and released the beam, hitting me square in the stomach.

As I hit the ground, I could hear one of the others scream out, and I watched as Nick stepped over me, just before everything went dark.

# CHAPTER NINE

I OPENED MY eyes to bright lights. I covered my face with my arm and propped myself up to sit on the bed. I was in the new infirmary. Oh jeez, I'd have to deal with Derek now.

"Annie?"

I squinted enough to see Jenny standing by my side.

"How are you feeling?" she asked.

"Blind."

"Give it a minute for your eyes to adjust."

"Or you can turn off the lights."

"Big baby," I heard her chuckle.

"What happened? Did he get away?" I asked.

"Yes, Andrew and I had to take care of you. We had no choice."

"What is it with me lately? I can't seem to get a good fight in."

"Stop complaining. You kicked major butt with all

of those guys," she said.

"What happened with everyone? Are they okay? Lisa was on the floor..."

"Everyone is fine. Lisa and one of the guards were tased. And the other one was shot, but he was wearing a vest." She put her hand on my shoulder. "The Lumins are fine. Their personal safe was missing all of the documents they kept inside, but their money and jewelry were left behind."

"Yes, I was there when they took the contents out."

"Nick has everything, then?"

I nodded. "It was in the backpack. We got his team, though, so maybe we can get Nick's location from one of them."

"That's not going to happen," she mumbled as she looked down.

"Why not? We captured them. Lisa can get the information for us."

"They're all dead," she said.

"WHAT? No, most of them were alive, we can get the info—" I stopped when she shook her head. "What are you saying?"

"They had kill chips connected to their hearts. When the team arrived to take them in, all they found were dead bodies with blood running out of their eyes. We found the chips. It looks like they were remotely activated."

"I can't believe he would do that! Next time—no matter who he hurts—we have to take him down, Jenny. We cannot worry about each other. If we keep letting him slip away, we're all going to be dead soon enough." I stared at my hands, lost in thought.

"What is it? Why are you confused?"

"I'm not…"

"I can sense you. Spill it," Jenny said.

"It's just that it felt like old times. He came to my aid, and we fought together against them." I jumped off the bed, making myself dizzy in the process.

"Hang on! Why would he fight his own men?" she asked.

"I don't think they knew he needed me alive. It's not like he expected me to be there."

"Right, he probably ordered them to kill anyone in their way if they had to." She shook her head. "No, I still don't get it. Wouldn't he have just ordered them to back off?"

"Yeah, I don't know. He didn't try to kidnap me, either."

"No, but maybe he doesn't need you just yet. He must need to follow up with the research notes before he has use for you."

"So why is Derek so sure he wants me now? This is the second time he could have just taken me with him but hasn't," I said.

"Well, after he hurt you, I guess he had to leave you so we could heal you."

"Yeah…But when we were upstairs he had the chance, instead of setting his men on me."

"Maybe they were supposed to take you," she said.

"Come on, he can't have thought they would have a chance against me."

"It doesn't matter. We need to get him fast. He killed all of his accomplices without mercy. We can't just leave him on the loose."

"No." I had ideas of my own, but I knew it was best to keep them to myself.

"Are you feeling okay now?" she asked.

"Yes, thanks for healing me."

"No problem. Actually, that was the easiest healing I've ever had to do. I didn't feel anything. I took from you and put back into you. I could do it in my sleep. I probably should have done normal healing, but I wanted to practice that again. Sorry."

"It's fine."

"I have to say, though, I'm glad it was his beam and not the fireball. I'm not sure even Derek would be able to heal you from that, and you know how good he is."

I winced. That didn't sound like it would have turned out in my favor. I didn't have long to contemplate that thought, though because, just then, Derek burst into the room.

"WHAT THE HELL WERE YOU THINKING?" he shouted from the door. He walked into the infirmary and shook me by my shoulders.

"Uh, hi?"

"Hi? You were reckless, Annie. You put yourself and Kevin in danger."

"Actually, if he hadn't been there, the Lumins would

have been in danger. We saved them."

"Don't give me that bull." He stepped back.

"You know it's true. And just because you want me locked up doesn't mean I intend to be."

"You will have no choice in the matter. Kevin has been reprimanded, and he understands that if he disobeys orders again, he will be sent back to training."

"It's not his fault, Derek." I jumped back up on the bed, agitated.

"No, it was yours. You should never have bribed Lisa to take you with her."

"Bribed? Is that what she said?" I asked.

"Yes, bribed. I'm not sure if she lied or not, but it sounds like something you would do," he said.

"It figures she would try to pass on the blame. Fine, I'll take responsibility for going against orders for all of us. I'm already on lockdown anyway, so you can't do much worse to me."

"So you think." He turned to Jenny. "Can you leave us alone for a minute?"

"Sure," she said, walking out.

"Being irresponsible or not, you did a great job. Lisa made it clear that you were the one who noticed the recording on the feed."

"She did?" Well, that made up some for making me take the blame.

"Yes, and I agree, it was a good thing Kevin was there. Don't repeat that to anyone! I can't have them thinking I'm praising you three after the way you all behaved."

"No, sir," I smiled.

"Now, you are going home and staying put. Understand?"

I rolled my eyes. "Yes."

"No attitude."

"You do know me, right?" I raised an eyebrow.

"I'll have some reports ready for you to go over tomorrow."

"Sounds exciting," I scowled.

"You need to trust me. I'm doing the best I can with the information I have. I know you want to be out there with the rest of the team, but for the safety of your friends and everyone else, it's best for you to stay put."

"I understand. I just hate it."

"I know. But right now, you are not in the position to be in the field, anyway."

"What does that mean?"

"This is the second time you've failed at your mission. Your guard is down or something, Annie. You're not your usual self."

"Technically, I failed only once. This was Lisa's mission. All I did was sneak my way in," I grinned.

"All technicalities aside, you are not good enough for the field at the moment," he said, and left.

That hurt. I couldn't complain, though. It was true. I kept messing up when it came to Nick. But what's a girl to do? First, I saw him last week after three years of him being gone, and then, he popped up again a week later.

Anyone would lose her senses if she had to fight against her ex-husband. Especially if fighting with him felt more right than fighting against him. I wasn't sure what was going on in my head. He had shot the beam straight at me, knowing darn well he would hurt me. I had to get that bastard. But *still*, I was glad he'd beamed me and not Jenny. Who would have healed her so quickly?

"Knock, knock!"

"Beth! What took you so long to come and visit me?" I asked as she walked in.

"Derek was being an ass."

*Pfft.* "As usual."

"You look good," she said.

"I've been better. Where were you today?"

"I was on lookout at *your* house, you know..." she stared me down. "It's the place where you left me hanging. You could have invited me to come join the mission." She shook her head.

"I didn't want to get you in trouble."

"You know, I got in trouble for letting you slip away. He thinks I let you go. At least if you had asked me to join you, I would have been in trouble for good reason."

"Sorry." I hung my head.

"Whatever. You chose Lisa over me, I get it."

"Stop it. She made me take the blame, anyway. I'm glad you weren't there, though. They're all dead. The men that work for him, he just killed them like they were trash."

She bit at her nails for a while. I knew she was about

to throw some kind of news at me, so I waited until she'd gathered her thoughts.

"Babe? It's okay if you don't want to hate him," she said.

"No, but I do. I hate what he is doing. I hate that he keeps hurting me, physically, emotionally, and he is hurting my people. I hate what he is doing so much."

"Yes, but you don't hate *him.*" She patted my arm. "It's okay, Jenny doesn't hate him either."

I looked up. "Beth, she told you that?"

"Yes, she thinks he's being framed."

"Why wouldn't she tell me this? I asked her to tell me what she thought."

"Jenny doesn't want to influence your decisions. She's nervous that he might have hypnotized her and that's why she can't sense him clearly."

"Well, that changes things."

"Not if he did hypnotize her," she said. "Which, let's face it, he probably did."

"Yeah, he probably did."

"Anyway, I came to tell you that Kevin is now free from his punishment, and you two can go home." She smiled at me. "He had to highlight our policy book from front to back so he doesn't forget to follow the rules again."

"Seriously? He is not in fifth grade." I followed Beth out of the room.

"You know how the big boss likes to show everyone he's in charge."

"Poor guy!" I said, thinking of Kevin.

We met up with him in the conference room, and he came up to me and gave me a hug.

"You're all right! I was worried that you might have been badly injured," he said.

"Nah, I'm tougher than I look. Sorry you had to do some highlighting."

"Oh, no worries," he grinned. "It was so worth it!"

Kevin was so weak after having to teleport so many people that we had Andrew use his portal to take us back home. I was once again stuck in one place, unable to help out. I guess it was for the best. Derek had a point, I was no good where Nick was concerned. I just wished I understood his actions.

I SPENT THE whole night reading all the files that Samantha had given to me, and I couldn't find anything new. The next day, I was so tired that I left Kevin playing video games and went to take a nap in the middle of the day. In my exhausted state, I smiled, remembering the old Nick.

*"Why are you crying?"*

*"I'm not. I don't cry," I said, sniffling.*

*"Okay, well...here, take this," he said, taking off his*

*sweater while standing in the cold in his white T-shirt.*
*"Your face is wet for some reason," he smiled.*
     *"I don't need that."*
     *"You have mascara running down your cheeks.*
*Come here," he said, and wiped my face with his*
*sweater. He was so gentle and caring and nice that my*
*tears betrayed me and poured down my face,*
*embarrassingly. He held me with my head against his*
*hard chest for a long while.*
     *"Oh, my God, why can't I stop crying?"*
     *"Don't worry about it, let it out. I'll hold you."*
     *I pulled away. "No, you don't have to. I'm fine.*
*Thanks."*
     *"So you punched her. You'll be all right."*
     *"No, they're going to kick me out for not controlling*
*my anger!" I squeaked.*
     *"I won't let it happen, Annie, I promise."*
     *I laughed. "What could you possibly do?"*
     *"I'll stand up as a witness. Lisa was pushing Beth*
*around, and you stood up for your friend. Loyalty counts*
*for Luminaries, you know."*
     *"Right," I smiled. Now, looking at him, I couldn't*
*believe I had cried in his arms. "Why are you so nice to*
*me all the time?"*
     *"I like you."*
     *"Ha! Don't you go thinking you're adding me to*
*your list of girls here."*
     *"You've been training with me long enough to know*
*I've stopped all that," he said, pushing my hair behind*

*my ears.*
*"So?"*
*"So, you and I will happen. My kisses fix everything,*
*by the way, so if you want to come closer I can—"*
*"Stop it, Nick. Not happening."*
*He touched the tip of my nose. "Not today, maybe."*
*"Not ever," I said, still feeling the memory of his*
*arms around me.*
*"Annie?"*
*"Yes?"*
*"I'm going to kiss you one day, I hope you know*
*this."*

I heard someone banging on my door and jumped
out of my bed in panic. I ran down the stairs and saw my
door crashing to the floor. And there he was, *again*. Nick
was being held up by Beth, and he was seriously hurt.
"Help me, Annie! He's heavy!" she said.
"What happened? What is he doing here? Are you
okay?"
"Yes, I'm fine, but Nick is hurt, Annie. I didn't know
what to do. I brought him here because I figured I should
let you decide. Should we call Derek?"
"HAHAHA, you might as well kill me now instead
of calling that idiot," Nick chimed in.
"And what? Save you from some well-deserved
suffering?" I asked.
He lunged forward and stared me in the eye. "If I die,
I want to go out looking into your beautiful brown eyes.

Go ahead, Beth, call that son-of-a-gun. I'm ready."

*Gosh, I'd forgotten how dramatic he was.*

"I'm not going to grant you any wish—" I started saying, but was interrupted by Jenny running in.

"Where is that bastard?" She caught sight of Nick and went up to him. "Oh, here. Okay, hold him down, Annie!"

As I did just that, I was surprised by the fact that Jenny didn't call Derek or try to hurt Nick. Instead, she started healing his wounds. I was frozen in place.

"There, are you better?" she asked him.

"Much better, thanks. But I'm still not healed completely."

"I would heal you more, but I want to make sure you're not going to run back out there."

I gawked at each one of them, refusing to believe my eyes. Derek was right. The people who I had thought were my friends were actually working with this psychotic killer. Weren't they? Maybe he was controlling them somehow. I knew I should trigger the alarm in my keychain, but I was too shocked and, quite frankly, too eager to kick Nick's ass myself. *Payback time, bitch!*

"Third encounter, huh, Annie? Wanna tango?" he smiled.

I ignored him and continued to hold him down. "Why am I the last person to know anything? Jenny? Beth? Why are you helping him?"

"He saved us," Jenny told me before she turned to talk to him. "I don't know what you're up to, but from where I stand, we seem to be on the same side. Now I'm going to ask you one big favor, Nick, erase my memory. I want nothing to do with this. Whatever Annie decides to do, I want no part in it."

"You bring him here and now you won't take responsibility?" I asked Jenny.

"If I take him in, we don't know what will happen," she said and walked up to me. "I had to bring him to you, Annie. This is your choice."

I understood what she meant, so I stood there while Nick hypnotized Jenny and sent her home. After she left, Beth and I took Nick to the basement and chained him up to one of the exposed support beams of my house. I hoped we wouldn't keep him there for too long, since the basement was my home gym, and I liked using it often. Obviously, with Nick here, that would be out.

"What happened?" I asked her.

"This idiot went back to Worldsafe and got caught between the armored door when it was closing. The guards attacked us all. They didn't care that Jen and I were with the Org. He's lucky I was there to save his ass." She tied his hands up behind his back with rope. "What about his feet? Chain or rope?" Beth asked.

"Leave them," I said, as Nick lowered himself down to sit on the floor.

I stooped down and back-elbowed him across his jaw. His head fell sideways, but not for long, he turned to watch me but said nothing. I got up and slammed a good kick to his side. He winced but remained silent.

"What are you up to?" I demanded.

"Killing."

"Why?"

He smiled. "It's fun."

"I'm about to call Derek, but I'd like to know what you're after first."

"Let me go," he said.

"Oh… you're *hilarious*."

"You'll regret keeping me here, Annie. I can't afford to be captured right now."

"Oh, RIGHT, what was I thinking? I should have called ahead to schedule an appointment for your capture. *I just didn't have your number!*" I watched him in disbelief.

"I don't have email or Twitter either. You know why?" His lip twitched. "I can't have *followers*."

I heard a chuckle from behind.

"Really, Beth? You're going to encourage him?"

"What? No, it was just… I thought it was…*funny,*" she finished saying in a low voice.

I turned back to Nick and was about to grab his neck when I realized being that close to him would not be a good idea. If I allowed myself to get that close to him, he could hypnotize me to let him go, so instead, I kicked him.

"Now you're just doing this for spite," he said.

"Yes." I kicked him again. "You started it at Worldsafe."

"What are you, ten? I pinch you, you pinch me?

Actually, I wouldn't mind pinching you..." I was about to slam him again. "No, stop. Stop! Your kicks are more painful than mine. Stop it."

"Any more requests? It seems you think you're in charge here," I said.

"Just, wait, all right? Don't call Derek. Don't let anyone know I'm here," Nick begged.

"Scared?" I smirked.

"When have you ever known me to be scared? Listen, no. Keep me here, tied up. Watch me all day, go back upstairs, I don't care. Just wait it out before you decide."

I leaned in close to Nick and asked, "Why should I?"

"Just think about everything that's been going on, and ask yourself if any of the information you have makes any sense. Go talk it out with your pals. Or at least come up with any questions you have for me. I'll answer them before you hand me over to your boyfriend."

Okay, what was his game?

"I can't do that. I know you, Nick, and I'm sure you're probably already planning your escape."

"I'm not, but you can always put me under with a tranquilizer from your fighting supplies," he offered.

"Please, Nick, you don't think I need a tranquilizer to put you out now, do you?" I saw the excited look in his eyes just before I clocked his ass. I bent down to make sure he was still breathing and said, "Well, we have a pulse!"

"I can see that." Beth's eyes danced as she fully

enjoyed the situation I was in.

We went back upstairs but didn't talk much because Kevin was around.

Later on, Beth ordered some food for us after convincing Andrew that it was okay to keep Nick in the house. After all, he was hurt, so where could he go? The house was being watched, and I had Nick restrained like the dog he was, in chains and out of sight. I went to the living room to wait for the food. If I were going to spend time with Nick, it had better be with food in my system. When it came, we ate in silence, each one of us lost in his own thoughts.

"You have yet to kill him like you said you would," Beth finally said.

"Not before getting some answers and beating the shit out of him some more."

She frowned, "More?"

"That wasn't enough," I said.

"And then you'll kill him?" The top of her lips trembled.

"Of course."

"Uh-huh." She gave me a full-blown smile this time. *Whatever—I'd show her.*

# CHAPTER TEN

BY NIGHTFALL, THE suspense was killing all of us, so
we went downstairs to give our prisoner some food and to
question him. We needed answers, and Nick was going to
give them to us. Andrew untied his hands from the back
so Nick could use them to eat his sandwich. His wrists
were still bound together, though. He took the food and
didn't say a word. He ate and watched all of us in turn as
he chewed slowly. He was doing this on purpose, I knew
it. I found it hard to have him in such close proximity.
The years had really done a number on him. He was in a
much worse state than I had originally thought. His wild,
rugged hair was dirty, his arms were burned, his face was
burned, and God only knew what had happened to his
eye. But if I was honest? Even in this disheveled state,
Nick still got to me, and I hated myself for it.

All this time, I'd tried to imagine what I would do to
him when I finally had the chance to get my hands on

him. But now? Seeing him like this just made me pity him. Of course, this was easier for me since I'd already knocked him around. Still, I had no idea what had caused him to go so dark, but the piece of nothing in front of me was a compilation of broken parts.

He finished eating and was sipping on a bottle of water when Beth couldn't stand it anymore.

"For goodness sake! Just tell us what happened to you to make you turn so evil," she shouted.

"I'm not evil. I'm just misunderstood," he said as his lip curled up.

"Of all times, is this when you should be joking?" Andrew asked him.

"If not now, when? This one here," his eye darted my way, "is going to murder me before the night is over, so I might as well go out laughing. She always did enjoy my sense of humor."

I stayed quiet and expressionless.

"You know what was funny? Those divorce papers she found on the kitchen counter the morning you walked out on her. Now, that was hilarious," Beth snapped.

Nick clenched his teeth. "That was my point. I had to be harsh so she would take me seriously."

"I'm here, you know. It's rude to talk about me as if I don't exist." I looked straight at Beth and admonished, "That is NOT what matters right now."

"Are you really with Derek?" Piercing me with his gaze, Nick waited for my answer.

"Yes. Derek and I are in a relationship."

"He is not good for you," he said.

"Nor were you."

"I know that," he turned to face me. "That's why I divorced you."

"Thanks for the favor."

"You don't love Derek," he said.

"My life with him is none of your business. Why are you here?"

"Uh...because your people kidnapped me, no?" He raised his eyebrow.

"You need to start giving us some answers," Andrew interrupted.

"Oh, yes, buddy. Answers: I'm not the bad guy," he said as he straightened his legs and crossed them at his ankles to get comfortable. "Is that good enough for you?"

"Don't treat us like idiots. We can and will hurt you if you don't start cooperating. The only reason you're still sitting here is because I don't want to kill you in front of Annie. We have orders to take you out, just so you know."

"Actually, if you don't mind, Andrew, I'd rather she kill me herself." I threw my coffee at him. "Ouch! That shit is hot, Annie!"

"Seems like you've had your share of burns. This one hardly matters."

He said nothing.

"You say you're not the bad guy. Did you or did you not burn down that building in India?" Andrew interrogated him with an even tone. How he was able to control his anger was beyond me. I was ready to explode.

"Yes," he looked straight into my eyes. "I killed all of those people. They had it coming."

"They had kids there!" I said.

"No, there weren't any kids there."

"Yes, they found little bodies. The report had a count of—"

"That's a lie," he growled. "Now, I suggest none of you get me too angry, I'd hate to turn your house to ashes," Nick warned, and gave us 'jazz hands.'

Crap, it was stupid of us to have left his hands loose. Beth got up to tie them behind his back again.

"You already hurt me," I said.

"Yeah, didn't you have your revenge earlier?"

"I'm not done."

"I knew you could take it. Andrew came after me before I could put out my beam. It takes way more control than I have." He shook his head and continued, "And since you were all blocking me, I had to choose one person to target, and Anniewee, you know that would always be you."

"Don't call me that."

"Would you have preferred I hit Jenny or Andrew? Face it, only you could have taken that hit and walked away from it in one piece. I knew Jenny would heal you. I wouldn't have hurt you if I'd had the choice."

"Ha!" Beth chimed in. "Only because you still have plans for her."

"Yes, I do." He smiled as my hands balled into fists.

It took everything I had to stay put.

"What about the Pentagon? What did you need from there?" she asked.

"Nothing. I wasn't there."

"The witnesses described you and even swore that the man they saw used laser beams. How would they know that?"

"Beth, it wasn't me. I have no reason to lie. You already know I killed those people in India, and yes, I also took Larry Lumin away, but I didn't attack the Pentagon."

"Why did you kill Dr. Lumin?" Andrew asked.

"I didn't. He recognized who I was and told me about his research. He said I needed to get them before…uh, someone else did, and even gave me the combination to his safe."

"And we are supposed to believe that?" I asked, incredulous.

"Yes, Annie, I'd think you would know if I were lying to you," Nick said, pulling me in with his gaze. He continued, "About a year after I left the Org, I went to find Dr. Lumin to ask him some questions. I found him hiding behind a dumpster, because he was being followed by some people. I saved him, and he asked me to take him with me, so I did."

"Why did you kill him?" Beth asked.

"I didn't kill him. He shared a lot of information with me, by his own choice. A few hours after we were safe, he was writing down locations for me to get into, including Worldsafe. He said they contained important information, and then his eyes started bleeding, and he just dropped dead."

Beth, Andrew, and I looked at each other.

"That's just like the others," Beth said. "So who is doing the killing?"

"He is!" I raised my voice. "Of course, he knows their eyes bleed if he's the one who put the kill chip in them."

"Whoa! Hey, hey. What kill chip?" Nick asked.

"The ones you had in all your buddies at the Lumins' house, and obviously, Dr. Lumin himself," Andrew answered.

"That was not my doing, and those were not my buddies. Annie, come on! We fought them together."

"Only because you didn't expect me to be there, and they didn't know you needed me alive."

"I was not there with them! Listen to me, guys. There is someone else at play here. I just followed Dr. Lumin's instructions. He told me about India, and also where to find the facility where these guys met to plan their moves. That's how I knew when they were going to attack."

"If you knew where the research notes were, why didn't you go before?" I asked.

"Because, darling, even if I did, these men would have no way of knowing the research notes were no longer there. I had to go at the same time as they did to prevent them from hurting Dr. Lumin's daughters. I'd promised him I would protect them."

"But you stole the notes," I said.

"Well, I couldn't let them take them, could I? Just like I couldn't let them hurt you."

I rolled my eyes. "Where are they? The notes."

"They are safe."

"That's it? They're safe?"

"Yes, Annie, that's it," Nick answered.

"What happened to you? Why are you so burned up?" Beth asked.

"I can't really control myself when I get angry. My hands start to heat up, and the fire just sprouts out of it and hits whatever is in the way, myself included," he said.

"You did this to yourself?" I asked.

"Yes."

"What about your eye?"

"In India. The building was actually a laboratory of some sort. It was in a deserted area because it was full of explosives and I'm not sure what other substances. Dr. Lumin assured me that they were preparing for terrorism. I went there on a mission to find evidence that would support what he claimed."

"So you just killed everyone?" I asked.

"Yes, I just up and killed everyone who was involved—can I finish?" He took a deep breath and continued, "I didn't do it on purpose. I stayed in the building overnight. I wanted to wait until most of the workers had gone before I destroyed their work.

Somehow, they knew I was there, so they put the building on lockdown. When I came out, everyone was still around. I decided to leave, but they were prepared for a fight."

"How many were there?" Andrew asked.

"There were no more than twenty employees, and they knew darn well what they were making in that facility. They were NOT innocent. The other eight were the guards who were fighting me. In the middle of all that, they brought…someone out whom I had taken with me. I didn't expect that." He looked down. "I lost control of myself and put the place on fire. That's how I blew up everyone and their work. I went to save my friend, and I got hit with a piece of burning metal in my eye."

"So you've been one-eyed for what? About one year?" I asked.

"Yeah. Look, you guys have known me for a long time. Do you really think I would go on a killing rampage if I didn't have good reasons?"

"What are those reasons?" I asked.

"You're not ready to hear them."

"Don't give me that crap, Nick, please."

"I will tell you guys. Heck, I'll show you. But not right now. None of you are ready to know the truth."

"Basically, what you're saying is that you are…what? Working to stop someone else?" Andrew asked.

"Yes, that's what I'm saying. Now, if you don't mind, I'm tired and want to sleep."

"What the—" I started to say some not-too-nice words.

"What? I'm used to running. Now that I have a chance to sleep in peace, I will. Goodnight." This asshole had actually dismissed us.

He was always so used to being in charge, he couldn't even play a nice hostage. It worked out anyway, because I had a tough time looking at him. Andrew, Beth, and I had to discuss what we'd learned and decide what to do with him. By this time tomorrow, he would be Derek's problem. I wasn't sure if he was lying or not, but I figured we could all gang up on him and push for more specific answers before turning him in.

We went back upstairs to find Kevin watching TV in the living room.

"What are you watching?" I asked him. I didn't need him questioning what we were up to. The last thing I needed right now was for Kevin to become curious about the basement.

"Movie," he mumbled.

"Are you still feeling sick?"

"Yes, guess I can't handle teleporting too many people at once," he said with a shrug.

"It was a lot to take on. Just rest up." I looked at Beth and Andrew. "I'm going to bed, guys, I need to… sleep."

"Good night, Annie," they said.

After I was done taking a bath, I took a bottle of wine with me to bed. This night required a decent amount of alcohol if I was planning to be a good girl and stop myself from going two flights down.

He was so much like the old Nick. Well, minus the new appearance. He was still making jokes, and he was still trying to be in charge, which was one of the reasons Derek had never liked him. Nick was always the lead when he was out on missions. Actually, he was very good at it. He never made a wrong call, and that never failed to annoy Derek. I could really see the old Nick in there, but if what he was saying were true, then that meant he'd never changed. And that couldn't be true. Could it?

If Nick had never changed, did that mean he had never loved me? Yes, we had gotten married young, but I was on top of the world for those two years that we were man and wife. Before that, even. We'd met at training when I was fifteen and he was sixteen, and I remembered his dazzling smile all too clearly. He had been a man-whore back then. He'd charmed girls into going out with him in secret, and he took advantage of the "no-dating" policy to see several girls at the same time. When I'd questioned him about it, he'd said none of them wanted to officially date because of the rule, so the way he saw it, he was free to kiss them all. I couldn't stand him then. He had been so full of himself. I'd considered it a good thing that he couldn't rely on his looks anymore. Karma is a bitch!

But Nick had a sweet side, too. It was a side of him that he didn't let others see very often. It was that side of Nick that made me love him. He was that arrogant ass everyone hated to love. He stood up against the bullies and always took the time to help train the weaker recruits, even when it was clear that they were not Luminary material. Training was like a fast-track high school. You got there between fourteen and fifteen years of age, and they taught all the necessary classes to get a high school diploma. That was the first year—after that, they focused on teaching martial arts, use of weapons, and all sorts of computer training. Depending on your progress, you were able to get your "Luminary injection" between the ages of sixteen and seventeen, and that's when the real fun began.

I was a fast learner. I'd passed all of my required classes within the first eight months of getting there. But after getting activated, I had gained a huge target on my back. I was breaking a lot of records for first time trainees, and who had come to my rescue? Nick. He'd stood up for me and made sure I held my head up high. I used to be so angry back then. Most of us were. We were all unwanted kids who had been mistreated growing up. We had either been taken out from orphanages or from foster homes when we were selected as winners of The Lake Scholarship. We were given a chance to turn our lives around. And me being a tomboy, I would normally have gotten into a fight with anyone who talked about me, but I wanted to fit in. I would have hated if they kicked me out because I couldn't control my anger.

Nick would let me use him as an outlet, and went head-to-head with me in secret fight battles to make me the best recruit I could be. Between him and Beth, they helped me keep my cool. Every morning, he would leave an origami rose by my window to remind me that he was thinking of me. It didn't matter to him that I wasn't interested in being one of his many girls. He was always so arrogant, he insisted that he would one day be my husband. Man, I can't exactly say that he lied...sigh.

# CHAPTER ELEVEN

I FOUND THE coffee already brewing when I got up. I opened the window over the kitchen sink to take a look and saw the van parked right in the front of the house. Whoever had been on guard duty that night wouldn't come inside for anything. The only two people with keys were Beth and Jenny. Andrew didn't need a key since he could just use his portal, and Kevin was sleeping, so who the heck made the…*no!* I turned around, hoping the realization I'd just had was wrong.

"Good morning, sunshine," Nick said, water dripping from his newly washed hair.

"How did you get out?" I asked.

He raised his hands and showed me his glowing fingers. "I burned off the rope and melted the chain. I would have waited for you to unchain me, but I really had to take a leak," he smirked. "And since I was out, I took a shower, too. I hope you don't mind? You didn't really think that I *couldn't* escape, did you?"

"YOU LET HIM OUT?" Beth screamed, running out of the portal from the living room. Andrew followed behind her.

"No, he let himself out," I said wearily as I rubbed my forehead. I wasn't sure what to do.

"Thanks for coming, guys. I used Annie's cell to text and invite you over."

"Ah, *thanks?* Should we tie him up again?" Beth's eyes darted to Nick then back to me.

"No use, he can melt his way out," I answered her.

"Guys, why don't you sit?" He pointed to the kitchen table and went on to pour and prepare our coffees.

"Why didn't you escape? Why are you still here?" I asked.

"As you can see," he lifted his bloodied shirt to show me his abs, "I'm still hurt, and I can't exactly defend myself out there."

Okay, so he wasn't exactly trying to show me the muscles that were popping out through his bruises, but that's what I was looking at. He'd always had an excellent body, the evil bastard.

"Injury didn't stop you from being on your own before," Beth said.

"No, but I also want to explain everything. Like I said, I'm not the bad guy. Some new clothes would come in handy, by the way. Do you still have my stuff around here?" he asked me.

"Storage section in the basement."

"I knew you couldn't get rid of me completely," he smiled.

"I hate you," I blurted out.

"I love you."

I stood up and slapped him.

"That's for not being man enough to face me when you walked out." I slapped him again. "And this is for having the nerve to say those words to me."

He didn't move. Didn't even flinch. Unless he did it with the covered eye?

At that time, Kevin appeared and took a good look at all of us. To any outsider, this would seem like we were all friends hanging out and drinking coffee. I freaked out, because what else would I do? Nick was out in the open, and now that Kevin had seen him, he would report us to Derek. Except…

Kevin walked up to Nick and gave him a hug.

"Sup, man?" he said.

"Kev! Dude, you are getting taller."

"Yeah, watch out or I'll beat you up for this one," he laughed, pointing at me.

"What's going on? Nick, Kevin?" I asked, the obvious question hanging in the air.

"Kevin here is my little buddy," Nick answered.

I turned to Kevin. "How do you know Nick? You're working with him! To do what? Spy and deliver me to him when the two of you see fit?" I slammed my mug down, breaking it *and* the table. Everything splattered, causing Beth and Andrew to jump out of their chairs.

"Calm down, Annie. Yes, I'm working with Nick, but he is a good guy, really."

"I'm going to wring your little neck out, you sneak!" I exclaimed as I walked up to Kevin.

"Annie, don't take it out on him. I know you find him adorable so let's not harm him. You're mad at me, remember that."

I snapped. "How, Nick? How is it that you have everyone around me working for you? All of you are nothing but traitors. First, Beth and Andrew, neither of you would tell me what Derek shares with you. Then, you save this ass." I shoved Nick to the wall. "And then you bring him here and Jenny heals him. JENNY! And now, Kevin, you know him, too? Why am I not in the loop? Do you really want me to kill you? Because I would!"

"Of course not, Anniewee," Nick said, clearly enjoying my freak out.

"Don't call me that."

"I—fine, but that's why I'm here. To talk to you and explain everything to the three of you." He sat down. "First of all, the person lying to you is Derek. Second of all, I can't believe you are dating that idiot, and third, there is a lot we need to discuss."

"I'm very interested in the third of all."

"Where do I start?"

"How about when you walked out on Annie?" Beth said.

"Right. Well, I was forced to."

"You liar! You stupid, selfish son-of-a—how can

you still lie?" I asked.

"I'm not lying. Since you don't want to listen, then at least look at this..." Nick turned to Kevin and said, "Get my laptop for me." It appeared in his hand, and he motioned us to follow him as he walked into the living room. "Annie broke the kitchen table so this," he pointed to the sofa, "might be the best place for the three of you to see." He placed the laptop on the coffee table and pressed play. What I saw next was completely unexpected.

*"The girl is safe, and she's getting stronger every year. If we continue to lower her dosage, there is no telling how we can harvest her powers."* A woman's voice came through, and I couldn't see her face, but the man...

*"We can't do that yet. Keep experimenting with the dose to see how she reacts. We will keep her off of it for a while, but if she gets out of our control we will make sure to double the next shot. The only problem is that husband of hers,"* the man said.

*"Is he that important? I think we should terminate him."*

*"I wouldn't worry about him. I have a plan for Nick Logan. He's leaving for a mission next week, and he'll be coming in for a shot before leaving. We are going to give him a sedative and will lock him up until we find a way to steal his powers."*

*"Hypnotizing people isn't that advantageous,"* the woman said.

*"You'd be surprised at how handy it is. Besides, he has a good weapon with that beam of his."*

*"How will we know the girl will work with us for sure?"*

The video stopped.

"So you were kidnapped? I can't believe *he* is behind all of this," Beth said.

"Oh, come on! You are not falling for his crap, are you?" I asked.

"No, I wasn't kidnapped." Nick ignored me. "After I witnessed their conversation, I figured that the best thing to do was to leave. Now you see who is really behind it all."

"You saved yourself and left me there in danger? I'm sorry I was such a heavy load of baggage for you to carry. So much so, that you couldn't take me with you. At least you got the divorce documents fast," I said to Nick, my voice dripping with sarcasm.

"Annie, it's not like that. I would never have left you if I didn't know you would be safe. You heard them. They need you to be healthy. I knew no one would harm you." He took a seat opposite us and continued, "The part in the beginning I didn't get a chance to tape. They are planning on using us Luminaries for some kind of project. It sounded as though they want to take over the government. I'm really not too sure. I left to investigate what they are planning and to make sure you are safe," he finished, looking at me.

"What's in Worldsafe?" I asked.

"That, I have no idea. All I know is that Dr. Lumin said I needed to get into that vault. The woman in the video? That's Jessica Smith. She is the third partner, and she is alive. I did not kill her. Jessica doesn't even know about the vault. I would have found out what's inside if you hadn't been there."

"Why me? What do they want with me?" I asked.

"Dr. Lumin said you are Kinetic. Your energy is beyond imaginable."

"What does that mean?" Andrew asked him.

"Annie is full of potential energy, *stored* energy, but when she starts moving, it becomes full-blown Kinetic, and that's why she is so super strong." He turned to me. "You are like an unlimited source of energy, and if they channel you right, one person can have multiple powers. I think that's something our dear bad guy wants. You would be his personal charger."

"That doesn't make sense. I ran out of juice when Jenny was using me to heal Beth."

"I thought that was because of the blood," Andrew said.

"No, I fainted because of the blood, but I still felt a little weak."

"Yes, but that's only because they've been giving us suppressant injections so they can limit what we can do. Since I stopped getting those shots, my powers have been more enhanced," Nick said.

"Apart from the fire?" I asked.

"Yes. I can hypnotize multiple people at once. I just

think it and it's done. I don't have to look at them like I had to in the beginning. My laser beam? I can paralyze people, shock them, or kill them if I put enough current behind it. I discovered that I have to be careful when I'm angry because that's when my powers are uncontrollable. My anger transforms my laser from a beam into fire. And controlling fire is the worst for me."

"I don't understand," Beth said. "Why are they giving us a suppressant? Don't we need the monthly boost to sustain our abilities?"

"Actually, Beth, we never needed any boost. We are born with the powers in our DNA."

"How?" Andrew asked.

"When we were in the womb, Dr. Lumin injected his formulas into our amniotic sacs daily. We were given our extra abilities before we were even born. We are simply the result of a scientific experiment—the Org's experiment to be exact—in order to create their own personal army of superhuman beings. Our mothers gave their unborn children up for this."

"I still can't believe what you're saying about the Org," Beth said in disbelief.

"Can't you? Think about it. How is it that the only people who can become one of us are from foster homes, or are runaways?"

"Because they don't want anyone to have to lie to their families or put them in danger?" she asked.

"No. Think about it, Beth. How come not one of us has ever been adopted? Don't you see? They've sabotaged all adoptions that had to do with a potential Luminary. They have people everywhere. All of us, we have always been a part of their plan, Beth, believe it," Nick finished.

"Tell her about us," Kevin said.

"Kevin and I, we're brothers. I found him by digging deeper into this whole Org scam. It turns out there's a reason most of us are from the streets and foster homes. If we have no family then there's no one to miss us or notice our abilities if we access them before time. They don't offer us scholarships out of the goodness of their hearts." Nick started pacing around as he talked. "They had a study group when they first found out that this drug can help enhance certain things and injected it into pregnant women throughout their entire pregnancy. They said all the mothers died from complications during childbirth, but I doubt that. Over the years, they kept some women alive and fed their drug habits as long as they agreed to have children for the Org. It looks like the body could normally only handle one pregnancy while taking the Luminary serum. Kevin here is one of the two who were born from a second pregnancy."

"Where is the second one?" Andrew asked.

"I don't know where the other kid is. I just know it was a girl and that she should be around our age. I can tell you that they turn the babies into the system because it's cheaper to have the government raise the children and to make sure we have a tough childhood. Then, of course, they become our heroes when we are hand-selected for their scholarship program. Little do we know that we have always been their puppets."

"No, I still don't believe that," Beth said.

"Believe it. I have records, and I will show them to you as soon as I can. They're not good, Beth. They want control of us, of the world. We need to stop them."

"But Jenny is a sensor. She found us!" I said.

"Yes, she found you because she can sense you, but also because it makes their lives easier to find the few Luminary kids who are stocked with the hundreds of regular kids. This way, they don't have to raise any alarms when they start questioning orphanages about specific stranded babies. They just seem to randomly choose youngsters to give them a better life. If they raised too many flags, the government would be onto them," Nick answered.

"You said kids can access their powers early? What happens to them?" I asked Nick.

"Yes, very few can display their abilities at an early age. Annie, you were one of them."

"Don't be ridiculous! I knew nothing of my strength until I got my first injection."

"They erased your memory."

"No way! I would—"

"What? Remember? How exactly would you do that? Hypnotizers and mind controllers are the most popular of Luminaries. Anyone could have changed your memories at any time. You've always had energy stored up. That's why you like fighting, it's an outlet."

Nick continued telling us everything he'd found out so far, but it was clear that he was still weak from his injury. Andrew sent him to get a change of clothes and to take a nap while he and Beth checked in with Derek to inform him that everything was normal over here.

Kevin came to sit next to me and handed me a bottle of water. "If you need anything stronger, let me know. A shot of tequila might just calm your nerves down a bit," he smiled. "Nick mentioned you're a tequila-shot-kind-of-girl."

"Was."

"So, I know this is a lot to take in, but I have yet one more piece of news that is going to devastate you. This," he waved his hands back and forth in between us, "cannot work. You were my sister-in-law, so I can't continue to give you false hope. Deep down, we both know my heart is meant to be with someone else."

He made me smile.

"Thanks, I needed that."

"What? No broken heart? I don't think you're assessing the gravity of the situation. I really cannot be your boyfriend. Bros before hoes, know what I mean?" he grinned.

"If you call Annie a ho again, I will laser your head off, got it?" Nick warned as he came down the stairs.

"So sensitive! You're supposed to be napping while I break your wife's heart, bro."

"Ex-wife," I clarified our current relationship standing for the record.

Nick gave me an awkward look and said, "I'm hungry. Kevin, can you grab me something from the kitchen? And I mean go in there physically and leave me alone with Annie."

"Okay…but do you actually need something, or do you just want me to leave—oh, okay," he said when Nick stared him down.

I looked up at Nick. He was wearing his usual jeans and white T-shirt look…oh, the memories. He was still somewhat handsome, eye-patch and all. He was 5'11", with a lean build but with some fine muscles, and even with scars, his dimples deepened as he smiled. I was glad he'd shaved when he'd showered that morning. The wild animal look wasn't as appealing... Okay, well, maybe a little bit. Now, if only he could get a decent haircut…ugh, maybe not. I would surely be in trouble if he did that. His hazel eye a tone deeper than Kevin's made me think that I should have noticed the resemblance earlier.

"I'm sorry," he said to me.

"About?"

"Leaving you the way I did. I thought it was better to keep you in the dark so they wouldn't harm you."

"You are a coward. Don't give me this crap about protecting me. You were saving your own ass. I could have come with you. Helped you. We were a team." I took a deep breath and continued, "At least, I thought we were."

"We were. We are! You and I are on the same side, Annie, and always will be. I didn't know what would happen when I stopped taking the monthly injections. And if there was any chance that I would die, I didn't want to risk *your* life."

"And then what? I would still have been in danger and wouldn't know what was going on," I said, exasperated.

"You think I wasn't prepared for that?" He picked up a candle from the stand. "I have a record of everything, ready to be sent to you—in your email, your phone, and even a USB drive to mail to you—if I go more than three days without checking in. It's encrypted, but I know you would figure out how to open it. I also have it being sent to Andrew and Jenny so they can help protect you. I never stopped loving you. I—"

"Don't. Please, don't you dare say that."

He brushed his hands through his hair. "Okay, I'm sorry. I just…I just want you to know that I kept you safe, and I knew that having you hate me kept you safe. The divorce was the only way I knew they wouldn't make me their priority because it left you free for Derek."

"Selfish move again."

He ignored me. "I'm glad you've moved on and that you've found happiness."

"You are, huh? Thanks then, I'm happy *you* are glad," I said.

"You and Derek really are together, then? It's true?"

"Yes, it's true, so stop asking."

"Good, we need you close to him. Now more than ever."

"Are you sure? He is so hot I can barely—"

"Okay, I get it. He is Mr. Perfect."

I jumped as Nick squeezed my candleholder into dust.

"How did you do that?"

"I channeled your strength. When I get upset, I have to channel anything I can to avoid fire." He started picking up some pieces from the floor. "Sorry about that. I'll pay you for it."

"No, it's okay. I just can't believe that channeling actually works. I mean, I know I've seen it before, but it's still a new concept."

"Yeah. I'm going to take my nap."

I spent most of my day going through all of the files Nick had stored on his laptop. The more I saw proof of what he was saying was truth, the less I believed it. It was difficult finding out that the place I called home, my safe haven, the one place that gave me purpose in this world, was so corrupt. All the blood that had been shed and all the injustice had just been for two people to gain power? In what mind does the need for such control make sense?

Nick thought that they were after control of the government by threatening our exposure through attacks, and that they were after becoming even richer and more powerful. I just thought they must have lost their minds with a huge sense of grandeur.

I couldn't believe who it was. His diary pages, which Nick had somehow gotten ahold of, showed how he had been so proud to be the only man with multiple powers for so long, he felt like God and loved the notion that so many people needed him for healing and helping them. Then stronger Luminaries came to be—me in particular—and he just couldn't stand it. He was being driven by jealousy. He wanted to harness a way to be the one Luminary with the most powers, and he needed me to give him strength.

Jessica had thought her work would make her famous and respected, and was happy that he'd offered himself as her guinea pig. But from what I read, once he got what he wanted, he would kill her and say that he'd developed all the powers himself, taking full credit for everything.

Our savior and hero, Dr. Derek Lake, had to be stopped.

# CHAPTER TWELVE

"KEVIN!" I CALLED.

"Yes?" I heard from upstairs.

"Come with me to the kitchen."

I stood staring at the van parked outside, wondering who was inside this time. I heard footsteps.

"How long have you been helping Nick?" I asked, turning around to face Kevin.

"Oh, I…why don't we wait for him? You are mad at him, don't forget." He tried smiling but realized it wasn't working.

"Kevin. You are under my roof," I said.

"OKAY, MOM! Can't believe you are pulling that on me. Fine. Over a year now."

"How did he find you?"

"I was in the accident I told you about. Remember? The one that made me forget my crappy life? Well, that's when Nick and Dr. Lake found me in the hospital."

"But you said it was only a few weeks."

He shook his head. "I was in the accident about a year and a half ago and met both of them at the hospital. Dr. Lake told me about the scholarship, and I was happy about it, but the night before I was to be discharged, Nick got me out of there."

"I see. How did Dr. Lake find you again?"

"I went back to the hospital claiming I was lost, and another doctor, who had been with Dr. Lake the first time, came to pick me up and acted like we'd never met before."

"Oh, and when you first met Nick, what happened?"

"He got me out of there and explained everything. He gave me back most of my memories. Turns out the reason my foster dad beat me up was because I scared him by disappearing into thin air. He was a drunk, regardless, so he thought he was losing his mind, but he still took it out on me."

"You had your powers earlier?" I asked.

"Yes, like you. I'm guessing they erased my memories and told me it was a side effect of the accident. Anyway, I stayed with Nick until I got this teleportation thing under control and helped him out when needed."

"You were the one who got him into my office?"

"Yes," he said, looking away.

"And Worldsafe?"

"Yes, and at the Lumins' also. That's why the man, Allen, thought he recognized me. I was waiting for Nick to scope the inside a few months back, and he drove by.

He saw me standing around and told me to leave."

"Nick's been having you do dangerous work. I can't believe how irresponsible he's been. Wait until he wakes up."

"He's been honest with me, Annie, and he's kept me out of danger. Well, except in India."

"Wait, were you the person they captured?" I asked.

"Yes, I panicked and didn't get out of there on time. Then I tried to get closer to Nick so I could grab him and go but was caught by a guard. He walked right into the middle of the flying metals so he could free me, and by the time he got to me, his eye was already messed up."

"Oh, Kevin. It's not your fault. You never should have been there in the first place."

"That's what he said, but still, I can't imagine he's forgiven me completely. I thought I had control of my power, but I freaked out," he said.

"Don't beat yourself up. Nick deserved that."

"No, he didn't," he objected as his brow creased. "How can you say that?"

"All right, not *that* exactly, but somebody had to show him he isn't almighty. He thinks he's the best at everything and nothing bad can happen while he's in charge."

"You're just bitter." Kevin walked away.

"Err, okay…" So what if I was? I had the right to be bitter. Had that young boy really just put me in my place? Whatever. Obviously, he would side with his brother over me any day. Besides, I could have Jenny fix his eye…if I wanted to.

AROUND SEVEN IN the evening, I was still busy replaying everything I'd learned in my head when the doorbell rang, making me jump. I called Kevin to go check with the guard to see who it was, since no one was supposed to even get to my door without notice. Kevin came back and put his finger to his lips, mouthing 'shhh' before disappearing, only to come right back. "It's Derek out there. I warned Nick. He didn't want to leave, so he'll keep quiet." He opened the door, and Derek walked in with two pizza boxes. He shot me a smile and walked to the kitchen.

"What the heck happened in here?" He flicked his hand and put the table back together. Show off. He put the food down and looked at me.

"Oh, thanks for fixing it. I was just frustrated about being stuck under house arrest. I don't like it," I pouted.

"I know, darling, but it's for the best." He walked over to me to give me a hug, but Kevin dropped his water.

"Oh, sorry, I just, uh…I'm going to grab some slices and go to my room. Is that cool?"

"Yes, Kevin, that's a good idea, actually," Derek answered, hardly taking his eyes away from me.

"Okay. Just remember…I'm one shout away!" Kevin walked out.

"Did he just take half a pie?" Derek asked.

"Yeah...I've been starving the poor kid all day. Don't be mad."

"I'm not. I'm glad he took enough so he won't come and interrupt us."

"True." I gave him a bright smile.

"You actually seem happy to see me."

"Of course, why wouldn't I be?"

"No reason," he frowned. He was obviously baffled by my behavior, but what could I say? I was trying to get under Nick's skin. He wouldn't expect that I would be hurting for him after all this time, when I had so obviously moved on. So much so that I didn't even know who Nick was. He hadn't crossed my mind since he walked out...not even on my mind in that moment, nope...

"So...is that a yes?"

"Ummm, yeah." *Was what a yes?* I had no idea what he'd said. I was too busy thinking about the guy I never think about.

"Really?"

"Yes, why not?" I asked, hoping he would give me a hint on what I had agreed to.

"It's just that even up to the other night, you were playing hard to get, and to agree now to go public as my girlfriend is awesome."

"Pu—public girlfriend, umm..."

"Don't be upset, not just public. I know you want to be with me, but have been trying to hold back because of the whole Nick business. I'm quite happy to make it serious, if just public bothers you," he said.

"I don't know, maybe it's not a good idea after all."

"Okay, we don't have to go public, it's just that if he is paying attention out there and he knows that you're mine, maybe he might want to back off. At the very least, he can roll in fire from being so jealous."

"Oh, come on, he wouldn't even care."

"Yeah, maybe not. But I don't want to talk about him anymore. I'm just happy you finally agreed to be mine." He came closer to me. "I've been dying to do this for so long," he said softly as he leaned in to kiss me, and the sparks were flying.

No, really. The sparks were flying from the stove, which just up and started all four burners, all by itself. Well, with some help from upstairs. *How did he do that?*

"Sorry, I forgot I was going to make tea when the doorbell rang!" I exclaimed, jumping up and pretending to turn the stove off. "Nothing," I said very loudly, "will interrupt us again."

I walked around to grab a piece of pizza and filled my mouth with it before Derek could fill it with his tongue. It's not that I didn't want to kiss Derek, it's just that I felt weird with Nick being right upstairs, which was exactly the other reason why I couldn't wait to kiss Derek. I was so complicated... maybe the whole Org corruption issue would be easier to solve than my love life.

"So, any news on what's going on?" I asked.

"I'm working on some leads right now, mainly from

Worldsafe. I'm trying to convince them that if I could talk to the owner, I would understand better why Nick was after that particular vault."

"Derek…who told you that Worldsafe was going to be broken into?" I asked him.

"My dad got a lead and he shared it with me. Why?"

"Well, maybe you should talk to your dad about this lead. He might be able to shed some light into the owner, or share with you how he got his information, maybe an email or phone number you can trace."

"Hmm, I hadn't thought of that. I guess I will be calling Dad soon. He's happy about us, you know. He said he always knew we would end up together."

"I'll bet."

"Come here." He pulled me to stand right in front of him. He wrapped his arms around my waist and drew me closer. He tilted my chin upward and kissed me. He simply caressed my lips at first and then deepened the kiss. He definitely knew how to kiss, I had to give him that…man, he was good.

"Oh, wow," Kevin breathed as he stared at us. "I'm sorry, I, uh…didn't know you were still here or that you two," he pointed from Derek to me, "were dating or whatever. I, uh, I'm just going back to my room. I'll leave you two to it." It was at this point that I became convinced Kevin deserved an Oscar for his acting skills.

"Good night, Kevin," Derek said, and turned his back on us to check his phone.

"'Night." Kevin looked at me, and in a theatrical

move, he grabbed his chest and motioned that I'd broken his heart. He gave me one last dashing smile and went back upstairs.

"Is everything okay?" I asked Derek when I saw him looking at his phone.

"Yes, just checking to see if I have any updates," he turned to me, "but nothing is important enough to distract me from you right now." He was about to put his phone in his pocket when it rang. He muttered something I couldn't hear and then picked it up. "It's Samantha, excuse me," he told me, and he walked back to the living room.

I washed the dishes and was throwing the pizza boxes away when he came back. "What's up with Samantha?"

"She was just updating me that the guard shift went off with no issues. Everything seems calmer than usual, so she's only sending one extra person to be on the lookout."

"Great, less people to fuss over me."

"Yes, but it's a must. Thanks for letting Kevin stay here with you. I feel better about it, not only for your quick escape if anything goes down, but also because he's had it tough, and being in an actual home with someone as caring as you might be good for him."

"Maybe he can stay here after our big problem gets resolved. I would like that." I knew that with him being Nick's brother, I couldn't let him go back on his own. Not knowing what kind of future Nick might have, the least I could do was protect Kevin.

"That's nice of you, darling, but if we're starting a life together, I don't think a third wheel is a good idea. And you're already dedicating most of your weekends to volunteering at orphanages and raising money for them. When would we ever have time alone?"

"It will be a while before we move on to the next level, Derek. I want to take my time, and we have to see how this whole thing ends, when it ends. By then, he'll be old enough to get his own place anyway. He is seventeen, isn't he?"

"Yes."

"There you go, then. He will have to go back to training, and he'll be busy, but I feel close to him so I—"

"How can you feel close to him? You only met him about a week ago," Derek snapped.

"I just do. We've been here locked up together for days, and we have a connection…I've learned a lot about him, and the guy deserves a break, ya know? He is here for me now, and I want to be there for him after this is all over."

"That's why I love you so much. You are so caring and generous. I can't wait to start my life with you."

"All in due time, Derek. Talking about love makes me uncomfortable. Please don't. Right now, let's just enjoy the moment and try not be too pushy, okay?"

"Sure." He went to get his jacket. "It's getting late and we both need to rest. I would love to spend the night here with you, but since you just made things clear for us to go slow before we even start, I'll leave now. I'm going to stop by tomorrow. Does that sound good to you?"

"Yeah. It sounds great…because you *have* to come here tomorrow."

"Yes, I have to." He smiled. "The birthday girl will need a birthday kiss, won't she?"

"But of course."

"You don't turn twenty-four every day," he said.

"Nope."

I WOKE UP late on my birthday. Really late, 10:00 a.m. late. And bless their hearts, the boys woke up a half hour later. It felt nice to have other people with the right notion of sleeping in. Nick made us coffee. I'd really missed his 'love coffee' as we used to call it. This was a great start to my birthday already. Nick stood by the stove and was staring at me.

"How did you light the stove from upstairs?" I asked him.

"I wasn't upstairs. I was looking from the corner. I wanted to turn Derek into ashes so badly my fireballs just formed," he said, shrugging. "So I aimed them at the stove."

"Don't be spying on me!"

"I was…thirsty? Would you believe that?"

I laughed, "No."

"I wasn't spying, I swear," he said with a smile.

"Right."

"I could have fixed that for you," he said, pointing toward my kitchen table.

"You? How exactly?" I asked.

"It was a clean break, nothing too hard. I think I could have fixed it with regular tools."

"Do you even own tools?"

"No, but I could buy some. It's just wood so it would be easy, anyway. Some glue with nails here and there and it would be like new."

"Uh-huh…just nail and glue…and what would happen to the crack, might I ask?"

"Tablecloth, my lady. A tablecloth would cover it right up." We were both laughing when Kevin announced that Beth and Jenny were at the door, so I went out to greet them.

"Hey, birthday girl!" Beth came in with two bags and placed them on the coffee table.

"Happy birthday, Annie," Jenny said, smiling. "Derek gave us the rest of the day off to spend with you doing girly stuff."

"Yes, we brought food, chick flicks, and we are going to make some margaritas later, but not before we use these mani/pedi sets I so lovingly have here for you two."

"She is obviously excited enough for the three of us together," Jenny said.

"I see that," I replied.

"Oh, come on, it's fun doing girl things," Beth said.

"You realize it's Annie's birthday and not yours, right?"

"Haha, Jen. I have to take advantage of any opportunity I get for us to act like normal girlfriends, don't I?"

"Thanks, girls, this is great. But, umm…Beth, are you forgetting something?" I asked.

"No, I went to the Sweet Orphan Home already. I dropped off the bags and explained you wouldn't be able to go for a while." She took a sip of her tea before she continued, "And I set up the order for cupcakes from the bakery. They'll deliver them monthly and everything."

"Thanks, Beth, but that's not what I meant. I knew you wouldn't forget *that*."

"What then? Andrew is bringing your cake later."

"She means Nick." I looked up in surprise at Jenny as she continued talking, "I didn't forget. Every night I practice healing on myself, and I've gotten so good at it that my body takes care of anything that isn't right."

I frowned. "And…you…what?"

"I think I healed myself from memory modification, and it's all clear again. Beth filled me in and—oh, hey." She ran over to Nick and gave him a hug. "I'm so glad to know that you were always on our side."

"Okay, so she believes you," I said as Nick picked up Jenny and set her down gently.

"You know I'm in a lot of pain, right? My healer

didn't want me to run away so…"

"Oh, come here." She put her hands over his ribs, and his paleness all but disappeared. "Better now, you big baby?"

"Oh, much." He took a sandwich wrap from a bag and took a bite. "I love you, did you know that?"

"Everyone loves me," Jenny said, smiling. "Now get out of here so we can have our girls spa-movie-drinking day."

At that moment, Kevin ran in and said hi to everyone and grabbed a couple of sandwich wraps before disappearing straight back up the stairs. Then he appeared next to me, almost giving me a heart attack, and gave me a hug and handed me one of the wraps he'd taken.

"Happy birthday, Annie, take this sandwich that I made for you with lots of love and mayo." He disappeared again and we were all alone.

We watched two of our all time favorite movies, *Dirty Dancing* and *Pretty Woman,* while Beth did some manicures and pedicures on us. It was around 4:30 p.m. when Andrew walked in with a cake.

"There is the birthday girl," he said, smiling at me. "I'm leaving this in the very capable hands of my lovely wife." He handed the cake to Beth and went around to give Jenny a kiss before coming over to me and giving me a bear hug and a kiss. "May I just say…how pretty your nails look?"

"I love you," Beth said with a sigh.

"Just saying it like I see it, honey. Where are the

guys?" With a small pop, Kevin and Nick appeared next to him.

"Called for us?" Kevin said, with a grin.

"Yeah, come on. Let's go make those margaritas for the ladies."

"What about us?" Kevin asked with excitement.

"Well, Andrew and I will drink beer, and you can have some orange juice," Nick said, smiling.

"You suck, bro." They all walked into the kitchen as the girls and I decided on calling for some Chinese take-out. As we were sipping our drinks and waiting for the food, my doorbell rang again. Kevin took a quick peek and immediately sent Nick upstairs, then he went on to open the door, revealing Derek with our food in his hands.

"Hey, guys. I got here at the same time as the food and decided it should be my treat." Derek walked over to the dining room and placed the food on the table, then came over to me and, kissing me full on the mouth, said, "Happy birthday, beautiful."

"Thank you," was all I could say with the burning eyes of my friends scalding my back.

"Well, you two don't waste time," Jenny said.

"We don't waste time? It took me quite a few years to get her to give me one date," he said, holding up his finger. "Now, I need a beer, too."

"I'll get it," Kevin volunteered.

"Yes, get one more for Andrew too, but no more for you, young man."

"For me?"

"Yes, you didn't think I would notice the two bottles here?" he said, pointing to the bottles next to our margarita glasses.

"Oh, sorry, man," Kevin said.

"I get it, don't worry about it. Just don't drink any more or we'll all be in trouble, young man."

"No problem, I have orange juice waiting for me anyway," Kevin shrugged.

We ate and enjoyed another round of drinks before Derek announced that it was time to cut my birthday cake. They sang for me, and we ate as he did some work on his phone.

"Good news, Annie," he said. "Since it's Friday and things have been on the slow side—for good reason, I might add—I think we can spend some extra time tonight...alone." He took another bite and started pointing toward Andrew and Beth. "You two do need to get your rest. I have some leads for you to work on, starting Monday. Tomorrow, you're back on bodyguard duties outside the house."

Then he turned to Jenny, saying, "And you...you need to get me that report about the incident that happened two nights ago."

"It sure sucks for your friends when you date the boss, huh?" Kevin said to me, stuffing his face with cake.

"Yes, it does," Derek answered for me, "so you, Kevin, get going to bed."

After they all left, we cleaned up and sat down to

talk in the kitchen while drinking a delicious wine he had brought for me.

"So what happened two nights ago?" I asked Derek.

"Nick made another attempt to break into Worldsafe, but I had some people standing guard, and in the process, he was badly hurt." I couldn't miss the satisfied grin spreading across his face as he talked. "I am pretty confident that he is going to need some time to recuperate before attempting to make another move."

"How did he get away?"

"How does he do anything? I don't know." He got up and walked around until he was standing right next to me. He grabbed my arm and pulled me up to stand. "I don't care about him right now, Annie. I don't want to talk about work either. Is that okay?"

"Of course," I answered while he spun me around to face him.

He lowered his head, staring at me, and gently but desperately kissed my lips. He continued staring, and I couldn't close my eyes. And as if helpless to resist, I found myself almost assaulting him for a more passionate and deeper kiss. I finally closed my eyes and gave in to this need to really be close to him. I pushed myself so that I had him pressed against the counter, his hands in my hair. I could hardly believe I was responding this way to him, but I couldn't get enough. I felt physically weak. His hands started wandering around my hips and pulling me forward.

"Let's go to the bedroom," he said, with lust in his

eyes. And I found myself responding with the same lust, so I let him guide me while kissing him. That's when his phone rang. Cursing under his breath, he placed me on the floor and took out the phone.

"Just ignore it, Derek," I heard myself whisper, while pulling his hands to go up the stairs.

"Yeah, okay," he said following me, and then the phone beeped. "A text message. Hang on a sec." He read the message and gave me a knowing look. "I'm so sorry. You have no idea how sorry, but I have to go."

"Noooo. Come on, you can go later." I was surprised by the desperate plea coming from my voice.

"There was another sighting. They are following Nick as we speak, I have to go. Remember, he's hurt, and this might be my only chance to get him."

"Fine," I said, disappointed.

"Come here, at least I can give you one more kiss." And so he did, making my world spin as he left. I never knew a kiss could leave you feeling so dizzy.

# CHAPTER THIRTEEN

"GOOD MORNING." I turned in my bed to find Nick staring at me. He was sitting next to me with a bottle of water. "How are you feeling? Any headaches?" he asked.

"Yes, actually." I took the two Advil he was giving me and swallowed them with one big gulp. "What are you doing in my bed?"

"You don't remember, baby?" He gave me a teasing smile.

"No way!" I took a peek under the blankets to find I had my clothes on. "Liar."

"Liar? I didn't say anything, I only insinuated something." He got up and walked to the dresser that had a picture of us on our wedding day. He picked it up and smiled. "This was the happiest day in my life."

"Like I said…liar."

"I can't believe you were going to bring him into our bedroom last night. How could you do that? Especially knowing I was in the same house. You do realize, don't you? I would have killed him before he got inside my bedroom."

"First of all, this is not *your* bedroom anymore. And second, what makes you think he hasn't already been spending some passionate nights in this very bed with me?"

"Because you wouldn't still have this little display of our love hanging around. No man would allow it," he said.

"You're right. I didn't even realize I still had it here." I walked over and snatched it from him and threw it in the garbage can. "Now, get out of my room."

Nick took one last look at the picture in the garbage and walked out. I went to take a bath to see if it would help ease the headache. I couldn't remember how I had gotten into my bedroom, and worst of all, I couldn't figure out why my last memory of the night before was of me being upset that Derek wouldn't spend the night with me. What had I been thinking? Sure, the man knew how to kiss, but I wasn't ready to take on a physical relationship with him. I must have been so drunk that I wanted to drive Nick crazy. Still, I knew he would have done something stupid, so what was I thinking? I remembered the reason Derek left in the first place and hurried to get dressed and confront the man in my house.

As I walked down the stairs, the scent of eggs and bacon hit me. In the kitchen, I found Nick taking some bread out of the toaster and putting it on a plate, then placing it on the table where Kevin was already eating.

"Come on, eat." He put the mug next to a plate, and I sat down to eat. Just because Nick was an idiot didn't mean I wasn't hungry. And if he was going to stay in my house, he might as well do something like cook anyway. He knew I was no good at it.

"What do you remember from last night?" he asked me.

"I had a great time with all the important people in my life."

"Okay, got the hint that I wasn't able to share it with you. But what about after the important people left?"

"I was having some fantastic moments with Derek when he got a call about some sighting of you. Which, of course, I'm sure you did because of what was happening in this very kitchen." I turned to Kevin, "And you are to remember that this is my house, and I do not appreciate you helping this asshole out to stop me from being with my boyfriend."

"I thought it was the right thing to do," Kevin said.

"Why? Because your brother said so?"

"No, because you were drugged." Kevin lifted his chin to Nick. "He had me spy on the conversation, and I saw Derek put something in your wine. You were fine for a while, but then you were all over him, and I didn't know what else to do besides tell Nick."

"Yes, Annie, that's why I made him take me to Worldsafe again. I needed to be seen and followed so I could stop Derek from taking advantage of you. When

Kev brought me back here, I found you sleeping on the stairs. We got you in bed, and that was it."

I had no idea what to think. I knew my behavior last night was out of order for me, and I did feel pretty dizzy.

"No, I don't believe you. I felt something last night. I wanted to be with him." The color drained from Nick's face. "Why would you lie for Nick?" I asked Kevin.

"Annie, you don't know me very well, but I'm here to help protect you. I would never lie to you, not for Derek and not for Nick. You are the only person who's ever wanted me to be part of their family because they care, not for money like my foster parents, or because they find out I'm their brother and they have to. You care. I heard you telling Derek last night, and it means a lot to me."

"I care about you," Nick said, hurt surfacing on his face.

"I know you do, but you have to because I'm your brother. She just cares, no reason necessary."

"Yup, that's Annie." Nick stared at me.

"So, no, I'm not lying to you," Kevin continued. "I saw Derek put something in your glass so I did what I thought was right. Excuse me. I'm going to finish this in the dining room." He stood up with his plate and walked out.

"Why would he do that?" I asked Nick.

"Derek? Because he wants things to move faster? To prove a point to me? He is desperate? Take your pick. Oh, and also, because you are incredibly sexy. That reason I'm sure of."

"Oh, come on, but he has to know I would question my actions," I said.

"Not if you were so drunk you couldn't remember. What's the problem, anyway? He is your boyfriend, right? Why does he even need to resort to drugs to get you to sleep with him?"

"He doesn't," I said.

"Then why haven't you?" He cocked an eyebrow.

"Too much going on. I want it to be special."

"Whatever." He picked up our plates and took them to the sink then turned around to say, "I hope you had a good birthday yesterday."

"Apart from being drugged, everything went peachy, thanks." I got up. "Hey, I've been meaning to ask you, why did you break into my office? You took our photograph."

"I went to download whatever information I could find from the Org. I used your computer because it was easier to crack the password."

"How come Beth was unable to open the door?"

"I channeled your strength. I found some notes on us leaving traces of our energies behind, and that was your personal office, so it was everywhere. I was shocked it even worked without you there."

At this point I decided to give up on the whole energy stealing thing. "What were you looking for, Nick?"

"I was trying to get into the network to see who else

is working with Lake."

"Did you find anything?"

"Besides our photograph? No. I only took it so I could leave you a note inside the frame, but Beth figured out someone was in your office, and I had to leave."

"Oh." What else could I say? He'd had no choice but to take it with him. I'd known it didn't mean anything to him.

"Here's a little something that will hopefully make your birthday better. One day later, but still..." He handed me a box that was so poorly wrapped I couldn't help but laugh. One of the sides was half opened, and it was covered in scotch tape. On top sat an origami rose. *Whatever*. Those roses no longer meant anything to me.

"I see you wrapped it yourself," I laughed.

"What do you want from me? At least I tried," he said, looking hurt.

I opened it, and I could feel myself stop breathing.

"I know we're divorced, and it probably doesn't hold any value for you anymore, but I hope you will accept it for old times' sake."

I had to stop myself before the tears ran down my cheeks.

"How did you find it?" I couldn't believe I was staring at the very first necklace he had given me for my sixteenth birthday. Actually, it had been my first birthday present ever. It was a thin chain with a pendant of a fake diamond. I'd never cared that it was a fake. It just meant a lot to me since it was also a promise that I would one day be his wife.

When Nick and I had grown close, we had shared stories about our lives growing up. He was luckier than I had been. He'd had a nice family that took care of him but who, for financial reasons, couldn't adopt him. Me? No one actually wanted to keep me long enough to reach a birthday, so I had never received any birthday presents in my life.

He had given me the chain back then and promised me that he would be the one to keep me always and forever. He told me to wear it as a reminder that there was someone in the world who would always want me. Even though that promise had been broken, I couldn't have been happier to have the chain back in my possession.

"Lisa had it. I found it in her desk." He snapped me out of my memory as he started to explain. "I was looking for any information I could find before leaving the Org. I wasn't sure if she knew what the others were up to, but I found this when I was digging around. I know I should have returned it to you, but it was something I needed to feel close to you. I'm sorry."

"So she was the one who stole it—I knew it. Didn't I tell you?"

"Yes, you did," he said, smiling. "But that was years ago, it doesn't matter now. And anyway, I know how much it meant to you when I first gave it to you." He brushed his hair with his hand. "I don't expect you to wear it, but, you know, at least you have it."

"Thank you," I said, choked up. "You didn't have to return it at all, but I appreciate it." I went to hug him, and what did I do that for? He hugged me, and the scent of him alone brought back so many memories. He pulled away and took a step backward. I didn't know what to do, so I just took a seat on the stool at the kitchen counter and stared at him. I know I should have moved away when I saw him coming back to me with a determined look on his face, but I couldn't. It was Nick.

He grabbed my cheeks in his hands, and I swear he pierced my very soul with his one eye. "May I kiss you?" he said, his lips so close to mine I could feel the heat of his breath.

"I don't think, umm, that's not what we…what I…ahh no, you know…it's, uh, not a good idea," I barely managed.

"It's not because my face is busted, is it?"

"Maybe." I smiled.

"Fine," he said, but didn't move. "I won't kiss you." He did, however, lower his head to my neck and slowly caressed my collarbone all the way up to my ear lobe and breathed hard against me. His hands were on my legs and my waist as I sat there, completely weak and overcome with lust. He gently bit my ears and moved to my lips. He bit me again, harder this time, and I cried out, making him laugh.

"Oh, just stop. I told you no, anyway," I said, frustrated yet still letting him hold me close.

"You didn't say I couldn't bite you."

"You didn't ask that," I said.

"You didn't stop me."

"I didn't say I didn't want you to."

"So you *do* want me to?"

"Would you believe me if I said I'm still under the influence of drugs?"

"If that helps you sleep at night...or better yet...with me, right now."

"Idiot." I pushed him away. "It's because of the chain and you know it."

"If that's how it's going to work, then you should know I have your wedding ring from the garbage, too."

I turned to face him so fast I walked right into his chest.

"You don't."

"I do." He laughed. "No pun intended since those were the same words I said during our vows. I do, darling, I do. You really have to stop throwing away the loving jewelry I give you." He took out a chain from his pocket and showed it to me. Hanging in the middle were both our wedding rings.

"That one I meant to throw out. Why do you have it?"

"I have it because one day I intend on putting it back where it belongs." He pointed to my left hand.

"Why, Nick? After everything?"

"I told you. I love you."

"You don't mean that."

"Of course I do. I will always mean it."

"You are a liar. You're only saying this now because you want something from me. What is it that you want?"

"This." He grabbed me and really kissed me this time. His lips found mine, and he lifted me right back on top of the stool. Then he pulled me close to him and stood between my legs. I found myself pulling him closer and closer to me and didn't budge when his hands found their way under my shirt to caress my back. I put my arms around his neck and then a rush of emotions came to me, it was all I could do to hold them back. I wanted to cry. My head was on his shoulder while he held me in silence. I wanted to stay there, letting him hold me, and I would have if Kevin's voice hadn't shattered the moment.

"Hey, guys, sorry, umm."

I moved away uncomfortably from Nick and looked at Kevin.

"I can come back if you want me to."

"No, go ahead," Nick answered.

"I thought you were with Derek," Kevin said in an accusatory tone, looking straight at me with a hostile gaze.

"You can hardly expect her to stay with him after he drugged her," Nick said.

"I am with Derek," I cut in. "I'm just being carried away by some old memories, but it won't happen again."

"You're not going to end things with him?"

"No, Nick, I'm not. End of story, I don't want to discuss this anymore, he is in my life now, accept it," I said, hoping he was buying my words.

"With friends like him, who needs enemies? You don't know what he is capable of doing next."

"I could say the same about you, Nick."

"Whatever."

"If you two are done, can I talk now?" Kevin asked, exasperated.

"Go ahead," I said.

"Jenny just called. She has a meeting with Derek's dad in the evening. He stopped by the Org and had some big fight with Derek, and the only thing she knows is that he demanded she see him tonight at his personal lab."

"This doesn't make any sense. Let me call her," I said, pulling out my cell phone.

"No." Kevin stopped me. "She can't talk right now. She got away to her office to call me to her, but she is being watched. She thinks they know she healed Nick, and she senses they think she is a traitor."

"That's crazy! How can they possibly think Jenny is a traitor? She would never—"

"Never what? Help me out twice? Heal me? Because she did, and now she's in trouble because of me. We have to help her," Nick said.

"But it could be a trap," Kevin said. "If they think she is a traitor, they would expect her to call you for help, and when you show up they'll have you, and can do whatever they want to you and her."

"I can't just leave her there. This is my fight, not hers," Nick said, rubbing his hands on his jeans.

"She said she would call me when she got home. She isn't sure if she's safe there, either."

"If they suspect Jenny," I bit my lips before finishing my thoughts, "then they definitely will be keeping watch on Beth and Andrew."

"Yes, don't contact them," Nick said.

"But they're not watching me, and they expect you to show up, so…"

"Annie, no! You are not going to make it so easy for him to get his hands on you."

"I have to. It's Jenny. Kevin will take me and bring both of us back if we need to save her." I turned to Kevin. "You can handle teleporting two people, right?"

"Yes, but no more. I'll need a day to recover from that."

"That's fine, as long as we can get out from there."

"You can't go missing," Nick said.

"They are watching the house, not me. And Derek won't even bother me because he'll be busy trying to catch you. He doesn't expect me or Kevin to come and help."

"I would rather you not. They are watching over the house for a reason, Annie. It's dangerous for you."

"They're watching over the house because they think you are out to get me. They have no idea you're already here with me, you ass!"

"Okay, but it really is dangerous for you. They want you to harness the energy you're carrying around inside."

"Yes, the same people who have me surrounded here

are the same people who would hurt me. If anything, I'm better off away from here."

"She has a good point, bro," Kevin said.

"Whose side are you on?" Nick asked him.

"Right now? I'm on Jenny's side. I agree with Annie that we should keep an eye out for her, but I disagree that she needs to come." He turned to me. "I can go by myself. They won't even know I'm around. The second I think she's in danger, I will get her out. I'll tell her to ask to use the bathroom and I'll get her from there."

"No, Kev, they'll know that you did it," I said.

"You can tell your boyfriend that Jenny confided in you and said she was experiencing odd things since you two exchanged energies," Nick said.

"You think he'll believe me?"

"If you continue acting like the loving girlfriend, he will just be so happy about the attention, he won't notice you lying." He got up and kicked a chair. "I guess this means that the best thing for you to do is to keep acting the girlfriend part."

"After he drugged me?" I asked.

"Isn't that the same point I raised earlier when you said you were staying with him?"

"Yeah," I frowned, "but I was just trying to get on your nerves."

"So, it's settled then?" Kevin asked, clearly annoyed.

"What's settled?" Nick asked while looking at me. "That she is trying to get me jealous when she supposedly doesn't care about me? Yes, it's settled."

"No, you ass!"

"I'm not sure how I feel about this new nickname you have for me," Nick said. "I liked 'baby' better."

"Shut up. Kevin, yes, it's settled. We will not be telling Andrew or Beth. You will go on your own tonight and save Jenny if you have to. And I will continue to pretend to be Derek's girlfriend so he doesn't suspect anything."

"As long as you don't pretend to sleep with him, I'm good," Nick said.

"Oh, don't worry…there will be no pretending when it comes to that." I winked at him, getting a grouching sound in response. "Come on, nothing better to keep him distracted than some good sex."

"You'd better be careful." He pointed to me.

"Yes, sir. I will be sure to use protection." I raised my hand to my head in a salute.

"Kevin, get out of here," Nick said, and Kevin disappeared. "You are a tease, aren't you?"

"Always," I said, smiling. "Which is how I know it will work when I come on to Derek."

"Are you serious or are you kidding? I need to know," he said, his face red.

"I'm serious. It's been a long time, and even if it was a drug last night, it really did wake up some needs I've been long ignoring."

"Then come here. If you have needs, I can meet them."

"Nah, this way it's two birds with one stone, ya

know?"

"Whatever." He clenched his teeth. "I can't tell you what to do. Just be careful."

He left me alone in the kitchen. This conversation totally had not gone my way. I assumed he really did care. He did, after all, have my precious chain this whole time. It had to mean something, didn't it? I did have needs, and gosh, he did know how to meet them if my memory served me right. Maybe I would take him up on that offer. I had nothing to lose, it was purely physical, and I could hardly be expected to want it from Derek after he drugged me. This way it would be what I wanted, and I would have the satisfaction of using Nick and taking the revenge I'd wanted for so long. This plan I liked…now, the question I had to ask myself was: am I ready? That was a whole other deal.

# CHAPTER FOURTEEN

I WAS STARTING to feel giddy with my menacing plan of using Nick for sex, but I knew I would have to put that on the back burner for now. I really had to concentrate on what was going on with Jenny in an hour. What kind of person lets themselves get distracted by sex, anyway? It wasn't like I was a man.

I tried reaching out to Samantha to see if she would tell me anything about Derek's whereabouts, since he'd ignored all of my calls and texts, but she acted as if nothing was unusual. She said that Derek wasn't answering her calls, either, and that she would surely pass on any message should he call her. Not helpful at all for being a personal assistant.

Oh, that's it! She was his personal assistant, which meant she knew more than she let on, and of course, she would protect any information. It was her job to do so. With that on my mind, and not sex at all, I went looking for Nick. I found him watching the news in the sitting room.

"We are going to have to kidnap Samantha."

He turned to look at me. "Okay, why?" That's one thing I liked about Nick, he always listens, no matter how stupid an idea might sound.

"She knows stuff. Maybe we can get her to see what's been going on, and she'll see that the best thing for her to do is to help us stop them."

"Annie, that's not a good idea."

"Why not?"

"Like you said, she already knows more than we do, and she has chosen not to do anything about it."

"Yeah, but maybe that's because she doesn't know who to turn to." I sat directly in front of him. "I'm thinking it might be worth a shot to feel her out. We can see if she might be more evil than good. And if not, we'll just have to convince her to work with us."

"What if you think you can trust her and it turns to bite you in the ass?" he asked.

"Then, my dear, you can just erase her memories."

"That. Or, I can just hypnotize her to give us all the information we need from the get-go."

"Or *that*," I said, defeated. He did have a better point.

"It's safer this way. Think about it."

"No, I know. I just hate using people without them knowing it." I sighed.

"Your problem is that you think everyone operates

for the good. If she knows what's going on and is staying quiet about it, then she can't be trusted. And please don't feel that we are invading her privacy. If she's on the bad side, then we're doing the right thing. If she's good, we are still doing the right thing, but we have all the reasons in the world to feel guilty."

"It's different now that I know my own memory was erased. I feel violated."

"If you want, I can make you remember," he said.

"You promised you would never hypnotize me."

"I know. I'm only offering to give you what was taken away from you."

"I don't know, Nick. Let me think about it."

"Sure."

"Do you know where Kevin is?" He nodded in response. "Is he going to be fine, you think? I really hate putting him in any danger."

"He will be perfectly fine. I've taught him to fight and stay hidden, and there is nothing to stop him from saving Jenny and himself if it's necessary."

"He told me he didn't know how to fight."

"He was keeping up pretenses," Nick said.

"Okay. But if he's caught, where will he go? He can't exactly come back here."

"Of course he can't, Annie, and he knows that. I have a cabin, and he knows where it's located. He will go there with Jenny if he has to. And he can always transport me to them so I can stay there if it comes down to that."

"You'll leave me again?" I asked before I could stop

myself.

"Yes. But only because they will all be here, and it will be impossible for me to stay."

"I can come, too."

"No, sorry."

"How can you leave me in danger? You realize they can hurt me, don't you? And if they find a way to do what they need me for, then they win."

"First, yes. I know you are in danger, but they won't hurt you because they need you. Second, I'm very confident in you and your strengths to hold you up until we can at least find out their plans. It's the only way, Annie. You need to be close so we can find out the details of their plans."

"You're just serving me on a platter to them," I said, bitter.

"Yes, I am."

"How can you not care?"

"I care," he said softly, holding me by my shoulders. "And I'm scared, but I will be keeping tabs and will be around you in any way I can. I'm not going to give them the chance to hurt you. The biggest problem—and you have to think about this, Annie—if they don't get to you, they will probably hurt someone else. They can choose just about anyone to test their experiments on, and if they choose someone too weak, the person might die. Can you live with that?"

"No. I didn't think about that."

"It's why you're a Luminary, Annie: to stop danger.

Why are you trying to turn your back now?"

"I'm not trying to turn my back!" I pulled away from him. "I'm mad at you for using me like just another piece in this game, and I'm afraid if they get what they need from me, that they would....that I would..." My mouth went dry at the thought. "I would hate to know that I gave them what they wanted so easily, and for innocent people to suffer because of it."

"It's a risk worth taking, I think." He tried to reach out for me again. "No, listen to me, Annie. You are a strong person, and I don't mean your physical strength. You yourself are a fighter, and you truly care. If someone else gets hurt when you could have done something with the information you're capable of getting, you wouldn't be able to live with yourself. Besides, you're already on this side of thinking, judging by your actions."

"What actions?"

"You decided to stay with Derek."

"Yes." I thought about it and came up with nothing. "What am I missing?"

"Same plan, Annie, different angle."

"How is it the same plan?"

"You are in danger's way, where they can get to you when they want, but also where you can get all the information you need. Be it with Derek or directly from his father, either way, you are already infiltrating them. You just have the power to infiltrate them even deeper."

"Right," I said, knowing he made some good points.

"Now, back to Kevin. He is at Jenny's place, waiting

for her to be picked up. Dr. Lake is sending a car, of course, so this way she doesn't have a way to escape if she wants to. Kevin is going to follow them and will make sure she is not harmed."

"Did Kevin eat anything?"

"Yes," he said, laughing. "Is that what you're worried about right now?"

"No, but it's one of the only things we can control at the moment."

"I get it," he nodded. "From what I gather, Lake doesn't expect her to be there for too long. He has a dinner with some government big shot around eight."

"Okay, that's good."

"Or bad," he said.

"Why would it be bad?"

"Well, if he is planning on detaining Jenny as a prisoner then he wouldn't need to stay there and chat."

We did some more research, both on the computer and on documents that Nick had been able to get his hands on, trying to cross-reference old and new information. Most of them Nick had already gone over, but we both agreed that I might be able to look at things from a new perspective. He had looked for anything that would prove they were up to no good so he could expose them. And I was trying to track and find their next moves to see if we could figure out their motives. From what we could find, they were certainly trying too hard to look innocent.

I was able to concentrate on my work once Kevin

called and told us that Derek was actually the person driving Jenny to his father's place. It immediately made me feel better. If he really didn't know what his father was up to—and Nick was almost sure of this—then we knew that Dr. Lake wasn't about to harm Jen.

About an hour later, Kevin quickly let us know that Jenny was on her way back with Derek. He said there was nothing for us to worry about right now and that as soon as Jenny was left alone at home, he would bring her to us so we could discuss what had happened.

I went to the kitchen to prepare some food. I had been so worried that I hadn't realized how hungry I was. I put some water on to boil for some pasta and took out some meatballs I had previously prepared to make with the sauce. I also went to start making some coffee since I knew it would be Jenny's first choice of drink—she was a bigger caffeine addict than I was. Nick walked in and took the coffee pot from me and started filling it.

"I do believe this part, right here, happens to be my job," he informed me as he finished setting it.

"Yes, you know my coffee sucks."

"You only think it does because you can't get enough of my love coffee," he said, making me chuckle.

"What are you doing?" I asked as he leaned into the kitchen sink and began running the water on his face.

"I'm washing my eye," he said, looking up. The eye patch was off. "It itches if I keep this on too long."

I stared. His damaged eye was closed, but I could see his whole face. It was a sad reminder of the old, handsome Nick. He was clean-shaven, but the scars on his left cheek and his puffed up eye made him look somewhat raggedy.

"Does it hurt?" I asked.

"Nah. Not anymore. It just gets sweaty and itches sometimes."

"Eww." I slapped my hand to my forehead. "Sorry."

"It's okay."

"Can you see through it?"

"I think so, the light comes through, but I can't open it. Does it bother you?" he asked.

"No, it's just so different."

"I mean, would it bother you to be with me? All disfigured?" He replaced his eye patch as he talked. This was obviously second nature for him, he didn't seem to need a mirror.

"That's neither here nor there, Nick."

"Why not?"

"Because I don't forgive you."

"Come on, you can see why I did what I did."

"No." I felt my blood boiling.

"But if you were to forgive me? Would my face bother you?"

"I'm not going to forgive you, so it doesn't matter," I said, staring him down.

The truth was, when I had loved him, it went beyond his looks. Yes, he had been hot and full of himself back then, but I'd learned that his arrogance was his defense mechanism, and that he would stand up for anyone who had been wronged, no matter what. I knew him to be a caring person. Nick got to the depths of my soul without my needing to say a word. He was the one who had taken me back to my old orphanage and who'd understood that I needed to be a part of those kids' lives. He grasped how much it meant to me to feel needed and wanted. So no, his new face wouldn't have changed how much I loved him, but the pain he'd caused me when I'd thought he didn't want me anymore…that would definitely stop me.

I had been mistreated growing up. I had been bullied when I was younger, and as I grew, I'd learned how to sleep with one eye open. It never failed, my loser foster dads had always tried to 'touch' me, but I had never let them. I was small, but I'd known darn well how to attach my knee to their groins, which, of course, had always ended with me being beaten more times than I could count. I had stood up for myself physically, but the psychological damage done by so many would never leave me. The wounds in my skin had long since healed. The wounds in my heart? There are none. Too many holes had been dug inside for far too long. Nick was that last shovel, and there was nothing left.

"I really am sorry, Annie," he said, and started walking away.

"NO. You don't get to tell me 'sorry'! You don't get to walk away, not again!" I grabbed a cup and gave it to him. "Throw it to the floor. HARD."

"The cup? Why?"

"Just do it."

He smashed it.

"You see that?" I pointed to the broken pieces.

"Yes," he said softly, not daring to question my moment of madness.

"No matter how much glue you use while trying to fix it, it will never be the same. No matter how many times you tell it you are sorry, it won't make a difference. The damage is done, Nick. You fixed me once, but it wasn't you who'd hurt me. This time it was all you. The cup is broken. I'm broken."

I grabbed another cup and threw it at him. "YOU BROKE US!"

I held back my tears and ran upstairs.

*I am not weak. I am not weak.* I promised myself I would not cry anymore for him. *God dammit, Annie, get ahold of yourself!* Deep breath. I sat at the top of the stairs for a moment.

*Breathe in, breathe out.*

*Breathe in, breathe out.*

I stood, held my head high, and went back downstairs. Nick was gone, but on the counter was a note:

*We all have cracks and missing pieces, but I do love you.*

I put it away and finished making my sauce. A few minutes later, I heard the door open and was happy to see Andrew and Beth walking into the kitchen.

"Hey, guys…. Uh…what are you up to?" Beth asked, giving me a side look.

"Making dinner, if it isn't obvious," I answered.

"Uh-huh, sure. Dinner, they call it. You two seem like…oh, there is some tension here," she raised her left eyebrow at me.

"Nothing to worry about," I said.

"Aren't you two supposed to be outside standing guard?" Nick asked, walking back into the kitchen.

"Yes, but since you are already inside and we are supposed to save her from you, we didn't see the harm in leaving the patio alone," Andrew said, grabbing some water from the fridge.

"Besides, we're part of this team, and we want to know how it went with Jenny," Beth said. "Kevin kept us in the loop, since they wouldn't suspect anything from him talking to us outside," she answered to the questioning look I shot at her.

Kevin appeared with Jenny by his side, and they filled the room with laughter.

"He is so funny!" Jenny said to no one in particular. "How are you guys?"

"We've been so anxious, Jen!" I said, giving her a tight hug. "How did it go?"

"It went…uh…okay-ish."

I smiled. "Well, from where I'm standing, Jen, you are here safe and sound. That alone makes this evening a good one for me. To make it better, I'm hoping you have some information to share with us."

"Oh, I do all right, I do," she sighed. "But I'm starving. Do you guys mind eating and talking? Oh, and can I have some coffee, too?"

"Anything for you, Jenny. Now you sit and I'll get it." Nick walked around the table. "Annie, darling, you sit too. You've been driving yourself mad all day, and I know you're exhausted." I rolled my eyes at him. He was still trying to be nice—whatever.

"I'll help get the food," Beth said.

I went to sit next to Kevin and asked him, "Are you okay? I'm sorry to have put you in the middle of all this."

"Come on, Annie, you know I was born for this, right? I'm good. No one saw me, if that's what you were worried about. But there is something that would make feel better," he said.

"What's that?"

"A kiss from each one of the ladies here," he said, grinning from ear to ear.

"Well, you'll get one from me," I pulled him to me and gave him a kiss on his head. "This is for you being so brave this young." When I let him go, Jenny gave him a kiss on his left cheek, and Beth followed suit and gave him a kiss on his right cheek.

"Awesome!" he said, turning into a tomato.

"Here you go, sweetie." Nick gave Jenny her coffee. And Beth gave each one of us a plate filled with food. After a few bites, Jenny looked at us and started talking.

# CHAPTER FIFTEEN

"DR. LAKE WANTED me to explain every detail of how I was able to transfer your energy into me so we could heal Beth that night. I told him that it took a lot of concentration and that it really took a toll on you… But then Derek, of course, jumped in and said that your weakness hadn't lasted long, so I couldn't really throw him off."

"Did it seem to you that Derek was in on his father's plan?" I asked Jenny.

"No, not really. He knows his dad is working on some great new advancement for us Luminaries, but he hasn't connected the dots. He also knows that his father is interested in Annie's power, but he doesn't suspect that it's for something bad," she said.

"Anything else?" Andrew asked.

"Oh, yes. They took my blood to see if our transference of energies had affected me in any way. Dr.

Lake wants me to do some extra practices at the training facilities to see if any of my senses are heightened. He also wants me to try and channel the abilities of other Luminaries."

"I don't like this, Jenny. You are most likely their test subject. We need you to please be careful," Nick said. "In Dr. Lumin's notes, there were a lot that were full of gibberish I didn't understand, but some of the notes clearly dealt with blood transfusions. He wrote that by finding the right formula, one can make up blood serums full of power. It will adapt to your DNA, and in turn, your body will hold on to all of those new powers."

"I don't know how else to be careful. I have to do what they say, you know how training is. They're going to put me in situations that will force me to react. They haven't said anything about giving me new shots, though, so that should be good, right?" Jenny asked him.

"Yes, I think so. If they do try to inject anything into you, don't allow it. Play sick, whatever, just don't let it happen."

"Nick, you're scaring me. It's not like our monthly shots that we're in charge of giving ourselves. But at least I have a week to figure out what to do. They need time to prepare for my training."

"Well, if we have a week, then we can try and figure it out ourselves. Let's try to get you training here and see if you're capable of channeling any of our abilities."

She considered what he said for a while. "And what if it works? They are going to love testing me to my limits."

"Not if you know that it's possible. Then you can train yourself to counteract the effects. I'm guessing you would have to concentrate to only react with your current powers, and not any new ones. It should be easy since it's basically being yourself. It all depends on what exactly they do to you," Nick said. "We'll need you to learn our abilities, but you'll also have to learn to avoid using them. We're all so in tune with what we do that it becomes second nature. It might happen to you with new powers, too, since you're a sensor."

"I can try...they said it would be just a few days of this testing with no other interference. But if I show no signs, then they'll introduce another stage where they'll pair me with other Luminaries who will concentrate on giving me their powers, instead of me taking them. If this happens, it will be hard to ignore the reactions. And if that doesn't work again, you're right, Nick: they actually are going to try to infuse my blood and Annie's into some kind of serum and test us that way."

"Wow, wait. How do you know this? I cannot believe they would just up and tell you that," I said.

"They didn't," Kevin answered. "I overheard Dr. Lake discussing the extra plans with that Jessica woman after Derek and Jenny left. They're very excited that they can test their theories on Jenny."

"We can't allow it," Andrew said.

"We have to." Nick turned to me. "For the same reason you have to continue playing your part with them.

We need to know what they want and if it works, so we can use it to our advantage."

"How do we know you aren't really working with Dr. Lake? Maybe you're just pushing us to do what he wants," I said to Nick.

"Seriously? Annie, are you really suggesting that I'm in the same league as those power craving maniacs?"

"I don't know you anymore. Maybe you're a power craving maniac now."

"If you truly believed that, you would have kicked me out of your house a long time ago. Actually, you would have turned me in to your boyfriend. I think the problem is that you are still angry with me."

"I don't know what to think anymore," I said, frustrated.

"You know what I say makes sense. I'm not saying that I have all the answers on the way to go. Nor am I saying that you guys have to follow my words. I gave each one of you all the information that I gathered, and I'm open to new ideas. The only reason I can think of these scenarios is because I've been after them for years, and I've been making little plans. The rest of you have to sleep on it, and if you have anything better than what I've come up with so far, then we can discuss it and vote on it."

"Well, I already have a better idea," I said smugly.

"What's that?" Beth asked.

"We can have Kevin attach some kind of bug or video camera in Derek Senior's house."

"Hard to do since they do a sweep for bugs almost daily," Nick said.

"How do you know that?"

"I don't know that for sure, Annie, but I'm assuming they do, since it's a routine they follow at the Org."

"Do they do the sweep at the same time every day? Because we can just remotely turn it off for a few hours before the sweep to make sure every connection is gone, and then turn it back on for the rest of the time."

"I doubt there's a set time. At the Org it was done randomly, but we can check on it. Kevin would have to stand watch for a few days to see if there is any set schedule or if there are other things we would have to worry about," he answered.

"Yes, and in the meantime, Nick, you can start training Jenny. If you don't mind, I'd like to attempt doing it, also," Beth said.

"Yeah, we can all train. Let's give it our best shot," he said, "… and hope that it works."

"I'm not a hundred percent sure we can trust you," I spoke up.

"After all the proof I've given you, why are you still doubting me?"

"You killed people!"

"I had Kevin and you to think about. Do you really believe I'm okay with taking those people's lives? I'm not, but it was them or you." He pointed to the two of us.

"How can you live with that?" I asked.

"I can live with it because I have to. It's simple—

you or them—I choose you. Always."

"But what about the transfer thing? You've always wanted it to work," I said.

"Why would I want that? And what do you mean by 'always'?" he asked.

"I don't know, why did you tease Derek about having me and Jen do the energy exchange?"

"When did I tease Derek? What are you talking about?"

"Your precious email that you sent to Lisa and Derek," I said.

"I have no idea what you're talking about, Annie."

"Are you denying the emails?"

Nick looked at me. "I will tell you straight up, I have never written any emails to anyone. I did think it would work if you tried to exchange your energies, but that's because I, myself, have tried and succeeded with it. Kevin can attest to that since he and I practiced."

"Yeah, it was cool, he—" Kevin started saying.

"Not now, Kev," Nick said. "Guys, I assure you that I have not shared this information with anyone prior to Beth's incident, and least of all with Derek. If there is an email out there that supposedly came from me, I would like to see it." He turned to me. "You are unbelievable, accusing me of hypnotizing or manipulating any of you. I respect everyone in this kitchen. I see each of you as valuable friends and partners."

I wasn't sure what to think, so I said, "Let me just get the email."

"Wait, one more thing, Annie. If you think I'm here with some devious, hidden agenda, then let me admit to it and leave it in the open: my only secret intention is to get you back by the time this whole thing is over. Because you *will* forgive me, you have to. You and I aren't a matter of ifs and whys. You and I are inevitable."

I felt so lost in the way he looked at me. "I—"

"And you see this?" He pulled out our wedding rings on the chain he'd shown me earlier. "I fully intend on putting it back on your finger. Got it? Now you have my full schedule laid out in front of you, What are you going to do about it?"

"I'll be right back," was all I could mumble after his little speech. I went to get my laptop and brought it to the kitchen. I opened up the file that had the copy of the email Derek had shown me and handed it over to Nick.

He looked at it and grunted, "You really thought I wrote this crap?"

"Yes, I believed it. I had no reason not to."

"Why didn't anyone question me about it before?" he asked.

"I have never seen any emails from you. May I?" Andrew asked. He took the laptop from Nick and read it before handing it to the girls.

"I didn't know about it either. Did you, Jenny?" Beth asked as Jenny shook her head.

"This means Derek has to know something. He's lying to you about this," Nick said.

"No, he has no reason not to believe that it isn't you.

It's anonymous," I said to Nick. "Think about it: if it's not you, then it means someone else is at play here, and Derek isn't thinking that far ahead. He is just obsessed with catching you and stopping your plans. It must have been his father who did it."

"I'm sure it was him," Beth said. "Jenny, I'm scared for you."

"Yes, I'm getting scared, too. I think I'm going to ask Derek to let me guard you for the next few days, Annie," Jenny said. "I'll tell him that I want to try to practice with you before I officially start my new training. I doubt he will say no, since he seems eager to try to please his father. One thing I can tell you for sure, is that he plans on popping the question soon," she said, turning to look at Nick.

"That's ridiculous! We've hardly dated," I said.

"He told me on the way home that it would be safer for you if it was known officially that you are his. Well, his wife, to be precise. He doesn't think anyone would try so hard to get the wife of the President of the Org."

"I'll kill him first." Nick's fists clenched.

"Is this a game to you? Like pride or something, or do you really care? I can't watch you hurt Annie again," Beth said.

"Ask her," he said, pointing to Jenny.

"He means it. I sense the love, and the anger towards Derek, as well as the fear of truly losing her." Her eyes moved from Beth's to mine.

I had no words. I had no idea how I felt. All I knew

was that, as of today, I was still mad at Nick. And I could only admit to wanting him physically and to wanting to get payback for all those tear-filled nights I'd had to make it through because of him.

"Jenny, are you ready?" Beth asked.

"Yes, come help me. Nick, we need you to come with us to the basement. I think Annie needs some space, anyway."

They got up and left while Andrew went back to the front to stand guard in case anyone else from the Org decided to drive by.

"Do you hate him?" Kevin asked.

"I didn't think I did until I found out why he left."

"But he left for good reasons."

"He hurt me. I had no explanations as to why he left. He made me feel like I really WAS the garbage my parents didn't want when they abandoned me as a baby. I put my heart in his hands, Kevin, and he crushed it. And knowing he left with 'good intentions' doesn't change the pain. In a weird way, I wouldn't hate him so much right now if he really had gone because he didn't care anymore."

"What do you mean?"

"Thinking he turned evil was easier to accept than to believe he would make me suffer so much by his own choice. He knew me better than anyone. He should have known what his actions would have done to me. He gave me a reason to finally be happy, and then he took it away—when all he needed to do was confide in me. Had he let me in on his plan, I would have been okay. Everything would have been okay."

"You wouldn't have let him go. You are so stubborn, you would have wanted to join him," Kevin said.

"True, but he could have left a note explaining all that shit with the divorce papers, no?"

He considered it. "But if he had, you would have gone looking for him. Or talked to Derek, or something else. And if you didn't act all brokenhearted, wouldn't everyone know you were still in contact with him?"

"So turning my life upside down was the only way? You'll side with him because he is your brother."

"No, I'm not saying he couldn't have done a better job at it. Like, maybe confided in Andrew to let you in on it later or something. Either way, it killed him, and he did what he thought was right."

"What makes you so sure?"

"You didn't see him a year ago. I did."

"And?"

"And that's between you two." His brows creased. "You are going to be okay. You were never garbage, and now you *know* the reasons why we were all alone for so many years."

"That's true, I guess. It's just hard to let go of the only feeling I've ever known while growing up."

"If you are garbage, then so am I," he said, smiling.

"You are not! Okay, fine, *we* are not."

"I never would have thought you were so depressed inside. You're always so cheerful."

"I have wonderful friends, I have a purpose in life, and I like putting a smile on other people's faces. My pain is my own. There's no need to share it around."

"They're coming back up," he said.

My head lifted in their direction, and then I think I might have drooled.

It's probable that my heart jolted back into place, too, because the only thing I could hear was the *ba-bump* pounding hard in my chest. Nick's face was back. Jenny had fixed him. Most of his burn scars were gone, but he still had a few, including a long slash going down from the corner of his left eye to his jaw. They were almost faded...I hadn't even noticed them before with all the burnt skin. They'd also cut his hair. His wild look was gone along with the patch, and both his beautiful hazel eyes penetrated mine with such intensity I could almost feel myself starting to swoon. I know, I know...I sound so shallow, but it wasn't because he was so cute, it was just that his full-blown smile took me back a few years. It took me straight back to our happy days when it was okay to love him.

"Oh."

"That's it? That's all our hard work gets us?" Beth asked.

"I, well...it's good. You girls did a good job, it's umm, good...healing, Jen."

"Bro, it's cool! I'm sorry I messed you up in the first place." Kevin slapped Nick's shoulder.

"You didn't mess me up, but yeah, it is cool. I can

burn the eye patches now. I hated those little fuckers."
His eyes turned to me.

"How come he still has some scars?" I asked Jen.

"I fixed them a little. I can only heal. I don't perform
plastic surgery, you know," she said, smiling. "He wants
to keep them, anyway."

"Why do you want to keep them?" I asked him.

"This big one here," he touched the longest scar,
"happened the same day I left. I wanted to turn around
and come back, but I knew I couldn't. In my frustration, I
fired a beam and hit myself," he answered. "I've done
enough damage to you and to the family of those people I
killed. The least I can do is carry my scar on the outside
too. Believe it or not, it pains me that I did what I did. I
don't deserve to be scar-free. I'm an animal, I should
look like one."

Darn right you are an animal. A sexy beast, to be
exact...*okay that's neither here nor there, get your mind
out of the gutter, Annie.* He might think it was a bad
thing, but man did it look hot!

After everyone left, I went straight to my bedroom,
leaving the kitchen looking like a disaster area. I heard
Nick and Kevin cleaning up, and as grateful as I felt, I
couldn't stay to help out, nor could I say another word to
them. I just wanted to relax, so I went and prepared a bath
for myself and got a glass of wine from the stand Nick
had originally put in the master bathroom. I made sure
my bedroom door was closed to avoid another morning
of being awakened by some man in my bed. I noticed

Derek had called me while I was discussing the issues with the gang, and decided to just send him a text message, telling him I was working out and that I would talk to him tomorrow.

I spent almost an hour twisting and turning, just thinking of everything that had happened that day. I held the pendant Nick had recovered to my chest and cried with abandon for the first time in many months, thinking of the pain he'd caused me when he broke my heart. I knew it was weak to wear it, but no one was there to see it, and I would take it off in the morning. For now, all I needed was the comfort it provided close to my empty chest.

A while later, I heard a gentle knock on my door and knew immediately that it was Nick. I could have pretended to be asleep and not answered him, but I decided to do what I wanted instead. Thinking too much could be overrated, I decided. I opened the door to find him there in sweat pants and no shirt, staring at me. The moonlight shining through the window reflected in such a sensual way on his chest and on his delicious abs that I felt my knees go weak instantly. He gently lifted my chin, and from the other side of the door, he lowered his head and gave me a soft kiss on my lips. When I didn't move, he put one arm around my waist and walked in, closing the door behind him.

"You are wearing my shirt."

"I always wear your shirts. They're all I had left of you."

"I'm here, you have me." He put his arms around me and whispered, "I'm home now."

Nick picked me up and wrapped my legs around him. We looked into each other's eyes as he walked us towards the bed. He pushed my hair away from my neck and began kissing it softly as he lay on top of me. His breath left a trail of intense heat on my breasts and along my neck, and then my mouth. Our lips met slowly at first, the taste, the feel, the sweetness of our memories fading into a passion that made me forget my name. His hands explored my body, and I pushed my hips into him as he took off what little I was wearing. His lips pressed into my neck as he took me, and I found myself moaning…we did not sleep until the sun came up. That night, we devoured each other completely.

# CHAPTER SIXTEEN

I JUMPED UP at the sound of the hard knocks coming from outside of my door.

"Annie?" I heard Kevin from the other side.

"Yes, I'm coming." I pulled Nick's shirt over my head as I went to open the door. "What's up? Are you okay?" I asked with heavy lids that were threatening to close on me.

"I'm fine, are you okay? You seem really tired."

"She's fine," Nick assured him as he came from behind me. "Did something happen?" He opened the door wider as I went back to sit on the bed and covered my legs. "You can close your mouth now."

"Err, no, I was just going to tell Annie that you had disappeared. I didn't know you were with her." He took in the scene in front of him. The bed was a big mess, most of the sheets were off, and the pillows were pretty much all on the floor. He gave Nick a big smile and a fist bump. "It looks like your little speech last night worked."

"Wipe that grin off your face. Nick and I were just practicing how to transfer our energies."

"Yeah, and we got it down…nicely." Nick shot me a smile.

"I'm seventeen, not stupid, guys. I'm going to make some coffee. Jenny is going to get here soon, so I'm guessing you'll need the caffeine. The way you people drink that stuff, you would think it's water." He took another look around the room before hanging his shoulders and shaking his head. "I'll make it extra strong."

Nick went back to his bedroom to get dressed while I cleaned up a little bit and got dressed myself. I went down to find Jenny and Kevin laughing together.

"So you must be exhausted, using up your energy like that," she said with a wicked smile.

"Empowered more like it. Trust me, she knows how to use all of her *energy*," Nick answered, walking past me to get two mugs.

"Bro, you have to teach me how to give speeches like yours."

"Shut up," Nick said good-naturedly as he gave Kevin a small tap on his head. "Breakfast, anyone?"

"Oh, actually, I brought bagels and cream cheese for us."

"Thanks, Jenny, you are the best," I said on my way to bring them to the table.

"Sit, Annie, I've got it," Kevin said. He made the

baggie appear on the table, along with plates and knives, and even butter.

"Yup, I figured I needed some food in me before training with Nick." She took a bagel from the bag and started cutting into it. "That's if you're up to it." She looked up at him as he sat down. "I'm not sure how much energy you have left."

He laughed. "No worries, I got enough energy from Annie to last me a few hours, but if I need more, then I'll just have to steal some more from her."

"Can I train, too?" Kevin asked.

"Let me concentrate on Jenny first, then we'll work on it with you and Annie. Is that cool?"

"I guess," he shrugged.

"Besides, we need you to check out Dr. Lake's place to see if we can bug them," Nick said.

"Okay."

I dropped the rest of my bagel down on the plate. "Yeah, you guys do that, and in the meantime, I'm going to just sit around and pretend I'm doing something important."

"No, I think you can go and work on Samantha like you wanted to," Nick suggested.

"But Derek will be mad."

"Not if you have Kevin pop you over there, and you use your charm on him. Just not too much," he said, frowning. "Your boyfriend won't be too upset if you're still in one of his safe zones. And if he's not there, then you can spend some quality time with Samantha."

"Okay, then. Let's get to it," I said.

Kevin took them, one at a time, to whatever secret location Nick had, and then went straight to spy on Derek's father. While he was gone, I called Samantha's direct line and, as usual, she was very pleasant. She informed me that Derek was indeed in his office and asked if I wanted to talk to him. I was about to say yes when Kevin came back, so I told her I would call him later.

"There's no one there, but I couldn't look around any place other than the lab. They have cameras almost everywhere. The lab is the only place where I didn't see one, though."

"When you say no one...not even the guards? Or—"

"Nah, the guards were there, and housekeeping also, but Dr. Lake and Jessica were not there," he said.

"Okay. When do you think they will be doing the sweep?"

"Not sure, but I'll check again in a while. No one seems to be preparing to do anything like that. At least, they seem like they won't be doing anything for a while."

"All right, then, can you take me to the Org now?"

"Yeah, let me just use the restroom, though. You people are a bad influence. I had way too much coffee this morning."

"And that was way too much information."

"Sorry," he said, walking away.

I decided to go put on some light makeup to hopefully help me stay on Derek's good side if I needed it. I knew he wouldn't be too happy with me just showing up. He always liked things to go according to plan.

"You look pretty." Kevin gave me two thumbs up. "You ready?"

"Yes," I said, and before I even finished what I was saying I was standing in the Org, right outside Derek's office. I turned to see Samantha's eyes widen at my sudden appearance.

"Samantha! Hi."

"Uh, hey, Annie. What are you doing here? Derek didn't tell me to expect you."

"I just thought I would surprise him. We're so lonely these days that I think Kevin and I were about to pop our eyes out of their sockets," I said, laughing, but I got absolutely no reaction out of her.

Kevin gave me a shrug. "Well, she is dull," he whispered.

"I'm going to call Derek, give me a sec." She spoke in such a quiet tone into the receiver that I didn't hear what she said. After she hung up, she looked up with a smile. "He's coming."

"Annie!" Derek said, opening the door. "What are you doing here? Did something happen?"

"No, no, nothing happened. I just got so bored, and then we didn't see each other yesterday, so I begged Kevin to bring me here."

"Oh yes, young man. What happened to following orders?"

"I made him bring me, Derek. Lay off him."

"What's to stop him from taking you out shopping or whatever you want? Apparently, he likes to break rules."

"I only agreed because she convinced me this was one of her safe zones. Or is it not?" Kevin asked him.

"Yes, it is, but watch your tone."

"I'm sorry, I guess I'm frustrated by being stuck in one place, too." He clenched his teeth as he watched Derek's arm around my waist, pulling me closer to him.

"Does Jenny know you're here?" Derek asked.

"Do you really think she would let me come without giving you the heads up? You know how she is. She just follows your orders with absolutely no deviations."

"Yes, I wish you would, too," he said.

"Oh, but I wanted to surprise you," I crooned. "I never get to do anything for you, and I really missed you. Here, I brought you something." I handed him a little bag and watched as he opened it.

"A bagel with cream cheese…uh, thanks?"

"What do you want? It's not like I can go out and get you something more exciting. My pantry is getting pretty sparse, and this was left over from the very generous Jenny. She said she would have gotten some groceries for me, but you've had her busy, as usual," I smiled. "Can I talk to you?"

"Yes, come on." We went to his office, and as soon as he closed the door, I turned and gave him a kiss. I really didn't feel anything but guilt after knowing I'd spent the night with Nick. My guilt, of course, was for Nick, not for my actual boyfriend.

"Hmmm, I missed you, too," he said, clearly surprised.

"Well, you know we didn't even get to talk yesterday, and you left so abruptly the other night. I had to come and see you."

"Oh, don't worry. I plan on finishing what we started. How about tonight?" he asked while taking my hand and kissing it.

"Yeah." Oh boy, I walked right into that one, didn't I? "Uh, what time do you think you'll stop by?"

"I'm not sure yet. I have a lot of work, and I have to let you go right now, actually."

"No, it's okay. I completely understand. I'm just going to hang out in my office for a while today," I said, brushing his arm with my fingers.

"Oh, honey, I think you should stay at home where I know you'll be safer."

"I'm glad you're worried, but I'll be fine here. I just need to get some things from my office and socialize a bit, and then I'll be on my way."

"Okay, come here first." He grabbed me and practically tongue raped me for what seemed like an eternity. He was a good kisser and all, but after reconnecting with Nick, I just couldn't get into it. I actually felt dirty. I went to my office with Kevin and sent him off to Dr. Lake's house. He was to check back with me every ten to fifteen minutes. This way I could tell Samantha that he was still in my office. I took some random papers and went back to see her.

"Hey, do you mind if I make some copies?" I asked her.

"No, go right ahead. Do you need anything? I'm getting something to drink."

"No, I'm good, thank you." I gave her a smile and proceeded to make my useless copies so I wasn't empty-handed when she returned, which she did rather quickly.

"Here," she said, handing me a folder for the papers.

"Thanks so much, you are a life saver. I can see why Derek keeps you around. You are really good." God, I'm bad at kissing ass.

"I do okay."

"Oh, come on, don't be so dismissive. Being the PA to the President of the Org is probably bigger than what we do."

She smiled in response.

"How many hours do you work exactly?"

"About twelve hours a day? I'm not sure, but I do love it, and when it's possible, Derek does give me extra days off. He is a great boss," she said, with a certain look any woman could recognize. "I really don't have many friends and, of course, no family so I don't mind working this much."

"See? At least you are busy. Me? I'm being so overly protected that I'm practically a prisoner in my own home. I'm going mad!"

"Yeah, it must suck." She gave me a sympathetic look.

"Well, I should be heading back." I took a few steps,

then stopped. "Hey, you don't have any new reports or anything else I can take with me to at least try to figure some things out, do you?"

"I can check if you want. I'll give them to Derek and maybe he can drop them by later."

"Oh, okay. Nothing I can check up on now? Maybe I can help you with some work. I don't mind typing up things for you if you need that," I offered.

"Wow, you must be bored out of your mind."

"You have no idea."

"I have to send some emails and finish something here. When I'm done, maybe we can grab some lunch, and I promise not to tell Derek."

"You are an angel." God, I was glad that I had a good relationship with Samantha. Most people dismissed her because she was socially awkward and didn't give much thought to her physical appearance, always with wrinkled clothing and messy hair. Sam wasn't a big girl, but she was a little on the curvier side, something I— having a stick-like, athletic body myself—found sexy and womanly. I even got to slap Lisa once for calling Samantha a fatty. She had made Samantha cry a couple of times, and this particular incident was something that I could use today to pull a favor.

I found Kevin sitting in my office, "Hey, what are you doing here?"

"They are doing a search of the full premises. I almost got caught."

"Maybe they sense someone is sneaking around?"

"Maybe. Either way, I think I'm going to wait it out for an hour before checking again. How did it go with you?" he asked.

"Not bad. She's finishing some work and then we'll have lunch together."

"That's good. Do you think I can go grab something to eat now?"

"Yes, sure, but the same fifteen-minute rule applies."

"Yeah, yeah," he said, waving me off.

I MET SAMANTHA in the cafeteria like she'd asked me to. When we sat down, I noticed Lisa walking by with a pretty big tray of food. This was new, since she was always eating salads and fruits or shakes.

"Oh, you don't know the rumors about her, do you?" Samantha asked me as we sat down.

"No, but do tell!" I asked excitedly. I wanted her to know I was interested in anything she had to say.

"Well, you remember a few months ago when she took that vacation and came back even bitchier than ever?"

I nodded.

"It seems like she either had some wild times or she is seeing someone and hasn't told Derek yet."

"How do you know?"

"Haven't you noticed her?" I looked at Lisa and didn't see anything strange, apart from her slight change in fashion. She was wearing a sweater dress that was baggy on the top with a short fitted bottom. She was really accentuating her legs, which was her usual staple. At my baffled expression, Samantha went on, "I think she is pregnant."

"Lisa? No way." I kept looking at her. "She looks fantastic."

"Yeah…in a glowing sort of way?"

"Well, no, but those dresses are very fashionable now."

"She is hiding her tummy," Samantha said, nodding.

"No, she is not!"

"Well, I think she is. A few of us think that, actually. She was found throwing up in the bathroom a few times, and she joked around saying she was hung over."

"But that makes sense, Sam, she does like to drink and party all night long."

"Yes, but she never jokes around or offers anyone an explanation for anything that she does. She could have easily made them forget what they saw."

"Okay, that part is odd. But she could have been drunk still and wasn't thinking clearly."

"She is also much more sensitive now," she said.

"You see that because that's what you want to see," I pointed out.

"Nah, she has been too nice lately. Even to you the last couple of weeks, don't you agree?"

"We've hardly talked. I don't know."

"And she has been wearing big tops or big jackets."

"You are so bad, I can't believe you, Sam!" I said,

laughing.

"I know, it's just that it would serve her right for being such a bitch. And you," she pointed at me, "stop finding excuses for her behavior. I like my theory, and I'm sticking with it, and anyway, we will find out soon enough if I'm right or wrong."

"Unless she has an abortion."

"Not likely. She would have done it already."

"True," I agreed.

"So what do you do all day at home?"

"Manicures and pedicures." I lifted my hand to show her Beth's job. "And talking to Kevin and watching TV. I already went through my reports on whatever Derek allows me to read. I think he believes keeping information from me is protecting me, but honestly, the more I know, the more I'll be prepared."

"Derek is not..." She took a deep breath. "He just really cares about you, Annie."

"No, I know. I just wish he would use my experience. I'm good at this, and if I really know what's going on, I can help them get the bastard soon. I want to tell him to use me as bait, but you know how he gets."

"That's a good idea, but Nick would know it's a trap, I'm sure."

"Oh, we would figure something out. Derek is a genius when it comes to making plans and traps."

"He is, but not when it comes to you."

"I guess," I sighed, "at the very least I can help out with searching for clues and investigating, but he won't even use me for that."

"About that, I asked him if there were any other reports I could show you, and he said he would talk to you about it directly."

"Of course he will," I said, slamming my drink on the table. "I didn't think you would ask him this fast."

"I'm sorry, I had to," she said, her eyes widening at my reaction.

"No, I know. I'm just so frustrated with this whole thing. I hope I didn't get you in any trouble with him."

"Not at all. He didn't think anything of it. Honestly, anyone in your situation would be asking for any help they could get. It's only natural. If I knew what was going on I would help. I hope you know that."

"You are a doll," I said, knowing this was a dead end. Samantha was very faithful to him. "I just don't want you to get involved. I'll piss Derek off even more. Thank you for asking him, though."

"Tell you what, if I hear anything that might be a little helpful, I'll call you and give you a hint."

"I love you," I said, and took a sip of my drink.

"Yes, sure, just use me for what I have to offer," she laughed.

"What you have to offer, my dear, is a friendly call here and there to fill me in on office gossip. That alone will save me from committing suicide."

"Oh, I sure will."

We finished up and then went back to our individual offices. We made another lunch date for Thursday since

Derek had a meeting. She was in full agreement with me, I would be just fine spending an hour at the office for a little bit of girl chitchat.

"Be careful with that one."

I looked up from my desk to find Lisa standing at the door. "With Samantha?"

"Yes."

"I think I can handle myself," I said.

"She is after your man. I wouldn't trust her if I were you. And she is so…I don't know, *annoying*." She rolled her eyes.

"Why? Because she eats?"

"*That* and I don't like her," she said.

"Do you like anyone, Lisa?"

"Nope, but trust me on this one."

"Yeah sure, I'll trust you the day hell freezes over."

"Go fuck yourself," she said before storming out. That was more like her…though the first part was definitely weird. She never offered advice. I wondered what she was up to.

# CHAPTER SEVENTEEN

THE NEXT FEW days flew by pretty fast. Nick and Jenny made some improvements, and it turned out she did have leftover power from me even with the distance between us. This was bad because it meant that Derek's dad would be able to do the same since he was also a healer and sensor. It must be easier for them than anyone else to tap into our energies and abilities. Nick and Kevin also started their training, and Kevin was able to create a type of current with his fingers, so we knew it wasn't only healers who could do it. He was also going back and forth quite often to casa de Dr. Lake, but no one seemed to be there, like, ever.

Nick and I continued spending time together, but we made a deal that we wouldn't talk about where our relationship was going. I hated to admit it but it felt like old times.

Derek came over two days in a row to have dinner

with me. He'd even had Kevin drop us off at his place the night before for a romantic dinner. I played the sweet girlfriend, and we did let things get pretty steamy. But I stopped him before his hands got too far, and when he would try to argue I just kissed him silly. I felt disgusted with myself, but no matter how much I tried looking at it on the upside that they were both hot and I was a single, grown woman, I still couldn't be at peace. I just couldn't do this to either one of them.

He did try to convince me that it had to happen soon since we were both adults and it was only natural to take things to the next level. I told him I needed to do some thinking and I would talk to him about planning a special evening together. This, of course, calmed him down. Before I knew it, Thursday came by, and there I was in the office, staring at Samantha's empty chair.

"Hello, Annie."

I turned around to find Dr. Lake staring at me from Derek's office door. "Hi!" I went up to him and gave him a hug. "It's been forever! How are you?" As much as I'd grown to despise him, I couldn't let him know.

"I'm great."

"What a surprise to see you here," I said.

"I could say the same. And my, my, you look great. You have truly grown into a—" he looked me up and down, making my skin crawl, "—beautiful and sensuous woman."

"Thank you."

He smiled. "My son is a very lucky man. Why don't

you join me in his office? We'll have a chat until Samantha returns. She is running an errand for me."

"Oh now, she's not your PA anymore." I shook my finger at him as if he were a little naughty boy.

"I know, it's a bad habit, but she is the only one who could do it. And I assure you, it's something quite silly, really."

I laughed as I walked past him into the office. I didn't have time to warn anyone that I was with him, so I could only hope that Kevin would discreetly check up on me. I turned to look at him just as Samantha walked up to the door.

"Annie! I'm so sorry, I didn't realize you would be early." She came over and gave me a hug. "How are you holding up?" She turned to Dr. Lake. "Annie is under house arrest," she said, explaining the question, which was weird really, since we all knew my situation.

"I've been good, actually. I've started a new workout routine and have gotten addicted to a few television shows. I guess, when in Rome…" I smiled, tilting my head slightly.

"And here is your very special wine." Samantha handed Dr. Lake a bottle and then looked to me, "I'm ready when you are."

"Oh, excuse me. I actually have a lunch date with Samantha. It was really nice to see you. Maybe we'll have a nice family dinner soon, huh?" I said, winking at him. Why would I offer that? That was stupid.

"Nonsense, you and I are both already here. I say we

have a lunch right now, and you can be the special person I share this wine with."

"Ah, but I had this—"

"I will not take no for an answer, young lady. You can come anytime to spend time with Sam over here, but when do you and I ever find ourselves in the same place at the same time?"

*When indeed?* "That's true, Samantha. Do you mind if we all have lunch together?"

"I'm sure Sam has a lot of work." He turned to her. "Don't you?"

"I do, actually. I don't mind, really. I can just get something and work through lunch," she said, giving me a sad look and mouthing what looked like 'this sucks.'

"Okay, then. Let me go get something from the cafeteria, and I will meet you back here. Do you want me to bring you something?" she asked us.

"Please, Samantha, you know I don't eat from those places," he said, not hiding the look of disgust on his face. "I happen to have food from a five-star restaurant. I'm sure you will love the food, Annie."

"I don't want to rob you of any food, though. You didn't plan on more than one portion and I—"

"It so happens, my dear, that I bought lunch for my son and myself. He is obviously not here so I don't see why you and I cannot enjoy this meal together. There is more than enough."

"Awesome," I said, following him to the little dining area in the back of Derek's office. I was starting to regret wearing a dress, but I'd thought it would be something Sam and I would have in common since she never wore anything but dresses.

"So, Derek tells me things are going well with the two of you."

"Yes," I smiled. "As well as things can go in this sort of situation."

He looked at me. "I don't follow."

"Well, he's so busy trying to figure this whole Nick thing out, and I'm very busy being locked up and protected from the evil that's waiting for me out there."

He gave me a smile, both of us knowing that I just so happened to be sharing wine and food with the very evil I was supposed to be far away from.

"This young man, Kevin—tell me about him."

"He is very fond of you," I said, smiling.

"Is he now? How so?"

"Well, you are pretty much his hero. You saved him from whatever horror his life was before. He feels…he owes you for this new life. Much like the rest of us, really, when it comes down to it."

"Ah…then." He gave me a nod as in understanding. "No one owes me anything. I am a giver as you well know, and I care for the future of this country. If I can bring a smile to any of these youngsters who have been through a lot, then my job is done. Bringing them to New York and placing a roof over their heads is a foot start I can give them. What they do after that is up to them."

"You have such a big heart," I said. He dashed me a

wide smile, completely missing the sarcasm behind my words.

"But about his powers?" His brows creased. "I understand he can go anywhere and transport objects to any location he wants?"

I took a big chunk of meat in my mouth, trying to buy time. This was not good. "Uh, you make it sound cooler than it is," I said, taking a sip of wine. "From what we can tell, he can go to places and take people or items." I paused as if thinking how to explain it.

"Go on."

"I don't really know. It takes a lot out of him so he needs to rest in between."

"With the right training, he would be able to do wonders," Dr. Lake said, looking up at the ceiling, "…many possibilities."

"Yes, I'm sure you're right. But I've been trying to train him and, honestly, it's not really working. Either he is too young or too weak. I personally think he doesn't have it in him."

"Interesting. You don't think much of him, do you?"

"On the contrary, I adore him. He is wonderful, but for the Org? I don't know, he needs many more years before we can tell."

"He is not like you, then? I do remember your abilities were extremely advanced for a newcomer. You have always amazed me, and I must say, in more ways than one."

"Thank you." I was having a very bad feeling about

this.

"No need to thank me. You are remarkable, and I'm only being honest. And please, don't take this the wrong way, but if Derek weren't my son I would be trying to steal you from under his nose," he said, laughing as if we were in on a conspiracy together.

"Oh, you're always so funny, you could be my dad," I said laughing back. I was so uncomfortable.

"Don't dismiss me because of my age. My experience is where it's at." He winked at me.

*Ugh.* "I'm sure you probably have a few lady friends trying their hardest to become Derek's stepmother," I laughed. "And my mother-in-law," I added for good measure.

"You have no idea," he said. "So this...relationship...with my son, how serious is it?"

"Very serious."

"Good, I don't want to see him get hurt."

*Then you probably shouldn't be hitting on me, you old fart.* Well, to be fair, he was a very attractive old fart. Derek took after him so much, he almost looked like a clone. "I wouldn't do that. I truly care for him."

"He wants to make you his wife, you know."

*Oh, crap.* "Really?" I covered my gaping mouth and opened my eyes big. I truly hoped my faked excitement would stop him from continuing to flirt with me.

"You seem happy with the news."

"I am! I really am." I was so bad at this, I'm sure I came off as either a chicken head or as a gold digger.

"After your past experience, I must say I'm surprised. Especially since Derek informs me that you are very intent on keeping things...*slow*."

"That's very personal. I don't think we should discuss this particular issue."

"Please, don't take it the wrong way, Annie. I'm only looking out for my son. If you really care for him, why make him wait? I was thinking maybe...you don't feel he has enough...what do you call it...experience." He stared deep into my eyes, but I did not flinch.

"I love Derek." Gosh, why did I say that? "It would make me very happy to be his wife, if that's what he wants. As for the other thing, I may not have explored that part of our relationship yet, but I plan to. I just want it to be very special. I am not the kind of woman who just sleeps around. It means something to me. I feel it's something only a husband and wife should share, and that's been my struggle." Lame excuse, I know, but I needed to get these two Dereks off my back, literally.

"Then, may I make a suggestion?" He took my silence as his go-ahead to continue. "Perhaps, you two should get married soon. And what is more special than a honeymoon?"

"But we just started dating."

"Sure, but if you love each other, then there is obviously no problem. Leave it to me, Annie, I will talk to him. He listens to me."

"No, really, that's not necessary," I insisted.

"Don't worry about it. You can thank me later. I do

want grandchildren, you know?" He laughed at what seemed like an inside joke.

When we finished, he walked me back to my office, and I had to endure the stares of everyone in our steps. The shocking part was seeing Lisa and finding her obvious hatred for me surfacing to her face. And if that weren't enough, she was quite rude, too. She didn't even answer when Dr. Lake said hello to her. She just rolled her eyes and walked away. I didn't see Samantha again after that, so I just went back home when Kevin was ready.

"Hello, gorgeous."

"Hey," I looked up at Nick and gave him a peck.

"I hope you had an interesting lunch."

"Oh, baby, you have no idea," I said, taking off my sweater and laughing when his eyes opened in total appreciation. "How did it go with you guys?"

"We had a breakthrough. Jenny is finally starting to control her reactions to the different elements and is stopping herself from using anyone else's ability but her own. But when she does use our abilities instead of her own, she is really good."

"Awesome! And you?"

"Me? I'm loving your arms. Working out really looks good on you."

"Oh, shut up. I'm always toned, even if I don't work out."

"Nah, it's a little different. Either that or it's the dress, I don't care. I like it all."

"Stop it. How are your controls?" I asked, grinning.

"Right now? They are non-existent," he said, raising his eyebrows and walking toward me.

"Nick!"

"Fine," he said, laughing. "I'm still finding myself throwing beams when I'm caught too off-guard. I've been trying for a long time and I've gotten better, but there is no telling how I'll react when things get, uh, interesting."

"What do you think it is? For you, I mean?" I asked.

"My trigger is my anger."

"I thought I was helping you with that," I said, flexing my arms.

"Oh, you are, baby. Come here," he pulled me to him and kissed me.

"You guys, really! Get a room!" Kevin said.

"People, chill out," Beth said from behind him. "I heard you had lunch with the enemy."

"Yes, I did…with Dr. Lake himself," I answered her.

"Wait, what? You... You what? Why didn't you tell me?" Nick asked.

"I didn't tell you, yet, because I was busy with your lips."

"Hey, guys!" Jenny came in. "I got your text, Beth, what's up?"

"Annie has to talk to us," she said.

I told them everything that happened, and they were as dumbfounded as I was. "I don't like that he is interested in Kevin. He might have known I was lying about Kevin's abilities, but I had to try steering him in the wrong direction."

"Kevin will be fine," Nick said. "He really got that...what's the word...*fresh* with you?"

"Yes, it was sickening. Calm down!" I said as sparks started flying everywhere.

"Nick, relax!" Jenny said as Nick disappeared.

"What happened?" I turned to Kevin. "Where did you send him?"

"I didn't do anything! I wasn't even touching him, but hang on, let me go get him."

"No, Kevin, stay right here. For all we know, he might be steaming off with his beams, and if you appear in the wrong spot you could get hurt."

"But Jenny can heal me."

"He'll call when he's ready," I said.

"Whatever," he said, standing and walking away.

"Wait, hey! Kevin, come back here. What's the matter with you?"

"Nothing," he answered with a short tone.

"Don't lie to me. You've been acting weird for a while now. Something is upsetting you, and if I can help you, I need to know what it is."

"It's not your problem," he yelled and disappeared.

I turned to look at Beth and Jenny at the same time that Andrew came in. "Hey, Andy, I haven't seen you since my birthday. I don't like it."

"Hey, Anniewee, I've missed you, too. Come bring it in here." He gave me a hug and then went on to kiss his wife.

"Jenny, do you know anything?"

"About what?" Andrew asked.

"It's Kevin. Something is bothering him," Beth informed him.

"I don't know what it is, but he's been in a bad mood since Saturday. He was good when he was at my place, but when he came to pick me up to bring me here I sensed his mood change. He is really conflicted about something, and is very sad and frustrated."

"Is it with anyone in particular?" Beth asked her.

"Yes, with Annie."

"Oh, I... I didn't know," I said, surprised.

"Try to remember, did you tell him anything to upset him?" Beth asked.

"If I did, I would know."

"Yeah, sorry, stupid question," she said as Nick came back.

"Hey guys, sorry I just had to—what's wrong? Why are you upset?" He looked at me.

"It's nothing," I said.

"Don't tell me it's nothing. I can sense you're hurt."

"What do you mean you can sense it?" Jenny asked him.

"Oh, I guess I'm very tuned to you and to Kevin. I got so angry, and I was thinking I wish I was at the cabin and then I was there. And now I feel pain in your heart, Annie." He turned to Jenny, "Is this what you feel?"

"Yes, it is," she answered.

"Wow, how do you do it?"

"You learn to control it."

"How?"

She laughed at him, "The same way you are teaching me to control everything else, with practice."

"So what happened?" he asked me.

"Kevin is mad at me for something. I don't know what, and I don't know what I did, but he is very sad. According to Jenny, I'm to blame."

"Where is he? He'd better get his butt here and answer some questions," Nick said, looking around. "I don't want to see you upset."

"Stop, Nick, stop!" I said before he stormed up the stairs. "That's the wrong thing to do right now."

"What do you mean?"

"Well, he's the one who's upset, so I don't think you yelling at him would help matters. And yes, I'm upset too, but it's only because I want to help him."

"Fine, but let me get him," he said.

"No, let him be. He's a smart boy. He will come to us, or me, when he is ready."

"Okay, what are we going to do about Lake?" Nick asked.

"Do we have news on him?" Andrew asked.

"Come on, let's go do some guarding outside, and I'll fill you in," Beth said, holding his hand.

"All right, later guys. Jen, you want me to drop you off?" Andrew asked.

"Yes, please!" she said cheerfully. "Bye, love birds."

"Bye," I said.

"And for the love of God, Annie, take him upstairs. His needs are very demanding right now. It's way too much for me." She looked at Nick. "Tomorrow when I come back, I don't want to feel any of this again, so control yourself, got it?"

"Yes, ma'am," he answered. They left and Nick turned to me, "Are you coming?"

"Yes, in a minute. I have to call Derek."

"What for?"

"To say hi and to make sure he doesn't call me in the next hour or so. We don't want him to interrupt something, do we?"

"Just make it quick, I'll be upstairs." He walked away, tiny sparks coming out from his fingers.

I called Derek, and he told me he'd had an interesting conversation with his father and that he would talk to me about it later. This, of course, was something I was not going to share with Nick until he needed to go hide. I went upstairs and found him staring out the window. I went and wrapped my arms around his waist.

It wouldn't be until a few hours later that we would get up, which was just in time to hear the doorbell ring.

"Why is that asshole here?" Nick asked.

"To have dinner with me."

"Must you?"

"You tell me. Do you want me to keep up pretenses and have him on my side while we can investigate this thing or not?" I asked him.

"Whatever—go. I'll clean up in here in case you need the bedroom for round two with stud muffin downstairs..."

"What did you say?"

"I don't know why I said that. I didn't mean it," he said, looking confused that he'd let his thoughts slip.

I was fuming. "Get out."

"No, Annie, don't be mad. Please."

"Just get the fuck out," I yelled.

# CHAPTER EIGHTEEN

I RAN DOWNSTAIRS after he left and went to open the
door. Derek stood there smiling. "Hi."

"Hey, you!" I tried to smile.

"Are you okay?" he asked.

"Yeah. Why?"

"You look agitated."

"No, I just rushed down the stairs. I'm fine."

"All right, good. I brought us some takeout," he said,
lifting up the bag of food.

We had a quiet dinner. We talked mostly about his
father and his excitement about us getting married. I
explained to Derek that while I would be happy to marry
him, I would be happier if we did it when all this
commotion was behind us.

"I really don't want to have a secret wedding and be
afraid that something could spoil our day," I explained.

"No, I understand, sweetheart. Don't worry. I'll just

have to catch that bastard a little faster," he said, smiling. His phone rang so he picked it up and walked away to the kitchen. I decided to go upstairs to check on the guys, but neither one of them were there. I assumed they must have gone to do more training or some more spying. When I came back to the dining room, Derek was there with a worried look on his face.

"What's the matter?" I asked.

"We still can't find Lisa."

I rolled my eyes. "What happened to her?"

"We don't know. She was at the Org today, but she hasn't been seen since this afternoon. Her cell phone is at the office, but she is not home, and she hasn't checked in with anyone," he said.

"Oh, come on, it's Lisa. She's probably just looking for attention."

"No, you don't understand. She is pregnant and things have been tough on her."

"By who? How do you know?"

"She confided in me," he said.

"Uh, why?"

"Don't look at me like that, Annie. The baby is not mine, I promise. She only confided in me because she was having complications and asked me to keep her out of the field. She says she doesn't know who the father is, but I believe she is just trying to protect him. Either way, she's been worried. She kept saying that someone was going to try to hurt the baby, and she asked me to help keep her and the baby safe."

"How are you doing that? Keeping her safe?"

"I haven't done anything, to be honest. I've been busy with you, and I didn't take her seriously because, well, she is Lisa, and she can take care of herself. And I thought it was like you said, she was just looking for the same kind of attention that you were receiving because of jealousy. Now, I don't know what to think." He shook his head.

"She's probably fine. What are you going to do to find her?"

"There is nothing we can do yet. We have to wait it out. She could just be trying to prove a point to me."

"Well, that does sound like her."

"Yes, it does." He sighed.

IT HAD BEEN over a week since her disappearance, and there were no clues as to Lisa's whereabouts. The positive side of this was that Jenny's testing had been postponed so she could help look for Lisa. As much as Dr. Lake wasn't happy about this, there was no arguing about it, since Jenny's special talents would allow her to sense Lisa from a long distance if she were around. At this point, she squeezed in very few training sessions with Nick, but she had pretty much gotten the hang of it, much faster than the rest of us. Nick assumed it was because her natural ability was to be in tune with everyone, so she was able to really control it.

Kevin, on the other hand, was still upset with me, but he didn't want to talk about it. He promised me that it was him and not me, and we all know how that goes. It was definitely me. His anger toward me allowed him to channel my strength better than anyone else. He even started bulking up quite quickly in just one week. It was freaky. He also learned to travel like Andrew—it was more stable and less stressful on his mind, but he preferred his way. So did Andrew, actually.

Beth was the only one of us who was having problems tuning in to anyone but me. Nick's theory was that she used her muscles to be fast, so that allowed her to relate more naturally to me. All in all, it always came down to the Kinetics of things. They all did better with energy transfers when I was around, making it easy to see why I was the target. Personally, I was getting really good at channeling Beth's speed and had learned to create fireballs like Nick. I had no luck on the mind control part, but I did manage to transport myself a couple of times, so I was right behind Jenny with learning the transfer control.

Since stopping our monthly shots, we had actually become better and stronger at our own individual powers. The drawback was whenever we overused each other's abilities, we would be wiped out for days. Jenny and I got charged up faster. She healed herself in about a day, and I just made more energy to keep me going in a matter of hours.

The only unexplained situation right now was Lisa's disappearance. The whole ordeal also helped keep the distance between Derek and myself.

As for Nick? We hadn't really talked since he'd insulted me. His mood had been so foul that he was acting cold and nasty with everyone. I pretty much just ignored him and only addressed him when we were in training. Otherwise, that ship had sailed for a second time. I was beginning to think that maybe I should just marry Derek after all. He, at least, respected me...well, if I didn't count that roofie incident. Which reminded me, I needed to find out why he had done it. *I'm still ticked off about that.*

I was getting ready to call Kevin so he could take me to the Org, but the only other person in the house happened to be Nick. I found him in the living room watching the news.

"The "F" train was hijacked about twenty minutes ago," he said to me with a worried expression.

I went to stand next to him to watch the report. "How do they know? There shouldn't be any cell phone reception underground for anyone to call..."

"Someone on the platform saw a group of suspiciously dressed guys with guns when the train pulled out from the 169th Street stop. The reports are that the train didn't stop anywhere else and already passed the Lower East Side stop," he said.

"Let's go."

"*You* can't go, Annie."

"The hell I can't! Watch me…" I said as I teleported myself to the top of a moving train.

A few seconds later, Nick appeared by my side and startled me. "Hardheaded woman! Stay here—let me at least make sure you chose the right train."

I watched him go and come back in less than three minutes. "All of the passengers are packed into the last two cars, and it looks like it's five guys. Two of them are with the conductors…the other three are guarding the passengers. It doesn't seem like they plan on stopping anytime soon."

"Okay, well…I'm going to give them a little hand," I said.

"Annie, we really shouldn't be here."

"Oh, come on. Don't you miss us working together?" I asked, placing my hands on his chest and staring into his eyes.

He raised an eyebrow. "Are you trying to manipulate me?"

"I wouldn't say *trying,* I'm just doing the right thing." The train hit a curve, and I lost my balance, making me fall into his arms. *He felt so good.* I held on tighter and kept eye contact.

"What you do to me," he said, shaking his head. "You win, let's do it."

I beamed, "Okay."

I ran all the way to the front of the train, channeling Beth's speed. Jumping about twenty feet forward, I stood facing the train. A second later, I braced myself for the impact as the screeching sound sliced my ears. The hot metal indented its way around my hands, pushing me backwards for a while. A minute of this and I felt myself almost being crushed. I had been training with other Luminary powers lately, and right now, tapping into Beth's speed was just draining me. *Shit!* I found it hard to focus, I was pretty sure I was going to be flattened by this train soon.

I thought of Nick and the love and the pain and how I would never see him again, and how poor Kevin was about to lose someone else in his life…then I felt this burst of energy surging through me. My hands lit up in such a beautiful light blue color. I heard the engine die, and I began to force the train to start slowing down. The rails sparked and screeched, but I dug in and was able to bring it to a complete stop.

I think I created some kind of electromagnetic energy that killed the engine almost immediately. It had to be something like that, because I know I didn't stop the train with just my body. *What the hell was this?* I didn't have time to worry about it. Once it came to a stop, I noticed I had an audience by the front window. I ignored them and lifted the first car off the tracks to prevent them from restarting the engine and taking off. I felt dizzy, but I seemed to have my normal strength back. Once I finished, I looked up and saw that one of the conductors had a gun to his head. Crap, the gunman seemed pissed.

I tried to transport myself inside, but I couldn't do it.

*Dammit, where was Nick?* I had to do something but felt myself ready to faint. I had to focus. I took a deep breath and jumped up, holding onto the top of the window portion. My elbow smashed into the glass and had it scattering everywhere, the gunman turned, startled. Quickly, I swung myself backwards and then into the car, hitting the gunman in the process. Before he fell, I grabbed him by the neck and threw him in the other hijacker's direction. That one was a fighter. He moved out of the way, and while his friend bumped his head on the door, he came at me with a knife. I slapped the blade from his hand and punched him square in the stomach.

While he fought to catch his breath, I asked, "What are you up to?"

"You…you…can have the money. Take it all, just don't hurt us," he said, dropping the knife.

"What money?" I waited for his answer as I ushered the two conductors to open the door and jump into the other compartment. "Go, you'll be safe. I'm not alone."

Still gasping for air, he answered, "The one from the bank…that's what you're after, right? We just…uh, we just robbed it. Have it, you can have it. I think you cracked…something."

"Thanks," I said, patting him on the head and looking at his friend, who was getting up. "Come here, buddy."

"No, no… I, they forced me. Don't kill me!" he said and started running towards the opening I'd made for my grand entrance.

"Sorry, not gonna happen." I spun on my heel and caught him in his rib with my right knee. It was as if he'd run into a wall. As he sat, dazed, I pulled off one of the metal poles from the center and twisted it around the two guys so they couldn't escape. When I turned around, I saw through the window that Nick was erasing the two conductors' memories.

He came to meet me and said, "I took care of the other three. They're sitting in the back, ready to confess."

"Did anyone see you hypnotizing them?" I asked.

"Yes, but they won't remember," he looked at my two guys. "These are the only ones left to forget today's incident."

NICK GOT US back home since my transporting skills decided to fail me. We called the cops and watched on the news as they talked about how the perpetrators had been miraculously captured...

"*It's still a mystery...*" The reporter finished saying. I sat on the couch as Nick massaged my shoulders from behind.

"How did you do that blue thing?"

"I don't know, Nick. I can't believe you saw the light all the way in the back, either."

"See it? For a second, all we could see was your blue, then we all fell backwards from the abrupt stop. I can't believe it... how?"

"I have no idea."

"That's all your stored up energy. Now that you're not taking the suppressant shots, you're really becoming…I don't know, something else. What were you feeling when it happened?"

"I got scared! I thought all my strength was leaving me, and I thought I was going to die and never see…" I turned to look at him, "…anyone again, and then my whole body trembled, and the light was there shining out of me."

"Are you still dizzy?"

"No, I'm feeling normal now."

"Good, you can return the favor when I'm done," he said as his fingers loosened up my knots in slow motion.

"Yeah, I can, if you want to risk me crushing the tension out of you."

"I might consider it, Anniewee. I just might." He came around to sit next to me.

I looked at him. I missed the ease we'd once had between us. I would love to let my guard down, but I just didn't know how. I saw him fiddling with a piece of paper when Beth and Kevin popped up in the dining room.

"Hey, guys," they both said, smiling.

"Beth, you'd better get outside before Derek gets here," I said.

Nick got up and threw something on the couch as he walked away. "Come on, Kevin, let's take a walk."

"See you later, Annie," Kevin said, following Nick.

I was expecting Derek to arrive at any time for lunch.

I decided I should change my dirty clothes so he wouldn't notice I'd had an excitement-filled morning. Debris was a dead giveaway that I had been up to no good.

I stood and noticed what Nick had made with the paper. Next to where I was sitting was an origami rose. I picked it up, smiling, and went up to change.

Fifteen minutes later, the doorbell rang, announcing Derek's arrival.

"Funny thing happened today." He walked in and slammed my front door. "Why did you interfere with the train?"

"I didn't do anything," I said, walking up to him and giving him a peck.

"You are supposed to stay in the house, Annie! You can't keep disobeying orders."

"Look, I'm not saying I was there…because I wasn't…but everyone on the train is safe, aren't they?"

"How the hell is it that they don't remember what happened? Last I checked, you couldn't alter memories. What's going on?"

"Derek, I have no idea. I saw the news on TV like everybody else, and I agree, it does look fishy." I turned around so he wouldn't see my face. I sucked at lies.

"So you didn't do it?"

"I've already said no."

He frowned. "All right, if you tell me it wasn't you, then I believe you. I'll drop the subject now."

"Maybe it was Lisa," I said.

"Not likely. Even if she weren't pregnant, she

couldn't stop a train."

I had to pretend being all-innocent. "Who said anything about a train being stopped? The news said no one knows why, but the men turned themselves in."

"They were tied up, in a very Annie-like way, but no one remembers anything. Not to mention one of the cars being 'moved' off the tracks, and indentations that look like hands might have been there."

Crap, I forgot about those. "Well, maybe you should go open an investigation on all of your mind-controlling people. See if any of them got some super strength." I smiled.

"I might have to. Listen, I'm starving. Can we eat?"

We went outside to the patio and ate in the sun. He kept shooting me suspicious looks, not that I could blame him, but I decided it was time to put him in the hot seat, instead.

"Derek, I have a question to ask you."

"What is it?"

"The night of my birthday, when we almost spent the night together…"

"Yes?"

"Did you put something in my drink?"

"Ah, shit." He tucked his hands in his pockets.

"You did!"

"I'm so sorry, Annie. I didn't know how to tell you."

"What the hell is wrong with you? Were you that desperate? Apparently, I can't trust anyone. You know what? I think you should leave now."

"No, it's not like that. Please, let me explain."

I didn't want to allow him, but with everything going on, I still needed to be close to him and his dad. "Explain."

"I was very confused about what I did. My dad had come to see me that same afternoon, and you know how demeaning he can be with me. He made me feel like a little kid."

"No, actually, I don't know. He's been wonderful with everyone." I tried hard to keep the sarcasm from my voice.

"He is great with all of you, maybe, but not with me, his own son. He always puts me down and insults the work I do. And with you, well…he thinks I'm just not man enough to be with someone like you."

"That's no excuse for what you did!" I pushed him, making him take a few steps backward.

"I know," he said. "Dad and Lisa are pretty close, so she knew what he thought of my lack of progress with you. She thought it would be funny to mess with you."

"What do you mean?"

"She hypnotized me to drug you," he mumbled.

That was actually more believable than the Derek I knew doing it on his own. "You are not lying, are you?"

"Come on, Annie, I would never lie to you. Keep information, yes, but I would never do something like that on purpose."

"How are you so sure of what happened?"

"Well, I knew I would never do something like that,

so I confronted her. Not sure if you've noticed, but there is a feeling you get when something is altered in your mind. She was the last person I saw before coming over, and it was the only thing that made sense."

"And she admitted to it?"

"Yes. She was scared that I'd figured it out, but gave in and confessed." He held my hand. "Look, if you don't believe me, you can ask her when we find her. She's been messing with me for months, and I had no fucking clue. Either that, or I ignored the clue. It has been a stressful couple of weeks. I knew as soon as she admitted to making me drug you—"

"I'm going to smash her nose in when we find her. You just wait."

"She is pregnant. At least wait until she gives birth," he said with a soft smile. "Anyway, now that she's gone, I can feel memories coming back, like my brain is healing itself. She must have been hypnotizing me daily for it to work."

"You say she's close to your father?"

"Yeah, she's been working with him on some project. I don't know, I didn't care as long as it didn't affect her work at the Org, but now she will be under suspension for her behavior."

"Right." I pursed my lips.

"I have to tell you something else. You might not want to hear it."

"Tell me anyway."

"I think the baby might be Nick's, and he is probably

with her right now."

"That's crazy, Derek."

"Is it? That bastard wants to do something with kids and their blood. And according to some documents we found when he got sloppy, he thinks a child from two Luminaries can help him with blood transfusion or something. Not being able to get his hands on more of our serum has made him desperate. Why do you think he needed Dr. Lumin's research?"

"What makes you so sure that kids are involved?" I asked.

"Because we found some bodies that had been drained of blood. He's left his dirty work for us to clean up. We had to bury two kids last month: one was a teenager, and the other one couldn't have been older than seven. The worst part is that more kids have been disappearing. Whatever he is up to, it's despicable." He pulled his hair. "Now Lisa might be his next victim, and her baby isn't even born yet. My God, he must be desperate!"

"I don't think it's Nick," I said in a panic.

"Don't you see? A baby with you makes perfect sense. That's why he wants you, too."

"Then it's definitely not him."

"Why are you defending him? I thought we were past him."

"We are, but I'm not defending him. Think about it. If it is him, how stupid would it be for him to leave me?" I asked.

"I don't understand."

"Well, if he wants me to have a baby with him, wouldn't it have been smarter to stay married to me? Chances are, we would have already been parents. This way is just stupid."

"Well, he is a very complicated man. Obviously he didn't think it through…or didn't come up with this plan until recently."

"I guess not." I wasn't going to get anywhere with Derek on this topic so I didn't continue with it. "There are a lot of missing cases of kids. What makes you think any of them are related to him?"

"They all follow the same M.O. The two bodies we found are from the same two orphanages that have been reporting kids missing. All of the kids complained of stomach bugs, and they disappeared while they were supposed to be sleeping it off during the day time."

"How many kids are we talking about?"

"About eleven of them," he answered.

"What? That's a lot! Why hasn't security been increased in these places?"

"There is security now. At first no one thought much of it, since kids run away from these places on a regular basis. But now that we've found drained bodies, we know better."

"They're all orphans like us?"

He nodded.

"Please tell me Sweet Orphan Home isn't one of them."

"I'm sorry, Annie. You've been here for the past month. You weren't informed before that because we weren't sure that we were dealing with kidnapping."

"Who are the kids?"

"I don't have their names on me, but it's only been three from there. Six are from NY Hope Orphanage and the other two are from New Jersey's Special Home."

"And the two who died?"

His eyes said it all. "I'm really sorry. I'll send you the names tonight."

"We have to stop this," I said, trying not to crush something.

"I'm doing all I can. I won't let you down, I promise."

LATER THAT DAY, I called everyone to come over. I needed to fill them in on the news.

"I'm not surprised," Beth said when I told them about Lisa. "It makes sense she would work with that idiot. They are both power hungry. She's probably with him right now."

"I think you're right. It would explain why we can't find her. Dr. Lake has the means to keep her hidden and away from any of us," Andrew said.

"No, we've been watching him. We would have seen her," Jenny told them.

"We might not have seen her," Beth insisted, "but that doesn't mean she's not working with him."

"No. I don't know about that. The only thing I've been sensing from her for these past few weeks is fear." Jenny frowned, "I know she wants Derek for herself, but I don't understand why she would want him to sleep with another woman."

"Because she knows I would never have forgiven him," I said. "She knows I would leave Derek free to be with her—if she ever managed to convince him, that is. Or she was working for Dr. Lake and they were trying to get me pregnant as soon as possible."

"I still don't know. I never sensed her doing anything so bad. She hasn't been herself, but if anything, she has been sweeter than normal. I just don't think she is in cahoots with Dr. Lake," Jenny said.

"I don't want to worry about Lisa. I have much worse news than her making Derek drug me." I told them about the kids.

"That's horrible!" Jenny said.

"He is a monster. We have to stop this! Maybe I should just go to him. We can't have him harm more kids," I suggested.

Beth came up to me. "Annie, no. You are not going to just offer yourself up to him. It will do more harm than good."

"I have to do something. They're in danger because of me."

"No, they're in danger because of him," she said.

"I can stop him. I just need to go there and take care of it."

"If he captures you, he will use you for all you're worth, Annie." Beth grabbed my shoulders. "And if you display the surge you just had, it will be over for the rest of us. Think about it, what do you think is going to happen to all the other young Luminary orphans still growing up? Nothing stops him from killing them once he has all the power he will gain from you."

"But you guys can come and stop him afterwards. I just want to save the kids he already has." The lump in my throat grew bigger and more painful.

"We might not be able to stop him," Nick said. "We don't know what formulas he has, or what the serums can do. Look at us, we don't have any of that, and we're getting stronger. Imagine his capabilities. He knows how it all works. We can't go up against him if he has you by his side. You'll be his personal battery."

*Sigh.* They were right and I knew it. "Derek said Lisa's been worried about her baby. Maybe she knows about his plans, and he's after her?"

"That makes more sense," Jenny said. "She might be hiding from him and not the Org."

"Until we know more, you two stay put," Nick said to Kevin and me. "In the meantime, we have to keep our watch on his moves."

They all scattered around and left me with Kevin.

"Why is it we're the ones always out of the fun?" he asked.

"Because they know we're the rebels," I smiled. "Want to go on an adventure?"

"Always. What do you have in mind?"

"Derek wants us to stay put. Nick wants us to stay put, so guess what we are NOT going to do? Are you in?"

He smiled. "You bet. Where are we going?"

"Not yet, silly. We have to make sure they're all really busy training and then we go."

"Okay, but hey, I'm not going to deliver you to the monster," he warned.

"What? No! We are going to the orphanages to see if we can get any information, and to visit the little people."

"Nice. Tomorrow?"

"Hopefully," I said.


TURNS OUT NICK knew us better than we'd thought. He kept an unusual and annoying eye on us for the next couple of days. And when he wasn't around me, he took Kevin with him to follow Dr. Lake's movements. I could have tried teleporting on my own, but I didn't want to risk getting stuck somewhere. I wasn't very good at it, anyway, so I had no choice but to stay locked up.

After a few more days, the guys decided that they couldn't plant any bugs since the scans were done randomly. Also, there were no unusual activities happening. Dr. Lake went out on multiple luncheons and dinners and also visited the different orphanages. This, of course, assured us that he was watching over future Luminaries. While at home, he would be on the computer, but there was no way of knowing what he was working on. Other than that, he spent long periods of time in the gym and sauna room.

I tried over and over to come up with that surge again but couldn't. The most I did when attempting that was suck everyone else's energy and leave them tired. Then I had to focus on sending them back energies so they could function. It was frustrating. I was lost in my thoughts when my back door opened abruptly and made me jump. I was getting ready to kick some ass when I saw Lisa standing there. She held her little bump, and rested against the door after closing it.

"You have to help me."

"Lisa!" I went to help her sit down. "What are you doing here? You're okay! Hang on, let me call Derek."

"No! Please don't call him or anyone. I just need to sit."

"Yeah, sure. Do you want me to get any food for you? Water? Anything?"

"Yes to both," she said as she put her head down to rest on the table.

I took out some leftover chicken and mashed potatoes from the night before to heat up. She looked so worn out, and I couldn't believe she was in my house.

"Here, drink some water while I heat this up for you."

"Disgusting!"

"Oh, I'm sorry. Can you not stand chicken?" I asked.

"No chicken is good. You are disgustingly nice. Stop it."

"Uh, okay. Why are you here?"

"Someone is after my baby, and I'm too weak to run. You're the only person I can trust to keep me protected."

"Right…"

"I'm serious. Look, your house is being watched…not that I saw anyone out there…but whatever. I can't go to anyone else. Everyone knows we hate each other, so they won't suspect I'm here."

"You said it yourself: we hate each other. What makes you think I'll help you?"

"Because I'm the bitch and you're the nice one, and once I tell you everything, you'll help me. If not for me, you'll do it for my baby," she said, rubbing her belly.

"How far along are you, anyway? You kept it well hidden."

"It wasn't easy, believe me." She took the food and started eating. "I'm twenty-three weeks."

"Do you know what you are having?"

"A girl."

"Aww, that's awesome!"

"I know," she said, glowing.

"Wow, okay, if someone told me that the two of us would be talking about this and being nice to each other I would have punched them."

"You and me both," she agreed as she ate the food. "So will you help me?"

"Only if you name her Annie."

"Over my dead body."

"That can be arranged." I went to get some water for

myself. "You have to tell me everything you know, okay?"

"Yeah, I will, but I'm so tired. Do you mind if I sleep first?"

"No, go ahead."

"But please, Annie, don't tell Derek that I'm here. I beg you. Let me explain everything first and then you can decide if you want me to stay. If not, just prepare some food and money for me and I'll leave. Just don't turn me in. Promise that you won't."

"Don't worry, I won't."

"Promise it!"

"I promise. Come on," I said, walking up the stairs, "you can sleep in my room and take a bath if you want to."

"Where is your guest bedroom?"

"It's occupied. Remember Kevin is here?"

"Shit! I... I have to go."

"No, you stay. I'll take care of it." I saw her biting her nails to calm her nerves, "At least stay in the bedroom and relax. He won't go in there. I don't have any big clothes, but I can get you some yoga pants and T-shirts while you take a bath."

"Oh, I just want to sleep."

"That's fine, but take a bath when you wake up. You stink." The musky sweat scent was getting to me.

"I probably do." She started sniffing her armpit.

I noticed she was still wearing the same outfit from when she was last at the office.

"I'll shower first."

"Towels are in the pantry in the bathroom. I'll leave the clothes on the bed for you. Oh, and you'll find an extra toothbrush in the bottom drawer of the vanity."

"Thanks!" she yelled from inside.

# CHAPTER NINETEEN

I DIDN'T PROMISE I wouldn't tell Nick, so I went down to call him to let him know she was here. Also, so he would know to stay out of her sight until we knew what was going on with her. We talked for a long while, trying to plan what to do about her, and we figured I needed to know her story first to decide whether or not to bring Nick and the gang to her.

Right before I hung up the phone, Derek was at the door ringing the bell, so I was able to tell Nick to send Kevin and Beth back to their posts.

"Hey, you," I said, flinging my arms around his neck.

"Hi, beautiful." Derek leaned to give me a peck and asked, "Where is Beth? I hope you two understand that she's here to watch out for you, not to do a girlfriend hangout thing."

"Yeah, yeah she's just—"

"I'm right here, I'm right here! Can't a girl pee?" Beth came running towards us and gave me an eye roll. "I'm going back right now, boss."

"Okay, I was just checking." He waited for her to go outside and asked me, "You're not mad, are you?"

"No, you know I understand how overprotective you are, and God forbid Beth fights off the bad guy with an empty bladder." I raised my hands at his change of expression. "Bad joke. Anyway, how come you're here?"

"I was in the area, trying to follow some trails that Lisa left, and figured I could pop in to see you."

"Aww, you are sweet." I pulled him into the kitchen. "So did you find anything helpful?"

"No, it looks like it was a false trail." He looked at the plate on the table, "So you already had some food…I was hoping we could have lunch together."

"We can. That was Kevin's plate."

"And he left it there for you to clean up? Where is he? This is not acceptable."

"Don't be silly, Derek, I told him to leave it. He is actually helping me clean the guest bathroom right now. I'd rather this," I pointed at the plate, "than that." I pointed upstairs.

"Good, that means he'll be busy for a while," he said, and then kissed me.

Kevin interrupted us. "Bathroom is done, Annie."

"You're not going to say hello?" Derek asked him.

"Hello," he said. "Can I go hang out with Beth since you are keeping her company?"

"Yes, go ahead," he said, staring at Kevin, who slammed the door when he walked out.

"What's with the attitude?"

"We are both just bored and frustrated being locked up in here."

"He has to mind his manners, though. I don't think he realizes who I am."

"He knows who you are, Derek. He is just a normal teenager. You remember those days, when our hormones were going crazy and we knew more than everyone else."

"My hormones are going crazy right now." He smiled. "And we do happen to be all alone. Are you sure we can't go upstairs and have a pre-honeymoon rendezvous?"

"Come on, you know how I feel about it."

"I had to try," he said, his shoulders sagging.

I laughed and turned to the refrigerator to make some sandwiches. "Is this okay, or do you want me to make something that will take longer? I'm not sure how much time you have to spare."

"A sandwich is perfect, Annie. I only have about half an hour."

"Okay."

"I need to ask you to do something, or rather not to do something."

"Shoot."

"But don't be mad."

I turned to stare at him with the knife in my hand and mustard in the other.

"Especially don't use either one of those on me."

I waved the knife around for him to continue.

"Can you please stop hanging out with Samantha?"

"Why?"

"I think she has feelings for me," he said.

"Okay, and?"

"You're not mad?"

"No, I know she does."

"How do you know? Why haven't you mentioned it before?"

"It's nothing. She's had a crush on you for years now. It's obvious from miles away, but she's always been a friend to me. I don't understand why I can't have lunch with her."

"All right, it's not just the crush thing. Since Lisa disappeared, I'm nervous about the security at the Org, and I don't want you around there. I keep thinking that it was too much of a coincidence that you were there the same day she went off the radar."

"Oh, that's it?"

"Yes, what else could it be?" he asked.

"I thought it was because I asked Sam to send me leads and reports so I can help out."

"You did?" He stopped midway to a bite.

"Yes, don't be mad at her. I practically begged her, but—"

"What has she given you so far?"

"Nothing, she keeps saying she has no information to report. I thought she might know more, being your PA and all," I said.

"She does know pretty much everything, and I'm glad she keeps it confidential. As for you, though? You really shouldn't put Samantha in this situation."

"I know, but she said she would run everything by you before giving me any information, so I figured that was a good compromise, even if she was just brushing me off, which now that I think about it, I feel a bit hurt."

"I'll have a talk with her."

"No, come on, please let this one go. I won't pester her for more information, I promise. I just need some time out, even one hour a week. It's horrible to be locked up here, and that's saying something, seeing as this is my own home, which I love."

He took me by the shoulders. "I don't think you're safe there. If Lisa can go missing from there, I can't be sure that you would be okay if you were to come by. From now on, I'm just going to be sending Beth, Andrew, and Jenny since I know they're completely trustworthy with you. No one else will stand guard. When this is all over, your friends are going to hate me."

"Okay," I said. As he was leaving, I noticed that Lisa was about to come down the stairs so I turned Derek quickly to face me. Her eyes were wide open while I did my best to keep his back to her. I kissed him as I pulled him to the door and closed it behind him.

"I'll talk to you later," he said, caressing my face.

"Bye, be safe!"

He waved and walked out to go talk to Beth and

Kevin. When he left, they came up to me and asked about Lisa. I told them to stay outside until I talked to her.

I went back into the house. "Where are you?"

"How could you?" She ran down the stairs. "I asked you not to tell him and that's the first thing you do. He thinks I'm sleeping, right? I have time to leave before he comes back. Give me some money and your car. It's the least you can do."

"Relax!"

"Don't tell me to relax. I thought you were better than this. You are a total bitch," she said.

"You mean…acting like you would in this situation?" I raised an eyebrow.

"Whatever, I…I need to leave now."

"You don't have to go anywhere, Derek just stopped by for lunch. He has no idea you're here. I swear."

"You're not lying?" she asked, tears in her eyes.

"Why would I lie?

"I don't know. It's the perfect time for you to take revenge on me."

"Revenge for what? You being a bitch to everyone for years? For getting Derek to drug me? Oh, you know what?" I pointed to her. "We are not getting anywhere with all these stupid questions. You trusted me enough to come here, so please, trust me enough to stay. No one at the Org knows you're here. Come sit down and breathe."

She followed me, but clearly not sure if she could trust me, she kept looking back towards the door. "What if Kevin comes in?"

"I asked him to hang out with Beth."

"But they can both come in at any time."

"If they do, you will be fine. They won't say anything if I ask them not to."

"Are you sure?"

"Yes. Now drink some more water." I gave her a bottle. "I'm sure all this running hasn't given you the chance to stay hydrated enough for your condition."

"Look at you, talking about pregnancy and hydration," she said with a weak smile.

"Well, that's the only thing I know about being pregnant…so be prepared for a lot of water and a lot of sitting."

"Thanks." She sat down, laughing. "God, I don't know where to start. Nick…he—"

"Let me stop you right there. Please don't lie to me. I know Nick has nothing to do with this."

"No, I know. I was going to say that he is innocent. I figured I should start by giving you a little bit of comfort."

"Oh, thanks."

"How do you know he's not behind all the attacks and killing?"

"Well, I don't know about that. I just thought you were going to say it was his baby. That's what Derek thinks, anyway."

"So he told you. I'm not surprised, you two look happy."

"We are okay."

"Don't get mad, but please don't marry him."

"Are you serious? You think he'll want to be with you now, after everything you've done?"

"No, you don't understand. It's not about that...I—just hear me out, okay? Just hear me out, and don't judge me, and please do not tell Derek anything. I know you won't believe me, but I can find proof for what I'm about to tell you."

"Okay."

"Umm, the father of my baby is Derek's father."

"Dr. Lake?"

"I refuse to call him doctor… Whatever. He kind of forced me, and—"

"Oh, come on, who would take advantage of you? You're strong and—is this for attention?"

"Annie, please. I asked you not to judge—"

"No, sorry. Go ahead."

"When I went on vacation in February, it was because he told me about this amazing opportunity he had for advancing our abilities. He told me I could be a part of something big, and you know me, why would I turn that down? Well, when I got there, he took me to this secret lab he has underground."

"How did you get to it?" I asked.

"Through the sauna in his gym, why?"

"Nothing, continue." No wonder everything seemed normal there. The guys never followed him into the sauna. I mean, who would want to see him naked?

"So he took me there and convinced me that having a

baby would enhance my powers. He gave me several injections, some new Luminary formula, I think. I didn't ask. He said all he wanted was for me to hand over the baby to him when I gave birth. I figured that was fine, since I didn't want the baby anyway, but as I got bigger and I saw the ultrasounds and I experienced the kicks…the life inside me," she looked me in the eyes, "and when I found out it was a girl, I just couldn't. This is my baby, and I want to keep her—and after what we went through, I just can't do that to her."

"I understand." I patted her hand. "It is weird, though, to see you being so motherly."

"Don't mock me, I'm serious about everything. You think I'm crazy, don't you?"

"Not at all. And I wasn't mocking you. I am honestly shocked that you are so caring for your baby."

She shrugged. "Oh, well, I guess I am, too. That day at the office, he kept trying to get me to leave with him. I think he wants me to stay with him until the baby is born." She snapped her head up. "And you? You have to be careful. I think he is after your child, also. That's why he's pushing for you to get married soon, and he's hoping you'll get pregnant quickly. Oh, God, you are going to be mad."

"About?"

"The drugging you mentioned, it's true. I'm sorry, I really am, but he made me. That asshole has been having me hypnotize his own son for a while now. And then he made me force Derek to drug you to sleep with him, too.

I was so happy when I heard your night got interrupted before you'd spent the night with him."

"How do you know I didn't sleep with him?"

"Derek told me, he was so pissed at me. I didn't know what to do. I just told him I was messing with you, but I would never do that." She took a deep breath. "You don't seem upset."

"Well, like you said, I knew about it. I just didn't know your side of the story."

"I'm sorry," she said.

"It's okay. My initial thought was to help you reconstruct your face, but I get it now."

She smiled. "But still, be careful with Derek. He is too eager to make his father happy. He might be working with him."

"I doubt it. Derek is too good."

"Yeah, I guess."

"Well, except lately." I looked at her, shaking my head.

Lisa bit her lip. "I know, sorry."

"Do you know what Dr. Lake is working on?"

"From what I remember hearing when I was drugged, he is using young Luminaries to enhance his powers. He tries to pull their powers into him, like a reverse healing process, but I don't think it's working too well. He has a partner, a woman scientist. She figured it might be more effective if he tried it while he was infused with their blood. Her latest theory is that the blood would be stronger if it came from a person whose parents are both Luminaries. That's why he and I conceived my little girl." She placed her hands on her bump.

"He won't get to her," I said.

"I hope not. The problem is, he's too impatient. His latest experiment involved him creating a formula with some of the kids' blood. While he was infused with it, he sucked their lives out of them while trying to absorb their powers."

"They found two bodies. Do you know if there were more deaths?" I asked.

"I don't think so. Since it didn't work, he didn't bother to try with the others, at least not yet. You know, he must be working on a new formula because once they died, he drained their bodies of their blood completely to use later on."

"How is it he confided so much in you?"

"He thought I was on his side. He promised to give me some new powers after he came up with the perfect serum. He doesn't know I would never allow him to inject me with anything that has other people's blood. Much less, blood from innocent children."

"You said you let him give you injections," I frowned.

"Yes, but it wasn't blood. It looked like our regular monthly ones."

"Do you know where he is keeping the other kids?"

"No, I just know that he has food supplies for them, so at least he is feeding them. I'm only worried about what their fate will be once he's done using them," she said and held my hand. "They talked a lot about you and your kinetic energy or whatever they called it. I think they are using us as practice. You'll be their biggest experiment yet."

"Which is?"

"The abilities in the blood are a bit weak still, since they're taken from kids, but with you, he can boost it once it's in his body," she said.

"I don't know how he can live with himself. Why not just get us to give him our blood? We are full-grown Luminaries. He is just destroying innocent lives. I can't even think about it without wanting to cry."

Lisa nodded. "Believe me, I've shed a fair amount of tears already. Being pregnant and overly sensitive doesn't help. What he is doing is absolutely heartbreaking, but he won't use us because we are capable of defending ourselves." She stopped for a moment, looking at me. "Wait, are you not going to question anything I said? He is almost your father-in-law, and you probably think he walks on water like the rest of the Org. I was so scared when I saw you with him the other day, I didn't know how to warn you and…well, here I am."

"Lisa," I squeezed her hand, "I am so sorry for what you went through. I believe you."

"Are you serious or are you making fun?" she asked, blinking furiously.

"I am serious. I wouldn't joke. I really am sorry, and I promise to do whatever I can to help you keep the baby. Jenny can help when it's time for her to be born, and—"

"No, she can't know! They can't know!" The panic in her voice rose with each word.

"Calm down, Lisa. You'll be fine."

"How can I be fine? Why do you believe me so easily? This isn't a setup, is it?"

"It's not a setup, I assure you. And I do believe you because I already know that Dr. Lake is working on his own agenda. We are investigating him and trying to figure out what he's up to. Thanks to you, now we know."

"Who is we?"

"Uh, please trust me with this, okay? I promise you that we're all on the same side."

"Please don't call Derek."

"I'm not calling Derek. Just FYI, I'm not really his girlfriend. Well, he thinks I am, but I'm just trying to be on his good side so we can be in position when needed. Anyway, do you trust me?"

She let her shoulders fall. "I have no choice."

"Okay, hang on." I took out my cell phone and dialed.

Lisa started pacing around.

"Hey, she's okay. Why don't you guys come so we can all talk?" As I finished saying that, Nick, Beth, Andrew, Jenny, and Kevin appeared in front of us.

"Ahhh! Oh, my God, I think I almost gave birth," Lisa said as she took in each person standing in my living room and her eyes stayed on Beth. "So all of you are...none of you will turn me in?"

"No, but it's not for lack of me wanting to, *believe me*," Beth said with a hard stare.

Lisa nodded and turned to look at Nick. "I have to say that I am shocked to see you here. So you two aren't really divorced?" She pointed from his direction to mine.

"We are divorced. I just have to endure him until we stop Dr. Lake."

She stayed quiet while I filled everyone in on what she'd told me. It was really strange to see her so humbled. "So if they are staying in the guest bedroom, where do I sleep?"

"With me," I smiled.

"God, no!"

"Oh, come on, you know you've always wanted to sleep with me. How else do you explain all the sexual tension?" I asked, laughing.

"Ha! You wish."

"I can't believe I'm seeing you joking around with us," Jenny said.

Beth snarked out a reply, "Yes, who knew you even had a smile?"

"Yes, I have a smile. I'm sorry I hardly ever used it with you." Her eyes filled up. "Sorry, it's this pregnancy, my emotions are driving me crazy."

Beth looked at her with suspicion.

"Do you mind if I check up on you and the baby?" Jenny asked as she walked toward Lisa.

"Go ahead," Lisa said. Jenny placed one hand on her belly and one hand on her forehead. She stayed there for a while, and we could see that she was healing her. "Ah, that feels better. You knew, didn't you? That I was pregnant?" she asked Jenny.

"Yes, I had to do some healing after Beth threw you to the wall, and then again after the Lumins' incident."

"Sorry." Beth bit her lip.

She ignored Beth. "Thanks for keeping it quiet, Jenny, I appreciate it… How am I doing after these past weeks of hell?"

"Good, just dehydrated," Jenny answered, and Lisa turned to look at me and laughed at our inside joke. "The back pain was from all the running. You'll be fine now. Just stay off your feet. Baby girl is doing perfectly, also."

"Thank you. All of you, so much."

"No problem, I have to get going. I have a big day tomorrow with Derek Senior."

"Uh, why? Jenny, don't go!" Lisa said.

"Don't worry, Derek is coming, and we'll be at training anyway. I'll let them explain. Kev? Can you send me home?" He nodded and she waved 'bye' before disappearing.

"We'll get going, also. Lisa, take care. Good night, guys," Andrew said, taking Beth's hand.

"No, hang on. I need to talk to Beth," Lisa said.

Beth looked at Andrew, then back to Lisa with a frown. "About?"

"I figured since I'm already sharing information, I might as well get it all out in the open."

"Okay, what else is there?" Beth asked.

"Your mother? Uh—she had gorgeous green eyes—like…like mine."

"Well, it figures one of my parents had green eyes, obviously one of your parents did too."

"No, Beth, your mother had *my* exact color. You and I have the same color."

"What are you saying, Lisa?"

"We are sisters."

"You and me?" Beth was incredulous. "You're crazy. You are a redhead, and I'm a mixture of some sort. Look at me, I'm shades darker than you."

"I don't know about my father, but I did see a picture of my mother, and I look a lot like her. That monster gave me my file to read to show how much he trusted me. After she gave me up, she got pregnant again by a different man. She was a prostitute so it's hard to say who, but I'm betting you took more to his looks, given your dark complexion."

Beth stayed where she was for a couple of minutes.

Andrew wrapped his arms around her. "Are you all right?"

"I don't know." She looked at Lisa. "Are you sure?"

"If the files were real, then yes. Look at us, skin color aside, we kinda look alike."

"That's ridiculous!"

"I have no reason to lie. Come with me." Lisa went and grabbed Beth's arm. She took her to the mirror that was hanging on the wall by the entrance. "Look." They stood next to each other, staring at what seemed to be every detail of their faces.

"NO! I can't be your sister. I hate you. You've made my life miserable! You made me feel like a piece of shit for too long, I—"

Lisa was crying. "I'm so sorry, Beth. I can make it up. Please?"

"I can't, I have to go. Andrew, take me home," Beth said, and they left.

# CHAPTER TWENTY

WE SPENT THE next couple of weeks sharing notes and investigating any leads we had. It wasn't all that bad living with Lisa. Once we found ourselves on the same side, we worked really well together, and she actually helped dissipate the tension between Nick and myself a little. Jenny had been doing some training, and as each day passed it got easier for her to control herself and react as she would with only her abilities.

I left Lisa resting in my room and went to the basement to use the treadmill. Running outside at the beginning of August would be brutal. Well, there was that, and it was not like they would let me go out anyway. Ever since I'd found out about the missing kids, my mind had been growing more and more restless. The only good news was that the added security had prevented any more kidnappings from happening. I had barely started warming up when someone came downstairs to join me.

"Thought I'd find you here."

"What do you want, Nick?" I didn't like talking to him unless it was absolutely necessary.

"I looked into Lisa's story about her mother while standing watch, and I broke out those documents."

"And?"

"It's true. But I guess we could tell she wasn't lying. They do look a little bit alike."

"Beth will be fine. I think she is warming up to it a little. She just doesn't know how to not hate her after the hell she put her through in training. Lisa bullied her pretty bad."

"She bullied you, too," he said.

"She's not my sister, though."

"True. I got something else."

"What?"

"Another set of personal documents. These I found in his bedroom." He showed me a yellow envelope. "These are your records."

I stopped and thought about it a moment. I wasn't sure if I wanted to know the details or not. "How are you with controlling your fireball these days?"

He cocked his head sideways with a frown. "Good, why?"

"Burn it."

"Annie, I'm not going to do that," he said.

"I don't need to know. It's in the past…well, unless I have a sibling, too. Do I?"

"No."

"Okay, then burn it." He shook his head. "Nick, you owe me this one, burn the darn thing. NOW."

"You're going to regret it."

"Fine." I got off the treadmill and snatched the envelope. I looked at it and closed my eyes to concentrate. I set it on fire myself.

Channeling Nick's fireball really came in handy. As it turned to ashes in my hands, I decided that I would let go of all my abandonment issues along with it. My past needed to stay there, and burning the beginning of it somehow felt like closure. I looked at Nick. If only I could burn our past away as well. I finished and went to the bathroom to wash my hands. When I returned, I found that Nick was still standing where I'd left him.

"That felt good," I smiled.

"Did it?"

"Freeing."

"You don't even know what was inside."

"It doesn't matter, I can't change it. But letting go frees me to choose my own path, and I now know that I'm in charge of my own life. I thought about what you asked me a while back, and I don't want you to help me remember whatever memory they erased when I was a child. I'm starting anew at twenty-four. I'm in control now. Dr. Lake or not, I burnt what he made of the first twenty-three years of my life."

"Okay," he considered this. "I'll be right back."

I got myself a bottle of water while I waited. I heard his footsteps coming down. I hoped he hadn't made a copy. It would totally take away from my dramatic moment.

"Here." He handed me a shot glass and raised his to mine. "To a brand-new, puppet-free life!"

"Cheers." I smiled and swallowed fast. "Gosh, I don't know the last time I had tequila."

"It has a kick, doesn't it?" he said with closed eyes.

"I'm assuming you read it?"

He nodded. "You want me to tell you?"

"I'm not sure. Is it bad?"

"If you hadn't burnt it, you could have found out," he teased.

"It's different. I can choose not to believe you. Haven't you heard? I make my own choices now."

He laughed, "Yes, I heard you two minutes ago." He took the bottle and poured another round of shots. "Here, this one is for…" he thought about it, "bringing down Lake!"

I clinked his glass and took my shot. We sat there for a long time and then had one more round. I'm not gonna lie, we got a little too drunk.

"So, anything you're dying to tell me?" I asked him. "I know I said I didn't want to know, but still."

"No, not much inside. The only thing I can confirm is that you have your mother's last name. So that's real, and also that you are part Spanish."

"Well, I knew that. Look at me."

"Ah, come on. You were never sure."

"No, you're right," I said, taking the bottle from his

hand. "So my name is real, that's good. Let's drink to that."

He was laughing so hard he could hardly talk, "Half of your name…the first part, well…be happy it's Annie now."

"Stop laughing! Okay, now you have to tell me," I said, feeling the effects of the alcohol.

"Your first name was originally Antonieta, hahaha."

"No, it was not!"

"Swear to God, that's what it said. I'm glad they changed it. I would have never married an Antonieta. You are most definitely an Annie," he said.

"I'm so glad I never took your name!"

"Why?" he asked. "You know that hurt my feelings, right?"

"Who cares about your feelings? It would have been too much paperwork to change it back from Logan to Fox after the divorce. And now I know I had something all along from my mother, so I'm happy."

"I don't know your problem. Annie Logan…it sounds nice."

"Better than Antonieta Logan," I snorted. *God, I'm a bad drunk.*

"It's not the first name, my love. Logan is just perfect for you."

"Ha! You would say that." I jokingly pushed him. Crap, the tequila made me forget to control the strength behind it, and I sent him flying. He landed on his ass and looked at me in shock before laughing.

"Ouch!" He got up and rubbed his backside. He turned to look at the weights right behind him. "Looks like I stopped in time. Those would have hurt if they fell on my head."

"Oh, you're fine."

"No, I'm not." He squinted and walked back to me. "But I'm gonna be."

"What are you doing?" I knew that look. Oh, hell, why not? I *was* drunk…

He grabbed my hair and pulled me towards him, his mouth coming down on mine. He roughly took my lips and pushed me against the wall. I ripped his shirt off, making him lose his balance, and he returned the favor while moving me away from the wall. He placed my hand on the elliptical to hold on as he left tender bites along my arm and shoulder, and then, grabbing me tightly, he tore my tights into pieces. He then moved on, leaving a trail of soft kisses from my jaw, to my breast, then below, and then more below…and then…stars were everywhere.

In the heat of the moment, Nick broke off one of the handles as he channeled my strength, and I was sure we would both wake up with some serious bruises the next day. He picked me up and turned me to face the elliptical's panel now that it was free to us. His hot tongue trailed my back while one arm wrapped around my waist. He moved up to kiss the back of my neck, then as he held on to my hip with his free hand, he made love to me.

*"Nick..."*

*"I love you."*

The passion we had that night was by far the best I had ever experienced. I don't think I'll ever look at my exercise equipment the same way again. The feel of his hands on my body, the way we fit so perfectly, and his animal side...who could complain?

After a second round, I made it back to the bedroom to sleep. While Lisa was busy snoring, I spent some time grinning and enjoying the buzz I still had left over from the tequila, and the sex. I still didn't forgive him, for anything. But it was so hard not to give in to my feelings and needs from time to time.

"Wake up!"

"What?" I opened one eye to find Lisa still shaking me. "You can stop that now."

"Sorry, I just...are you okay?"

"Yeah, why?"

"You have some big bruises, look at your leg."

"Oh, shit." I looked down and pulled the sheet over me. "I'm fine, I was...Nick and I were...fighting last night."

"He did this to you?"

"Yeah, it's fine." I sat up. Clearly I wasn't going back to sleep now. "We were channeling each other and practicing...stuff."

"Oh, okay. Sorry I woke you."

I yawned. "S'kay, I'm getting up anyway." I walked like a zombie to the bathroom and hunted down a couple of Advil from the medicine cabinet. This hangover was not going to be fun.

"Good morning," Beth said when I went downstairs. "I heard you had an interesting night."

I looked at Nick, but he was busy pretending to read the newspaper. "Yeah, where is the coffee?" I wasn't sure if she'd heard from him or from Lisa.

"Maybe you should try a Red Bull. I heard it helps with hangovers," Beth said. Her eyes were smiling. She knew what I had been up to. *Whatever. I can do what I want.*

"Thanks," I mumbled as I took it from her. "Glad to see you're ready to come back over here."

"Yeah." She looked at Lisa. "I've had enough time to come to terms with…things."

"As long as you accept that I'm the pretty one, we are good," Lisa said, trying to bring their relationship back to a lighter state.

"Ha, you wish!" She went to sit across from Lisa. "You're older, the first draft. Me? I'm the masterpiece."

"Oh, you are lucky I'm pregnant or I would smack you upside the head," she smiled.

"Oh my God, I'm going to be an aunt," Beth said, grinning.

"Yes." Lisa reached across to hold Beth's hand. "We are going to have one more addition to the family, huh?"

"I'm so going to spoil her. And you can't say no. It's my job as the aunt."

"Works for me. Somebody has to change the

diapers."

"I'm not helping you with that. It's your punishment for being so mean." They laughed and continued chatting.

Nick looked up at me with a raised eyebrow and smiled. I turned around and made my way into the living room in a heartbeat.

"Why are you running away?" he said.

Of course, he'd followed me. "I'm not."

"Right. You wanna talk about it?"

"Nothing to talk about."

He held my hand. "Why? Last night was—"

"You think I'm a slut!" I exclaimed, pulling away.

"I was angry, I didn't mean what I said. I'm so sorry."

"Last night changes nothing, Nick. Let it go."

He came close again and looked into my eyes for what seemed like forever. "If you're sure that's what you want."

"I am."

"I'm going to check on Jenny before she leaves for training," he said before disappearing.

During Jenny's training that day, they took some more blood from her. She wasn't told what the first blood work results were, but we figured they were just trying to track any changes in her DNA that would indicate any extra abilities. We weren't sure yet if channeling each other changed anything in us, but since we couldn't do it for too long without burning out, we figured not. Beth had gone on a mission, and Andrew was standing guard outside with Kevin.

While they were all gone, Lisa and I were trying to track down any new bodies, either of kids or women who had recently given birth. Jessica had talked a lot about 'the next set coming up,' and Lisa was almost positive that she was referring to other babies. She knew she wasn't the only woman Dr. Lake had impregnated.

"Oh my God!" Lisa snapped.

"What? Are you in pain? Come here, let me check." I had gotten good at the healing business and at tapping into other Luminaries even when they weren't around. It didn't last long, but still, I could do it.

"No, I'm fine. I just can't believe I'm so stupid."

"Well…"

"Shut up." She smiled, "I forgot to tell you guys…ah, that Worldsafe thing?"

"Yes?"

"It was Dr. Lake's."

"We know."

"Okay, well, he closed it out. That's where he kept most of his concentrated blood serums."

"How do you know?"

"He went to my last check-up, and he was talking to Jessica about it. They moved everything back to his place. Maybe we should just destroy it, burn the whole place down."

"We can't do that," I said.

"Why not?"

"We don't know if he is keeping the kids there. I'm

so frustrated. We need to find some clue soon as to where he's hiding them. We can't let anyone else die."

She nodded. "Too bad the lab has so many cameras. The guys can't even pop in to look around."

"Luckily, you knew that, or they would have already been caught."

"Right," she said right before the doorbell rang.

Kevin ran to the door and gave me a puzzled look. "It's Samantha," he said.

"Okay, take Lisa and these things so she doesn't see them," I said.

It took him two seconds, and when he came back, we got the door. "Samantha! Hi, girl. I'm so happy to see you!"

"Hey, Annie. Hi, Kevin. I brought lunch," she said, smiling. "I figured if you can't come to me, the least I can do is come here and bring you some outside food. It's from the Org, though, sorry."

"I'll take it!" I grinned.

"We have pizza, soup, and rice pudding."

"Perfect! How come you got away?" I asked.

"Derek has no idea I'm here, don't worry. Neither one of us will get in trouble," she assured as she winked at me.

"Phew!" I faked a sigh of relief. I hadn't talked to her since Derek had asked me not to. It's not like she had been full of information, anyway.

"What?" I asked as she beamed up at me. Clearly, she was bursting to tell me something.

"It looks like Nick is the father of Lisa's child."

"No way!"

"Yes, think about it. How else do you explain that she can't be found? Just like Nick…I'm just saying…"

Here I go, fake Annie in full mode. "Oh goodness, they are probably together. Disgusting."

She talked the whole time, she told me about who was seeing whom and how Derek and his father were both excited to start planning our wedding and how she could see how happy I made Derek. She also told me that she had started seeing this guy in her apartment building, and that even though he was a little older than she, he was wonderful in bed. We laughed a lot, and she asked if she could come back in a couple of weeks when she knew Derek would be gone at a business meeting in Washington. The one big piece of news she did confirm for me was that the Worldsafe account had been closed out after the attempted break in.

"She is fat," Lisa said, coming down the stairs.

"Stop it! She is not fat, she is curvy and beautiful."

"Come on, Samantha is getting bigger as we speak."

"At least we know the bitch in you is still around."

"I don't know, I just never liked her," she said.

"You've never liked anyone."

"Not true. I've always liked both Nick and Derek." She winked me off. "And one of the greatest mysteries in life is why they both picked you instead of me."

"Maybe because I'm not such a high-maintenance know-it-all?"

"Nope, if it were that, then they would have gone for Beth. You and Jenny are okay, but we're pretty much supermodels. I don't get it—you're short and annoying."

"I'm annoying?"

"Yes. You are *too nice* annoying."

"Fantastic..." I left it at that and continued doing more research.

"I got something," Lisa said after about an hour, I looked up for her to continue. "It looks like there was a druggie who was found dead shortly after giving birth. They think it might have been an overdose but no one found the baby. They're assuming the baby is also dead from the drugs. It happened last month...near Worldsafe."

"Print it out so we have a record. Do they know the name of the woman?"

"Yes, her name was Destiny Star. They say here she was a stripper, and that's the only name they have for her. No one claimed the body, and the club she worked for said they had no official records because they respect their dancers' privacy."

"I'll bet. Any pictures?"

"None in this report. I'm going to do some more digging and see if I find one."

# CHAPTER TWENTY-ONE

IN THE NEXT month, we found several more bodies of women who had recently given birth. Some had died from drugs, some from childbirth, and there was even one suicide. The babies were all given a place in orphanages. Probably the future generation of Luminaries. This had to stop.

Jenny was displaying very minimal reaction to other powers. It was impossible for her not to react once in a while, though, so they knew something was working. Dr. Lake tried to convince her to go back to his lab for a week, but instead, she asked him to let her rest for a few days because she felt exhausted. Nick was sure that Dr. Lake wanted to test everything on Jenny first since she was a healer like himself. After much convincing, Dr. Lake agreed to give her some time but told her he might want to try a new formula recently developed. Then he said resting before trying his new plan was a fantastic idea. Jenny was scared out of her mind, and she was thinking of running away.

Beth was getting good at healing, or at least learning as much as she could so she could serve as midwife for when Lisa's birth came around. They still had their moments when they fought, and Beth wasn't as forgiving as she pretended to be, but the baby did bring them closer, and they spent a lot of time planning for their future as sisters and talking about how much they would spoil baby girl.

Derek and I kept seeing each other, and now that he wasn't being hypnotized, he was less possessive. Luckily, he respected my decision to wait until we got married, and didn't push for me to sleep with him. I actually grew pretty fond of him and felt like I could develop real feelings for him. Nick being around me opened my eyes and, in a way, gave me the closure I'd really needed when he'd left.

He had been cold and had had a short temper with the rest of us since our last night together. I couldn't care less that I was the reason for his bad mood. I just knew that I didn't need to be with someone who did not respect me. I'd slept with him and gotten him out of my system, and I was good now.

Kevin was still keeping his distance from me for the most part, until one day when he knocked on my door.

"What's up?" I asked.

"Nick and the others are at the cabin training," he smiled. "I know this is no train-stopping, but still want that adventure with me?"

"Hell yeah! Let's get outta here. Give me twenty minutes and meet me by the stairs."

I took a quick shower and threw on my favorite pair of jeans. I didn't have time to do much with my hair so it was stuck in a ponytail, making me look extra young. To people on the street, I'd probably look like I could be Kevin's girlfriend.

"Where do you want to go?" he asked when he saw me.

"I want to go visit my little buddies at the orphanage." We appeared about a block away to make sure we could stop by the local supermarket and buy some candy for them. While I was busy in there, Kevin left to scope out the area. We weren't sure what type of security Derek had in place, and the last thing we wanted was to get caught.

Kevin sent me a text saying that the guards were not Luminaries, so there was nothing to worry about. We spent a couple of hours with the kids, and I was happy to see that Kevin enjoyed them as much as I did. We tried prying for information on the kidnapping, but no one could tell us anything. Memory modification was obviously at play here.

"I guess we have to go back now," I said when we walked out.

"Unless..."

"I like the sound of this. Unless what?"

"You think we can practice lifting objects? I'm

curious to see if I can pick up a car…"

"Yes, but I'll be next to you in case you need my help."

We made it to a junkyard and went to the most isolated area we could find. There were piles of cars everywhere, which was perfect for what I had in mind.

"Okay, here I go," Kevin said with a big smile. He got a car halfway up before being startled by a pigeon and dropping it with a loud thud. "It was the pigeon! The car wasn't even that heavy."

"You're right. That one is not going to cut it. Allow me to assist you," I said with a grin.

We walked around, and I found some large pieces of metals and bricks that I collected and put into the back of a pickup truck. I filled it up as much as I could, and then I lifted the car next to it and stacked it on top of the pickup.

"Annie, you are crazy if you think I can lift that."

"Try it first. I'm already eyeing that set over there for you." I pointed to his left.

"That set has four cars. You are out of your mind."

"Oh, come on, those are empty. And anyway, I'm right here, dude. Just pull from me, you can do it."

Kevin went to grab the pickup from the side and failed a couple of times. Right when I was ready to lighten his load, I felt the pull from him, channeling my inner strength. He started slowly balancing the pickup so the car on top didn't fall off and made it all the way over his head.

"This is cool!"

"Stay there, let me get a picture for you," I said, snapping away with my phone.

"You got it?"

"Yeah, it came out really nice."

"Okay, help me now. I can't put it down," he said, his arms trembling.

I went to the other side and gently placed it down. I decided training couldn't be over so I lifted the pickup and threw it toward him, and his eyes widened as he disappeared, letting the truck fly past him into a pile of discarded car parts. *Ouch.* That metal crashing sound was not the most pleasant. I frowned.

"Sorry, I freaked out," he said, appearing a couple of feet behind it.

"No worries," I said, walking towards the pickup once again. I looked at Kevin and decided to kick it in his direction, instead. I saw the panic in his eyes again, but this time he stayed put, and stopped it with one leg.

He grinned. "You gotta see this. I left a dent!"

"Haha, that was frigging awesome! Good job, Kev," I said as he ran to me, laughing, and gave me a high five.

"Not that I want to ruin this fun, but I have to talk to you before I chicken out," he said, and teleported us on top of the pickup to sit.

"Okay, go ahead."

"Annie, I'm really, really sorry. I've been behaving poorly lately, and I honestly have no excuse."

"You've been upset with me."

"Yes," he looked away, "but I realize I really have

no reason or right to be."

"You have the right to feel the way you want. I'm not sure if I can help it, but why don't you tell me what it is that's bothering you, and we'll go from there?"

"It's really silly now that I have to say it out loud."

"Tell me anyway."

"When I first met you...I liked you right away. We got along really well, and I could tell that you wore your heart on your sleeve...and I really trusted you. But then I saw how you were able to be with Nick and Derek at the same time, and even though Nick knew your situation with Derek, well, you were practically cheating on them both. I started thinking that maybe you were sleeping with Derek and fooling Nick."

"I wasn't. I'm not."

"I know, I know. But at that moment, I thought if you could fool one then you could fool the other one, too...and maybe you were fooling me."

"You?"

"Yes, maybe you pretended to care so you could have your revenge on Nick or something. You know...that you were using me."

"I would never use you!"

"I know, I thought you were using me to get to Nick. And that maybe you were using me against Derek, too. Like trying to keep your distance from him by having me—the child—as an excuse to not marry him."

"No. Kev...you mean so much to me, I would never dream of using you."

"I shouldn't have made *me* the center of everything. It's just that no one else really cared for me before and you do. Well, you know exactly how I feel, because you went through it, too." He took a deep breath and said, "I know I'm almost an adult, but I thought it would be nice to have someone I could always count on as my family or even my home. Derek made it clear to me on one of his visits that my friendship with you would be over once Nick was caught."

"He did what?'

"He told me that a teenager had no place in a young married couple's life and that you just felt sorry for me— just like you feel sorry for the other orphans."

"I don't feel sorry for you, Kevin. You're right, I've been where you are. I also went through the pain of being unwanted and mistreated. We are family. If not by blood or marriage, or ex-marriage—whatever—then through our life experience. You are my family, Kevin, and don't let anyone tell you otherwise."

"How did you do it? How did you get rid of all the hatred? I can't seem to snap out of it, not since I got mad at you, anyway, and almost all of them are carrying around resentment and are bitter in some ways. I don't know how you did it. I'm betting someone was there for you…like you are for me?"

"Yes."

"Who was it?"

"Hmm…" I sighed before telling him. "Nick."

"You mean the same angry, full-of-hate person I

know? He gave you hope?" he asked.

"Yeah, before he took it away."

"But you still seem okay." He turned to me again. "I thought he just broke your heart when he left you, but really? Nick helped you?"

"Oh, he was a different person back then…" I smiled at the memory. "He was the first person to pick me as his partner when I got to training. He liked to joke around and," I turned to Kevin, "actually, he was a lot like you. I can't believe I didn't notice that before…"

I continued, "Nick was in the first group of kids I met, and he was the teacher's assistant…as you can guess, his ego didn't need that, but he kept me challenged and helped me rise up pretty quickly to be the best newbie that year. I was eager to fit in and for them to want me. Beth was my roommate, and since luck wasn't fully in our favor yet, we had Lisa as our coach. She kept telling us that we would be sent back, and as much as I hated her making me so afraid, I suppose I should thank her. Between Lisa and Nick, I was more than motivated to exceed. Anyway, Nick was a cutie back then, and he was so full of himself that he was seeing several girls, but once he met me, he paid them no mind. He swore up and down that he would marry me."

"He did," Kevin said, smiling.

"Yeah, I would have bet against him if I'd had to. I was sure he was just messing with me because I was so shy, and I didn't take him seriously. Not until my birthday." I paused, remembering and reliving those days.

"Anyway, he never left my side. He found out somehow that Lisa was trying to get me kicked out. She said I was cheating and that Nick was covering for me."

"She is such a bitch," he said.

"Was, Kevin. She isn't anymore. You see how much she's changed. Look, even Beth forgives her, and she bullied her like crazy."

"So what happened?"

"Nick stood by me and requested that they do a hearing and have me try out in front of everyone for them to witness how good I really was. They didn't want to," I shrugged. "Why listen to a student when a coach had no reason to lie? It didn't stop Nick, though. He gathered a few other students and two coaches—Jenny and Andrew—to walk out of there if I wasn't given the chance. I was mad at him, but in the end, I proved myself. I was ready to walk out. After all, I was used to it. He will always be the first person who ever…loved me."

"He's never stopped."

"Right…is that why he doesn't respect me?"

"About that, Annie, I don't know how to say it." He took my hands. "I hope you forgive me. I was the one who was thinking that you were, uh, screwing Derek. I was so pissed at you. It was right after Derek had told me I was nothing to you. I was so hurt that I kept feeding doubt into Nick's mind. I told him you were just playing him, just like you were playing me."

"You…you what?"

"I messed with Nick's trust. He'd been jealous with

you spending time with Derek, but you know him, he was playing it cool and being supportive. But it was killing him. And then I came and fed more doubt and…he was so mad at me for insisting you were not to be trusted. After everything happened, I wanted to tell you it was my fault. But he figured it was better if you thought it was all him."

I sat in silence, thinking about what he'd just said.

"Annie, say something."

"I don't know what to say. You're not covering for him?"

"No, Annie, you know I wouldn't. Nick, he didn't want you thinking that I disrespected you like that. He said it would break your heart. I tried telling him that you hated him instead, and all he could say was that he'd already lost all rights to your heart and that he wouldn't let me get involved. I wanted to fix you guys, Annie, I really did. He just insisted that he was the one responsible for ever hurting you, and that I deserved your full heart."

"I would never hate you, Kevin. I would be upset, sure. But I get where you are coming from. It was so much worse with me thinking it was all Nick…I can't believe he took the blame. I mean, I know you didn't force him to say what he did, but still."

"He was just angry. We do stupid shit when we're angry."

"Language, Kevin."

"Sorry." He looked down. "He is the first person to ever love you, but I'm his brother." He looked into his hands and, as if realizing it for the first time, he asked, "Do you think he loves me, too?"

"Do you doubt it?"

"All the time."

"Why?"

"I thought maybe he just felt responsible or guilty." He turned back to me. "I guess he really just loves us both."

"I guess."

We went back home and were quite happy that no one found out about our secret outing.

WITH EACH TRAINING session that went by, the rest of them still felt drained when they used someone else's power too much. So even if we could have multiple abilities, it just didn't last long unless it was their very own. Nick's studies of Dr. Lumin's notes showed that it was all tied to our emotions, and wasn't sure what formulas would fix the problem, unless they had some kind of recharging DNA to study. Obviously, that meant me. The sad thing is, it was true: I was able to recharge all of them pretty quickly after their sessions. I just couldn't escape this Kinetic shit.

The only drawback was that I was more prone to getting sick, and slept for days after recharging everyone. But then I would see hints of the blue surge. Jenny thought it was like her healing. I used it up and recharged, building resistance and, in a way, healing the energy and making it come back stronger. I felt stronger…if only it lasted longer.

After Jenny went back to the Org's training facility, she started to display major abilities. Nick made her show how strong she was. I tried to argue against him, but he had her convinced this was the right thing to do. He insisted that it was either that or being injected with the serums that were made of innocent blood. He thought maybe Dr. Lake would let those kids go since there was no reason to create new formulas made of blood and enhanced DNA. All that was needed was for Luminaries to tap into each other's energy.

They were suspicious of her new powers, of course, but she told them that all she'd needed was to rest and to get a boost from me. We knew this was something that would make Dr. Lake happy, but in the end, Nick decided it was worth it. We were accomplishing what he was dying to have just by practicing and refusing to take their debilitating monthly shots.

I hated Nick for it. He crossed the line putting Jenny in such danger. I wanted her to stay hidden at the cabin, but she was so brainwashed by Nick that she followed his every word.

Samantha kept visiting me every other week for lunch and even admitted to being engaged. She did seem to be getting bigger as Lisa loved to point out, but I didn't feel comfortable asking her if she was expecting or not. Better safe than sorry. Insulting Samantha was not part of my plan. I actually had to ask her if she could look into the identities of some of the girls' bodies we found for me since she had full access at the Org, and she'd agreed to do it, no questions asked.

I got a cup of coffee and went to sit on the couch, thinking that maybe watching some TV would get my mind off things. Samantha had just left me, and she'd talked so much, my head was spinning.

"Wow, is Sam pregnant?" Nick asked, interrupting my thoughts.

"I don't know, I didn't ask her."

"You don't think…" he frowned and turned his head sideways.

"What?"

"She wasn't taken advantage of, was she?"

"No, don't be silly. She's seeing some guy in her apartment building. Well, actually they got engaged last weekend."

"Oh, good. I just don't know with Lake. If he was able to keep Lisa, of all people, quiet about what happened, there is nothing stopping him from taking advantage of sweet little Sam."

"Um, I didn't think about it, but I'll try to press her for more information next time I see her."

"Or Kev and I can do some spying," he suggested.

"No, that's not cool. She's a nice girl. I'll just ask her next time."

"What if she is in danger?"

"She seems way too happy to be in danger," I said.

"Okay." He sat down. "Is your boyfriend coming

over tonight?"

"I'm not sure yet. Why?"

"Can you do me a favor and tell him not to come if he invites himself?"

"Sure, but you still haven't told me why."

"You really don't know?"

"Nick, please just tell me." I gave him a dramatic begging gesture.

"It's my birthday."

"No, it's not. You were born in March."

"They told me I was born in March, but remember how I found my birth records? I thought you read them. Anyway, it says I was born on October 8th."

"Uh, I guess... Happy birthday?"

"Thanks. Do I get a hug?" he asked, walking over to me.

"Just because I'm still talking to you doesn't mean that I care."

"You care, come here." He pulled me in and gave me a very tight hug, and when he pulled away, he looked me in the eyes and I could feel my knees melting.

"Happy birthday," I whispered.

"Thanks." He leaned in to kiss me.

"No," I pulled away. "You don't get to do that. I have a boyfriend."

"A fake boyfriend."

"You fake something long enough...it becomes real."

"You're serious?"

"Yes." I shrugged and turned my head before my frigging eyes gave me away.

"Whatever." He turned to walk away before stopping abruptly. "I don't understand. You know I didn't actually mean that comment. I never, ever, thought any less of you. I am so sorry I said that, but he just made me so mad at you."

"I'm supposed to believe that?"

"Kevin told you himself," he said.

"Right, because he wouldn't lie for his brother." I knew it was true. I just couldn't stop being mad at him.

"Let's talk about this."

"You can talk all you want, Nick, I don't care."

"Have you slept with Derek?"

"That's none of your business," I said.

"Do you love him?"

"Still not your business."

"Please, just tell me straight up if I truly don't have any chance of being with you again."

I felt myself drown in his eyes. "I can't be with you, I just can't."

"Why not?"

"You..." My voice trailed off as I walked back and forth. "I just don't know. I hate you. You are a killer. You are an asshole who hurt me. You threw Jenny into the lion's mouth without a second thought—she could get hurt, Nick."

"Look, I am sorry. About everything. I'm going to the lab."

"Which lab?"

"Dr. Lake's. I'm going to do a quick check for those kids. Nothing we're doing is working."

"They're going to see you."

"That's fine. I'll have enough time to send the kids into safety. Kevin is a good teacher."

"Okay. That sounds good. You can probably come back with them."

"I don't have that much concentration, Annie. I'll probably only be able to send the kids to safety, if they are there. After that, if I get away, I promise you'll never see me again."

"What do you mean?"

"I'll get out of your hair," he said.

"Good," I said in anger.

"I'll just go say goodbye to Kevin first."

The lump formed in my throat as he walked up the stairs. Midway up, he turned around and sprinted back to me.

"No, you know what? Before I go, you need to know. Yes, I hurt you. I'M FUCKING SORRY. I had to. I had to leave you to keep you safe. Yes, I'm a killer. I HAD TO KILL THEM TO SAVE MY BROTHER! Yes, I sent Jenny to danger. I just needed to take the attention from you and the kids as long as possible. I keep thinking I can figure out how to stop that monster before he kills again, but the problem is, I don't know what other powers he has. I would do anything for you, Annie. If that means putting our friends in harm's way, then so be it."

"That's crossing the line!"

"I DON'T CARE! I'll redraw the line many times over where it concerns you! Jenny can handle herself. She is better at this than any of us," he said, pushing his hands in his pockets. "I'm walking away, Annie. I just need to tell you one more time that I love you. Thanks for loving me back." He took out my wedding ring and placed it in my hand. "Well, back then, anyway." He sighed and said, "It used to be the best feeling in the world."

He did go upstairs this time. I'd barely had time to drop a tear when I heard a loud crash from the kitchen.

"Where is everybody?" Beth yelled. She had teleported right on top of the table and was jumping off when I walked in, the guys and Lisa behind me. "Jenny is gone."

"Where?"

"He took her. She's been gone since this morning."

"No, she's just resting at home," I said.

"No, I was talking with her when she rushed me off and told me she would call me back. I had some work to do so I didn't think anything of it. I figured she was sleeping or something. I just stopped by her house, and her cell phone was on the bed and it looked like there had been a fight. She's gone."

"Well, we have to go and get her. Dr. Lake probably has her at his house." I turned to Nick. "Go check." He left, and it seemed like he was gone forever. When he came back, the whole gang was in my kitchen. We hadn't notified Derek because we knew he would call them all in, and we just wanted to get her back safely.

"Guys," Nick said when he got back. "It's not good. She is there, in handcuffs and pretty drugged up. I tried to get it off her, but the chains and cuffs would send a shock into her every time she struggled with it. "They left her in there, for now, but she is not the only one. We have to plan this efficiently. Annie, you're the energy pro. You might be the only one able to pull that electricity into yourself while I beam it off her."

"I don't get it. Why can't she just teleport?" I asked.

"They have some strange control with the chains and the current. It's almost like its connected to their skin or something. She tried teleporting, but the shock dragged her back down. They are really advanced. I really hope you'll be able to try your new trick, Annie. I'm counting on you pulling the electricity away, but you haven't exactly managed it fully since that incident."

"I'll try. Let's go," I said.

"No, we can't go yet. We have to plan this out. There are several women there, some clearly pregnant. The kids are also chained in another room next to theirs. We have to get everyone out."

"Yeah, we won't leave them there. Let's go."

"Annie, honey. We have to prepare better. I'm sure he saw the camera feed, and he'll be ready for an attack."

# CHAPTER TWENTY-TWO

"HELLO, HELLO!" WE heard a voice from the front door. Everyone in the kitchen disappeared as I went to see who it was.

"Samantha! Did you forget something?" I asked.

"Two things, actually."

"Oh, sorry." I looked back at the door. "How did you get in?"

"I have my ways," she said, laughing. "I forgot to ask you earlier: how is Lisa?"

"Lisa?"

"Yes, I know she's here." She smiled. "Actually, between you and me? I knew she was here the whole time. The bitch doesn't even know she has a tracker chip under her skin. Ha!"

"Does Derek know she is here?"

"No, he doesn't know." She smiled for a second before her sweet expression was replaced by one full of hatred. "Not your Derek, anyway. But his dad does, we figured you were both exactly where we needed you. It's time now."

"For what?"

"For you two to come with me," she said.

"You're working with him?"

"Of course. I would be a bad fiancée if I didn't, don't you think?"

"We are not going anywhere with you," I said.

"Ah…now, Annie, don't do anything stupid. We have something to encourage you." She threw her phone at me. "Recognize her?"

"Jenny."

"Yes, if I don't come back with the two of you in thirty minutes, she is going to suffer. And believe me, it's going to get very ugly if you don't comply. Lisa!" she called.

"Let me go get her, she won't come out on her own."

"Stop. Where is Kevin?"

"I'm sure you saw him outside with Andrew. It would be stupid for you not to check out your surroundings before coming in," I said, hoping she would take the bait.

"Of course I saw them. Just make sure they stay where they are. Give me your cell phone."

I took it out, but knowing I had texts and emails I didn't want her to see, I just dropped it in the full cup of coffee I had forgotten on the side table. "There, it won't work now."

"Fine, but don't try anything, Annie, I'm warning you."

"You have Jenny, so you have my word. Lisa is sleeping. Let me just wake her up and get some proper clothing for her. Can you go to the fridge and get us some bottles of water, though? She gets dehydrated very quickly, and that's not good for the baby."

"Do I look like I care what happens to her or her baby?"

"No, but Dr. Lake cares what happens to them while they are in your care."

"Fine, hurry up."

I went up to the bedroom where everyone was waiting and told them what was going on. We all agreed that Lisa and I would go and they would come to help us out once they were able to form a plan. Before I left, though, I asked them all to hold each other's hands, and I transferred all the energy I could into them. I knew they would need the boost for later.

I turned to Kevin. "You need to tell Derek what happened. If he seems to be in on it, come back here. If not, stay with him so you can take others to help us out there. Stay in contact with Nick so you can all know what's going on." I held Lisa's hand and left them.

We went through the front, passing by Andrew and Kevin, who went out to make it seem like they knew nothing.

"Annie, Lisa…what's up? Hey, Samantha!" Andrew said.

"Sam is taking us to Derek. It's all right, he knows Lisa is here," I told him.

"I can drop you guys off, if you want," Kevin said.

"NO!" Samantha snapped, and I turned to look at her.

"Derek doesn't think it's safe for Lisa in her condition. But you know I'm in good hands with Sam," I smiled. "I guess if you guys want to go and rest, you could. No need to keep guarding the house. We'll be gone for a while, I'm assuming?" I turned to Samantha.

"Yes, don't wait up." We followed her to the car.

She drove in silence for a while.

"Okay, so I have to ask," I said. "Are you pregnant?"

"Obviously, I'm pregnant."

Lisa laughed. "Huh, I wasn't really sure. You seem like the same big, fat pig."

"Lisa! Stop it," I said.

"You do realize she is the enemy, don't you, Annie?"

"Sam is not the enemy. She is doing what she is asked to do, right?" I turned to her from the passenger side. "Are you being manipulated?"

"Haha, Annie. You're so stupid. I can take care of myself. I love him and he loves me. And I hate all of you fucking full Luminaries. You think you're better than me because you're out in the field. Well, guess what? I have more power than any of you because I have all the knowledge. Who do you think gave him the idea to steal all of your special abilities? Me—I'm smart. I've been trying to steal them myself for a long time, but I needed his help to come up with something that would make it easier." She seemed pretty proud of herself.

"I've always known you were smart, Samantha."

She smirked. "Right, smarter than you. I bet you had no idea I was playing you this whole time."

Crap, it didn't look like I was going to get her on my side. "No, you got me there," I said softly. I couldn't get Jenny and the kids off my mind.

We said nothing more until we got to his house. She went straight to a side door that led to the gym area and continued to the sauna room. Once in there, she pressed what looked like a second light switch, and the back wall slid away to display stairs going down.

We followed her to the bottom of the stairs and found Jessica waiting for us with two guards. Behind them, we could see a big lab and two glass rooms. In the first one, I could see the kids sitting linked to each other in chains. And in the second room, I could see Jenny sitting on the floor next to three girls. Their hands were in cuffs that were linked to individual chains that reached up to the ceiling. One girl kept trying to loosen her grip, but the electricity kept shocking her. The other girls were clearly pregnant as well. I stared at Jenny, and she opened her eyes to look at me and quickly shut them back.

Dr. Lake walked past me and took both Lisa and Samantha with him. Jessica pulled me and we followed him, I watched in horror as he injected both of them and put them both in handcuffs.

"What are you doing? Mom, stop this!" Samantha screamed. "I'm on your side! Stop!"

"You've been a good girl, but now our use for you is done," Jessica said.

"But I'm your daughter."

"Yes, but right now, we only care about my grandchild." She smiled at Dr. Lake, who turned to Jenny and made me jump backwards as he slapped her in the face. The sparks from the electricity jolting all of the girls made their screams earsplitting.

"Stop it! You are harming them and the babies!"

"Annie, Annie…it doesn't matter. I need them for my experiments. And don't worry, I don't really need them alive. All we need is their blood, isn't that right, Jess?"

"Yes."

I swear I was about to puke. "You two are sick…she is your daughter. And what did any of those girls do to you?"

"It's what they can do for us." Jessica smiled. "They are going to help us become the strongest Luminaries in the world. Them and you, my dear."

"Speaking of you, I don't think I want to wait until you marry my son and decide to give me a grandchild. Your investigation was getting too close for comfort. Samantha informed me you'd found out my little secret. But I'll admit, it makes me a bit happy."

"Why is that?"

"Well, now I get to impregnate you myself." He

looked me up and down. "I've always admired your sexy little body. My son is an idiot for not taking what he wanted, and now it's going to be mine."

"What makes you think I'm going to let you lay a finger on me?"

"You see, I thought you might ask that question. Let's demonstrate, Jessica, shall we?"

Jessica came from behind me and used her fingerprint to unlock the computer. She typed something, and I watched as water fell on Jenny and the girls, making their bodies shake uncontrollably from the shock they were receiving. The screams were so bad, I ran up to the glass, but before I got there, Dr. Lake pulled me back.

"That was just a small fraction of a volt on the chain. If you try anything, it will be worse for her and the others. And I doubt you want me moving on to the kids, do you?" he asked.

"No, please don't hurt them."

"Now, as you can see, the best thing for you to do is to follow me to my bedroom and do as I say." When I didn't move, Jessica typed some more, and I watched as one of the girls received a shock so strong her body turned purple, and she was killed instantly. I screamed out. He smiled and said, "Now, come on, darling, don't be shy." I went with him as he took me to his bedroom. I could hardly feel my own legs.

"Why are you doing this?"

"Because you are very delicious-looking."

"You are a monster."

"I've been called worse." He went to a bar he had close to his window and poured some red wine in two glasses. "Here you go, love, why don't you relax?"

"No, thank you."

"Annie, it would be a lot easier if you did as I say." He turned to get a remote control and turned the TV screen on. I saw the girls in the glass room, along with Jessica jumping over the dead girl's body. She just lay there, motionless. As he pressed a button, Jessica looked up to the camera, smiling, and jiggled Lisa's hands in the cuffs, shocking her. Any move they made resulted in them receiving a shock. *I had to get them out.*

"I can make them suffer the whole night if you don't do everything I say. Or you can be a good girl and allow them a good night's sleep. What's it going to be, baby?"

"Don't call me that," I said as I took the wine and took a sip. I had to buy some time. He didn't seem to know that Nick had been in the lab earlier. This was good.

"Good, you finish that glass, and I'll answer your questions as we have some food." He went over to a table I hadn't noticed before, and I saw there were some plates with covers on them. I took a bite from the bread and took another sip. He smiled and continued, "So you want to know why I'm doing this."

"Yes."

"For power," he said, as if it were so simple.

"Right, but what are you going to gain from it?"

"Control, money. I'll have the President of the

United States eating from my hands."

"Still don't get it."

"Well, I like power, Annie. It's like a drug: the more I get, the more I want. Being full of abilities, along with yours, I will just be absolutely indestructible. Do you know how annoying it is to become so weak after an amazing moment of power? I am the first Luminary, so I get more exhausted than the rest of you after going through a surge."

"Why do you need blood from my...child?"

"If I can enhance my own DNA with yours, it will be easier to become like you."

"Take my blood. I'm right here."

"It doesn't work like that, sweetheart. Young Luminaries are still developing powers. If I get it from an infant, I can manipulate it enough to give it the abilities I want. Your descendant should make it easier for me to become Kinetic. In the meantime, I can reverse my healing gift and absorb the energy from you as I need it. I hate having to depend on someone else, however, so if you and I have a child, I'll be able to adapt better to the changes, since it will have both our genes. And then I won't need you or anyone else anymore. I'll have enough stored energy to boost my own ability and steal more powers."

"None of us will just stand by and let you do that," I said.

"I know. That's why I'll kill all of you when I'm done. I just love power," he laughed.

"I see the appeal. You can use my energy all you want."

"Coming over to the darker side, Annie?"

"No, no matter what you try, you won't be able to keep my strength or my energy forever. It wears off. I just plan on enjoying myself when I see you behind bars forever."

"Oh, now, now. Play nice."

"Why try to make me marry Derek if you wanted me all along?"

"He is my son. I love him, and he loves you. I didn't see a reason to keep him away from you while I got what I wanted from you two."

"But now?"

"Now, you were shoving your nose where it doesn't belong, Annie, and I don't like that. You were getting too close. I'm glad you trusted little Samantha enough to ask her to look into those bodies for you, otherwise, you would have messed up all my plans. But no matter, complicating them or not, this is far more exciting. Now I get to have you."

"What about Derek?"

"Derek will do what I say, don't worry. He doesn't have a backbone when it comes to me. He tries so hard to make me happy, he'll probably think this is the best idea…to have you as his stepmother."

"What about Samantha? Why punish her if she's on your side?" I had to keep this man talking for as long as possible. Everyone else should be arriving soon.

"Forget her, she is of no use to me anymore. Not now that I have you. That's enough. I need you to go change into this." He threw a bag at me. "And I don't want any complaints. Either you wear it, or someone else dies. Or even better, I will keep tormenting them until you do as I say. Oh, by the way, I love sex. I especially like it when they struggle, so feel free to fight me if you want." He licked his finger, making me gag.

I took the bag and walked into the bathroom. I was really praying that Nick or Derek would show up soon. I would kill him before letting him get close to me. The problem was, Jessica was ready to push those buttons at any moment's notice. But then, if she didn't know he was dead, I could sneak up on her and get to her before she hurt the girls again. So I made up my mind, I changed into the red lingerie set he'd given me and went out, ready to kill him.

"Annie! I am so happy to see you in my clothing."

I scowled. "You call this clothing?"

"If you don't like it, there is no need to worry yourself, I'm going to take it all off very soon," he said as he touched himself.

"What makes you think I will allow you to touch me? Jessica is in the lab and would have no idea if you were dead."

He jumped, excited. "You see this?" He pointed to his watch. "It's connected to the computer downstairs. If my pulse stops, they are all dead." He gave me another glass of wine, "But don't worry, nothing will happen when my pulse speeds up." He gave me a tap on the ass.

There had to be another way. I took a sip of the wine and walked around. Maybe I could try to hypnotize him…but I had never really been good at it, and no one was here with me so I couldn't tap into them. Lisa was too far below, and I was still recharging after transferring energy to the others before coming. I knew it wouldn't work.

"Come here." He sat on the bed and patted the spot right next to him. Knowing I had no choice until I could figure something out, I decided to go and try to push him off for as long as I could. I sat next to him and kept drinking the wine. "That's a good girl, you like the wine?" He rubbed my leg.

"It's fine." I cringed as he brushed my hair to the side.

"Look at me," he said as he started to lean in for a kiss. I could feel him draining my power. "Oh, it is amazing, I knew you had energy like no other, but this." His eyes widened, and he smiled hungrily at me. I tried to fight his pull, but he was stronger than the others.

"Stop right there!" Derek's voice came from across the room. I had never been happier to see him in my life.

"Son! I am so happy to see you. Look, meet my new lover."

"Dad, step away from her. She's mine."

"Now, come on. Why would she be with second best when she can be with a real man? I'm so far above you that you could never reach my accomplishments. Living in my shadow is the only thing you're good for. Now, walk away if you know what's good for you, Son."

"I will not allow this, Dad."

"And I will not allow your insolence! I would rather not hurt you, Son, but I will if you don't listen to me. You think you can save her all by yourself, do you? Look at this," he sneered as he showed Derek the life feed of the prisoners in the lab and had Jessica demonstrate what would happen if we resisted. "Now step aside, you little boy, and let the man do the work." He pulled me onto his lap and started kissing me in front of Derek. "Or you can watch," he said before Derek launched himself at us.

I was thrown to the floor, and they were both rustling on the bed.

"I will not let you hurt Annie or anyone else, Dad."

"Unfortunately, you have no say, Son," he said as he raised Derek off his feet with my stolen strength and blasted him with a beam from his hands, much like Nick's. "Looks familiar?" he said, and turned to me as Derek shrieked with pain in the air before falling hard on the floor. "I was able to get ahold of your beloved's blood before he left us. I'm happy with the way his powers turned out. What do you think?"

"I'm thinking since you would enjoy me struggling a little bit, that you can handle a good fight. What do you think?"

"I like it." He threw his beam at me, and I jumped quickly to the side, tapping into what I'd learned from Beth, and I was behind him in a second. I strangled him from behind, before he mentally threw objects at me. I was able to destroy most of them before they hit me. Grabbing my arm, he pulled me from him and slammed me into and through part of the floor.

"Get off her!" Nick said, the rest of the gang appearing all around us.

"Ready to die?" Beth asked, taking the scene in.

"No, don't kill him. If he dies, they die," I pointed to the screen. In that moment, Dr. Lake teleported from the room and was instantly in the lab. We all did the same and followed him.

Kevin reappeared beside Jessica, who held the control. Without even blinking, she sent a shock wave to him. He fell.

"You like that?" she asked Nick as he lunged towards his brother.

"You bitch," Kevin said, getting back up.

"It's the same shock waves hurting the whores in there. It's my gift." She smiled as she sent a wave to Andrew, but he dove away before she got him. "And you," she turned to Kevin again. "I'm your worst enemy, boy. I can also control a magnetic field that stops teleportation, that's why your friends can't escape. I bottled up my power, and it's all over those chains," she said, laughing.

At that same moment, Dr. Lake and Nick started shooting beams at each other, dancing all around the room.

"Be careful not to kill him, Nick," I said while Beth,

Andrew, and I went to the glass rooms.

"I'll do what I can, but I don't promise anything," he said.

"There are other lives at stake," I yelled. He nodded my way and then threw himself at Dr. Lake to get into a physical fight instead. I was worried Lake was strong now, and I was fighting the feeling of being drained. Out of the corner of my eye, I saw Kevin taking on the guards. He was able to teleport since Jessica was too busy with the others to try and stop him. He appeared and disappeared, sending kicks and punches in between.

Andrew and I made our way into the glass room with the girls inside since they were in more danger, currently, than the kids. Beth left us to that while she blasted her way around with her speed, trying to break the glass where the kids were chained. The glass was made of something too hard for her to break.

Jessica went up to her and started firing electric waves, but with Beth's speed, she kept missing. Eventually, Beth lunged and tumbled on top of Jessica. Jessica's head crashed to the floor, and Beth went back to get the kids. After I broke down our glass door, Andrew concentrated to tap into Nick's beam to cut off the chains, and I ran to help Beth.

"Go to the back of the room, NOW!" I told the kids. As they stepped backwards, crying, I spun on my feet and gave the glass a kick, breaking it on impact. I was barefoot, so the pieces stuck in my feet and left a trail behind me as I went back to the girls.

At the sight of their bodies convulsing with electricity, I turned to see Dr. Lake burst through Nick's fire and backhand him, sending Nick flying. The older man's clothes were in flames, and he turned to me and smiled. "This is power, Annie. This is what I have always wanted." He began ripping the burning clothes from his body as he walked toward me.

I didn't have time to ask Andrew whether or not he could start freeing them. Their screams were absolutely horrifying. I held on to the main chain, and I absorbed most of the electricity waves, feeling my body tremble as I continued to pull. Andrew was busy beaming the chains off the two girls first, since they were weaker than Jenny and Lisa. He was able to free just one of them before he lost his balance. He was too weak from tapping into Nick's beam, and whatever Jessica had done to these chains was much too strong for him.

I saw the girls' skin starting to change colors, and I got so angry, I barely noticed when the blue surge came out of me and began pulling all of the electricity away. I turned to Andrew, "Come and take some more from me and get the chains off them!"

"Annie, you have to stop before it kills you," Andrew said.

"No, keep going. Get Jenny and Lisa." He stood and placed one hand on me while sending beams with his other hand towards the chains. Through my almost closed eyelids, I could still see what was happening outside. Beth was almost done freeing the children and Andrew was beaming off the last chain, when I felt a hand grab my shoulder and send me flying back.

I hit the ground hard and watched Dr. Lake stalk toward Andrew, who was swaying with exhaustion. I wouldn't let him hurt my friends. I wouldn't let him hurt anyone anymore. Next to me was a massive generator. I gripped its base and flung it at the power hungry doctor. It hit him in the back, sending him into the wall.

The rubble moved, and Dr. Lake pushed the hunk of metal off of him. Several cuts along his chest and arms were bleeding. He looked crazed. "Yes, this is amazing, now that I know all these years of struggling and failing were worth it." He started running. His speed picked up—he must have pulled from Beth. He grabbed me by my throat and slammed me into the ground. I grabbed his arms and tried to pull them from my throat. He had become so strong.

"I am the true Luminary, Annie. I am greater now than any of you. I will have the power, all of it."

I was frantic. Black spots were forming in my eyes as I began to lose consciousness. Then it happened: the blue light started to form around my hands, then up my arms. "You want all the power, you bastard, then take it." I pushed it into him, all of it, as much as I could send, and with the blue light, it was a lot. He started to shake, his eyes rolled back, and the veins in his arms began to bulge.

"Wha- what have you done to me?" he said, falling to his knees.

"I gave you what you wanted, *power*. But you are weak. You are not me, Lake. You are not Kinetic." I kicked him, sending him flying into a support beam. He convulsed a few more times and then lay still. I went back to help free the girls.

Jessica, having regained consciousness in time to see what I had done to Dr. Lake, screamed out at the sight and, picking up a couple of large pieces of glass, she went toward Beth and the orphans. Beth's back was to her, so she couldn't see Jessica walking along with the guard who had come to assist her, gun in hand. Andrew ran off to stop her, but I could barely stand. I fell to my knees. I couldn't stop, though. Samantha was still chained in, and Jenny was trying to heal the other girls, who were convulsing violently.

Before Andrew got too close, Jessica electrified him and he fell. The guard raised his gun, pointing it at Beth's head, and Lisa ran towards him. The sound of the shot barely registered in comparison to the loud drops of blood splattering out from Lisa's body. This happened simultaneously as Jessica went to shove the glass into one of the kids' back. I watched like a statue as Nick appeared in front of her and the glass went right through his chest.

I think I heard myself scream just before everything went black.

# CHAPTER TWENTY-THREE

SEVEN MONTHS LATER, I found myself walking on the sandy beaches of the Bahamas, Derek's hands taking me in slow steps to the altar and whispering in my ears.

"You know it's okay if you've changed your mind."

"No, stop it. I want this."

"Sure?"

"Yes." I smiled and gave him a hug before he placed my hand in Nick's.

"Dearly beloved, we are gathered here today…"

Nick and I were being married for the second time on May 1st, 2009, which would have been our fifth wedding anniversary. I couldn't help but be thankful for all of our blessings. I had been able to save the kids, along with the pregnant girls who were in the cell that day. Their bodies, being weaker than a Luminary's, hadn't been able to keep the pregnancies after all the electricity that had been volted into them. Nick took care of their memories, and they were now back with their families, living a happy life.

Jessica was now in custody, and Samantha hadn't made it. She had been the last person left to be freed when I thought I had lost Nick forever. She'd received such a strong blast that she was dead in a second. Jenny was able to handle the blast since she was used to transferring energies back and forth. It turned out that she and Lisa had helped me by sending their electricity to me that day, and I still wasn't sure if I was happy about that or not. *That shit hurt.*

All of the kids were back at their respective orphanages. Their memories were also modified. Living a life with that terror hanging over them was not worth it or needed. I visit all three orphanages regularly. Between the gang and me, we've been able to make a slightly happier life for them.

Little Elisa was born that same night, at just thirty-five weeks. Lisa was able to hold her baby girl and kiss her goodbye before we lost her for good. It all happened too fast. Jenny tried her best to heal her, but the bullet had nicked the baby, and she was fading along with her mom. Lisa's last wish had been for her daughter to live. We still mourned the person she had become. I'd lost a friend, but Beth had lost her sister—a sister who gave up her life so she could live—right after finally starting to get close. The only consolation she had was that her niece now lived with her and Andrew, and she still had someone to claim as part of her family. A real family.

Kevin stood next to Nick as his best man and was beaming with happiness that I was going to officially stop kissing other men. Behind him stood Andrew, who was so emotional that he kept sniffing and crying the whole time. He kept looking behind me to his beautiful wife, my matron of honor, Beth, who was standing, hands linked to my other bridesmaid. Jenny's sun-kissed hair flew around while holding Beth and her bouquet. There were burns on her wrists, a painful memory of all that had gone down, and like Nick, she wore the scars in honor of all the blood that was shed.

On that day, Derek had regained consciousness just in time to help save Nick's life. Apparently, he'd never given it a second thought. He worked on Nick as though his own life depended on it. Derek told me later that he wasn't sure if Nick was bad or not, but he had to try saving his life for my sake.

I owed him. Thanks to him, almost everything was well again.

We had a beautiful ceremony and reception. I couldn't help but notice that Derek and Jenny were spending a lot of time together. They said they were closer because of little Elisa, since she was Derek's sister and Jenny's Goddaughter, but the sparks that were flying were much more than just baby sparks. I was just happy to see them finally getting a shot at something real. They were both such compassionate people and true rule followers that I wondered why it had never happened before. Okay, so I might have had something to do with that, but still.

Nick took me to our honeymoon suite that night, and after a wonderful lovemaking session, we lay in each other's arms. He was my husband again.

It was always Nick.

Almost losing the person you love forever can change anyone's mind. Thinking he'd died while saving the young boy had made me understand the drastic measures he'd taken when it came to me. I got it now, because thinking I'd lost him had made me realize that saving the one you loved would be above anything else. And if you acted like a heartless lunatic in the process, so be it. He did what he'd had to in order to keep me safe, and I would return the favor in a heartbeat if I had to.

In that moment, I forgave him. I would do anything for him…including taking his name. Gosh.

"Mrs. Annie Logan. See? It sounds wonderful," Nick said.

"I love you."

"Music to my ears," he smiled.

I kissed him. "I love you, I love you, I love you!"

"How did I get so lucky twice?"

"God must love you," I said, teasing.

"He sure does."

"Not so much, though. Tomorrow we have to get back to work," I said.

"Why so fast? I thought we had a whole week here."

"We did…but this morning Derek gave me the information we were looking for."

Nick frowned. "The rest of his father's team?"

"Yes, Jessica finally talked."

"Well, time to do what we Luminaries do."

"Yeah." I smiled, showing him the blue surge in my hands. "Let's do this."

*Loved Kevin?*
*His story continues…*

# ACKNOWLEDGMENTS

IF YOU ARE me (and I am) you wouldn't pass on the opportunity to thank all the amazing people who've offered immense support in your journey to fulfilling your dreams. So here I am humbly saying thank you. Without you this book wouldn't be what it is. So if it sucks, then I also blame you.

To my kids, I love you guys to pieces, even if chances are high that I would have finished writing this sooner without your sweet interruptions. Your hugs and kisses make my days brighter and for that, I thank you.

To my husband, thank you for supporting this crazy dream, even when you weren't sure if you still had a wife somewhere. Still, you hung in there and as always believe in me and in everything I do. You made this possible along with so many other wonderful and incredible things that make up our love. Maybe someday I'll allow you to read it, but for now, thank you.

To my parents, you made me, so you get big puffy hearts for that. You've always been supportive and have taught me to follow my dreams no matter what. Thank you.

To Debra Ann Miller, you kept me sane and cheered me on. I owe you wine and gummy bears, like a lot of it, mostly for allowing me to vent. Your words of encouragement and insight on things are absolutely priceless. Thank you.

To Brandon Ax, you pushed me to my limits. The good news is even when I wanted to strangle you, I still loved you for it. You have a gift with words and I appreciate you sharing your genius with me. Thank you.

Special thanks to Regina Wamba of Mae I Design, Raina Campbell of Grapevine Book Tours, Lynda Dietz, Melissa Gray, Kate Koller, Brenda Williams, Laura Wells, Jeff R.S., P. Olarte, Julie Daly, Ana Tariq, Hilda Carranza, Amanda J.H. John, Z. Danny, Tim JOY, Jenny Anjanie, Bee Mitchell, and Shanny Seewald, without you this book would not be possible.

# ABOUT THE AUTHOR

S. K. ANTHONY IS A writer, a reader and a make-stuff-up-er who lives in New York with her husband and toddler twins. She is a wine connoisseur, which just really means she knows she loves it, and a caffeine addict. When she isn't busy with her family she finds herself being transported into the world of imagination. Well, either that or running away from spiders…she is convinced they are out to get her!

www.**skanthony**.com

CPSIA information can be obtained at www.ICGtesting.com
Printed in the USA
LVOW01s2042061013

355647LV00020B/239/P